A Thomas Family Novel

# perfect harmony

## ZEA KAYLEIGH GALAN

Perfect Harmony

To you,
Perfection is an illusion. Love is real magic.
The one that understand the difference between the two is worth chasing.

# Listen to the Official Playlist

Bryson Tiller — Don't
GIVĒON — All To Me
SZA — Garden (Say It Like That)
Miguel — Use Me
Sabrina Carpenter — When Did You Get Hot?
Wale — The Need to Know (feat. SZA)
dvsn — Too Deep
Becky G — Shower
SG Lewis, Dornik — All Night
Bryson Tiller — Open Interlude
Snoh Aalegra — I Want You Around
KAYTRANADA — Intimidated (feat. H.E.R.)
Elmiene — Someday
Alina Baraz — More Than Enough
SG Lewis, Louis Mattrs — No Less
Sinéad Harnett, GRADES — If You Let Me
Bryson Tiller — Autumn Drive
Olivia Dean — So Easy (To Fall In Love)

**Listen on SPOTIFY!**

# PERFECT HARMONY

# Join the Newsletter

Never miss an update about Zea Kayleigh, newsletter exclusives such as freebies and giveaways, first looks at new books, upcoming series, and events.

## SIGN UP HERE!

A Thomas Family Novel

# perfect *harmony*

# CHAPTER 1

## Korra Thomas

"That was tonight?"

I trail a line in the water between the cobblestones behind the club with my strappy heel while he shuffles around on the phone. Early fall rain has come and gone. Enough for it to cool the weather but not enough to skip on a good heel for a special night out.

*Deep breath in.*

As calm as I can manage, I remind him, "Today is my birthday. Of course, it was tonight."

*Okay, maybe not as calm as I would have liked.*

"Oh, Kor, it must have slipped my mind. I already brushed my teeth though. I'm not gonna be able to make it. We'll do something tomorrow night. Okay?"

I pick at a nail and immediately stop. I very rarely paint my nails anymore since they all chip off anyway. *This was a birthday treat.* Allowing him to ruin my manicure is not allowed.

"You have something planned?" I ask, filled with hope at the idea that he might have something better than a night clubbing to celebrate. He's the type...

*I think.*

"Not exactly—look it will be good. I promise." There's the trilling from his nightstand alarm clock that notes it's time for him to go to bed. "I gotta get to bed, so I can get up in the morning. You understand, right?"

"Yea…"

I thought he would have done something, anything, to celebrate me and I guess I was wrong. Maybe, I'm just expecting too much.

I look down at my phone, utterly dejected.

*How does your own boyfriend forget your only birthday though?*

Turning at the sound of the club door opening, my sister's best friend is standing there with a hand on her hip. "What are you doing out here? There's a whole party going on inside. You need to be in there!"

The harsh lighting from the street lamp illuminates Malaya's face beside the club's side entrance. I don't miss her look of concern.

Raising my phone for her to see it in my hand, I say, "You're so right. I was just on the phone with Palmer telling him good night."

She rolls her eyes. "Come on. That's enough of that." Malaya and Kasey both hate Palmer, but I know they just don't see him the way I do. *Outside of tonight*, he really is a good boyfriend.

The burly bouncer at the door steps aside to let us through. My friend never loosens her grip on my hand and she dances her way through the crowds and onto the dance floor. A perfect moment of all the moving bodies swaying more passionately when a hit song comes through the mix.

It feels good to let the swish of my hips move the fabric of my dress in a careless manner. I debated on wearing this dress tonight. The slinky forest green fabric is too nice for work and definitely too nice to get dirty on the weekend. But the club is the perfect place for me to show it off. Falling to a rhythm that heats my blood and makes it race, the smile on my face is genuine.

I'll be the first to admit that I prefer to be at home. This feeling is not one you can get in your living room though.

My friend raises our joined hands above our heads and we both dance to the beat with lights flashing and flickering over us. My spirits lift even higher as my sister comes to join us and then it's the three of us, belting the lyrics to the next song and then the next.

*This is what I needed.*

A carefree night with my girls and fruity cocktails that I don't have to watch because my brothers are here to make sure we get home safe.

Speaking of which, I search along the bar top tables at the far left for them. I spot Zach first since his hair is the biggest and he is the tallest. He looks around uncomfortably with a beer, I know he hasn't drank, in his iron-like grip. Lee is not looking too much more comfortable with his scowl on the dance floor scary enough to skin a cat with no tools.

When the sweat on my skin feels a little too dangerous to the carefully applied makeup I've chosen for tonight, I drag my sister and Malaya away from the dance floor and over to our table again.

Several men try to stop us on our way out. The shortest of the group, though he is probably the most attractive of the them, leans close to my ear to ask, "Can I buy you a drink?"

Palmer's face flashes in my mind and I say, "No, thank you though maybe my sister wants one." *I can at least be a good wing woman if nothing else.*

He doesn't seem deterred that I'm passing him off, but Kasey doesn't even let him try. Before he can open his mouth, she holds up a hand saying, "No," in capital letters.

Malaya doesn't let him get anywhere either with a quick point to the table we're headed towards. Lee is ready to jump over the balcony at this point. They bow out of the race, likely not wanting any of the smoke Lee is promising them with his glare.

I can't help but think—I should be pointing to Palmer over there. Or better yet, he should be here to ward off the advances to begin with.

*I'm not single, but you'd never know it.*

Kasey reaches the table first taking the seat next to Zach. I plop onto my stool, grabbing my rum and pineapple with fervor, downing what's left of it. I fan my face, "Why do they make these things so small? I'm going to melt. It's so hot in here." I lift my curls off my neck, trying to get some air flow back there.

"It's not meant to be gulped, you guppy. You ever heard of alcohol poisoning?" Lee chastises.

I stick my tongue out at him and casually scratch my nose with a middle finger painted boldly yellow. "Gee, thanks for that assessment, Doctor Dick. Just for that, I'm going to order two more. Have fun carrying me."

Lee rolls his eyes, "Yep, and I'll be sure to drop you off at home, so Dad can take care of his baby."

"Ah," I point at him, feeling victorious in catching his slip up. "Nia's not here. I'm the oldest at present."

"No, that would be me," Kasey corrects, primly drinking her sauvignon blanc. "By four minutes."

I wave her off. "We're twins, for argument's sake we're both the oldest."

"Got you both beat by four years," Zach says. "And I'm not carrying anyone home. Only rescues I do are from burning buildings and I'm off tonight."

I look to Malaya, "Please, tell your boyfriend that he is required to take us to our flat. That was the deal, right?"

She tilts her head from one side to the next. "Babe, I love you but you will not be cockblocking me tonight. I had a long day. Can't you get Palmer to do it?" She sips from her beer. It's not one of the light ones that Zach ordered for the table, but a dark stout. There is a moment of silence before she winces. "Sorry, I forgot. I mean what's up with that anyway?"

"What's up with what?" A deep, yet familiar voice asks from behind me.

I whirl, letting out a yelp as I hug my best friend. "You made it!" I yodel. It takes me a second, but I realize that I'm the only one embracing here. With my arms still around his neck, I ask, "Bryce, why aren't you hugging me back? Those are the birthday hug rules. Well, the hug rules, in general."

"Take a step back and you'd see," he says and I do just that.

Through slightly tipsy goggles, I look my friend over from top to bottom. His hair cut looks fresh, with the curls still in place on top and a taper up to his ears. Honestly, I think his curls are looking better than mine after all that dancing. He only has a slight shadow on his jaw from a shave this morning. His suit jacket is long gone, but he's wearing a pressed — actually more crumpled now from how tight I hugged him — button-down shirt and slacks. He must be coming from work and didn't change. I know for a fact that he owns casual clothes, clubbing clothes. These aren't them. His shoes are still shiny enough to reflect light by the time I make it there. "What am I seeing?"

His arms extend and I spot the light colored cocktail with the short black straw first. "Ooo, a—"

"Pineapple juice and rum, yea. And…" From behind his back he produces a brown paper bag and hands it to me.

"Um." I'm moments from shaking the bag before he stops me with a hand and an amused look. "What are you doing? Just open it."

"Right," I say, setting the drink down on the bar top. My sister catches my eye, but she says nothing with her lips twisted to the side and eyebrow raised. It's a look that tells me she's clocking something that I'm not. I *usually am not clocking what she's clocking though.*

Twin intuition fails me, yet again. I've got no idea what the face is for.

Using careful motions, I remove the sticker sealing the top and the tissue paper underneath. A whole heap of crinkled packing paper litters the club floor as I open the nondescript box in the bag.

With that out of the way, I catch the glint of the smooth glaze over crackle pottery.

"You didn't!" I yelp.

Everyone is leaning over the bar table to see what I'm making such a fuss about. I take a look around to show off how smug I am at the most perfect gift I've gotten this year.

Saying that isn't a big thing— Bryce gets the best gifts every year. Since I met him in the tenth grade, no one has ever topped him in that department. Not even Kasey and sometimes it's scary how well she can spot things. Don't get me wrong, her gifts are pretty great.

I don't know how he does it either. They're always the kind that make you think, "*Wow, I didn't know I needed this until you got it for me.*" Bryce takes the cake. Every time.

Carefully, I remove the pot from the box to show everyone what he purchased. I turn back to Bryce with all thirty-two teeth on display and the flash goes off.

I've come to expect his candid photos. Arguably, a gift in itself. He just has the natural ability to capture great moments. "Let me see," I say as he turns the phone around to show me. "Oh my goodness!" I bounce in my seat, "I look so good." Bryce and I look through the photos while my family is still trying to figure out exactly what my friend got me.

"Is that a cat?" Zach asks, with a shudder. He's got a bit of beef with them. Ever since a freak accident led to a broken arm. He had to save someone's neurotic cat who gave him grief in a rescue. Honestly, I didn't know why they send firefighters to help with those kinds of calls anymore. Most cats can get themselves down. They just don't want to.

"Awe, it's laughing," Malaya says from under Lee's arm. He looks completely unimpressed, but that's the little brother he is. I'm glad he isn't sharing a snarky remark because I would have to fight him.

Taryn's Pottery makes only small batches of these pots. The little cat's face looks paused in laughter. Excess water from the soil inside will drain through a small hole under the eyes that makes it look like the cat is literally cry-laughing. It's so niche and kitchy, but I love these pots. They cost way more than I can afford, especially for the one plant that I'm in a constant cycle of rehabilitating.

"This is the one, right?" Bryce asks, biting a corner of his lip. He scratches the back of his head. "You were always giggling at the videos. I didn't know if you just thought it was funny or if maybe I should have gotten the pig. I—"

"Ahh," I cut him off, placing the planter carefully onto the table next to my drink and jumping to hug him again. "It is purr-fect." I lean away from his chest since I barely reach, even in high heels, to look at him. "Get it? Get it cause..."

"You've been hanging around your brother too much," he says, shaking his head with a wide grin on his face. Lee is known for his animal puns. It started as him teasing our Dad because he thought they were cheesy and now he can't stop. Sometimes it's hard to take him serious when there is some hidden dog pun thrown into the mix. "Happy birthday," he says, finally releasing me from the hug. He looks around and then looks back at me. "Where is Palmer?"

*Well shit.* If Palmer has no haters, Malaya, Kasey and Bryce have all died.

President of that hate-club is my best friend.

I grab my drink, murmuring into the straw, "He couldn't make it." Speaking as fast as possible, I add, "He's got work early, so he needs to rest tonight."

Bryce blinks once and then he blinks again. He raises a finger, mouth open to go off about my boyfriend but then lowers his hand. Patience is not my friend's forte. Especially not when it comes to Palmer.

Pinching his nostrils quickly and then deciding on, "He didn't take the day off? He's a dental assistant and it's," he checks his watch that catches the colorful club lighting. "Friday. I came right after being in court all day, several meetings and driving from the city." Bryce points across the club to the north, "He's right down the street!"

My drink is half gone, but he presses down on the glass until I let him return it to the table. Grumbling, I say, "Really thought you were gonna let it go..."

"Let. It. Go. You can't be serious." He looks at my sister, "Is she serious?"

Kasey is no help, adding, "I don't think she has been for a single day of her life. No."

I glare daggers at my brothers, they better not add to this ribbing.

"Hey! It's my birthday. Let's get back to the celebrations. I think the DJ is finally back to playing something I can break my back to!" For that I'm grateful. I need this subject change like an emergency exit right now.

Malaya finally gives me a life line to hold onto by agreeing that she'd like to dance, too.

"Sitting this round out," Kasey says, swirling what remains of her wine. "I'm ordering nachos."

Zach pipes up, "Make it three, sis."

She scans the little QR code on the table to pull up the ordering system. "Oh, good," Kasey looks at Zach, "It's on your tab already. I'll add some wings, too."

"Oldest privileges," he says, nursing that same beer. There might be more beer in the bottle than when I first spotted him from the dance floor.

"Good plan!" I say. Holding a hand out to Bryce, I ask, "May I have this twerk?" Exhibiting a move that absolutely would not qualify as twerking of any kind, Malaya joins in, mimicking my movements.

He chuckles though I know he's still pissed about Palmer. But, he can't resist my antics. "You may."

# CHAPTER 2

## Bryce Hampton

"Isn't that Jillian?" Korra asks.

I look at where she's pointing.

*Damn.*

Harmony Hill has grown exponentially since I first moved here in the tenth grade, but all the space in the world couldn't keep me from seeing my ex.

*Small towns never get big enough.*

You know how they say "the one who got away"?

Jillian Geier is the one who I can't escape.

Korra hops up to catch my attention. She's shorter than me by almost a foot at my six-two height so she's putting in effort to actually block my view. I must have been boring holes into the side of Jillian's face.

"Hey, are you okay? You wanna go?" She asks, looking a bit panicked. The woman is unable to see people upset around her. It's something I've told her is a problem. You aren't responsible for other people's feelings.

I know it well. It's why I think I'm a better attorney than most. I don't let my own emotions cloud my judgement in that way.

But for Jillian...

I'm grinding my teeth and am unable to respond just yet. "I'm actually all twerked out." I can still sense Korra's discomfort as she shifts back and forth next to me. "C'mon." She grabs my hand and uses as much strength as she can in the little pin-needle heels she has on to pull me away from the dance floor.

I'm torn between going and saying something to my ex or not. She's dancing on this guy who looks as unsuspecting as I once did.

*Good luck to him.*

"You think the wings are here yet?" I have to lean close to her ear for her to hear me with the volume of the music. A few roaming spotlights catch in Korra's curls making them glimmer around her face. She keeps it short and gelled into a curly afro. She doesn't like to let it get too long.

The easiest way to tell the Thomas twins apart is in this way. Kasey wears her hair long. Korra's is always short.

It's been many years since I was mistaken on who was who. They are about as different as they come. Where Korra is quirky and peppy; Kasey is serious and untrusting. With one word it would be abundantly clear who was who.

She nods emphatically and I allow the flimsy excuse to leave. This is my best friend's birthday and I'm not going to make it about me.

I'd gotten here late and I already felt like I was letting her down. The case I was on had wrapped up in good time, but it was my planning that made it so I could leave straight away and get here at all. Her gift arrived last week in the mail and she only drinks one thing anytime we go out. The fact that I had nailed both gifts is the temporary balm I needed on how guilty I felt for being late tonight.

We walk up the steps to where everyone is sitting. The music is a little less loud though the bass vibrates the liquids on the table. It looks like the food had arrived and only a few remnants of the nachos remain though there are plenty of the other items they ordered. I take the empty seat next to Korra with Malaya on my left and Lee on the other side of her. Zach and Kasey or on the other side of the table and it's just like it always is at their house, minus Nia.

I always admired how close they all were. Going over to their house was like being another part of the family. I liked that too.

I barely get to enjoy getting off my feet before Lee asks, "Hey man. Isn't that Jillian over there with Terry Alexander?"

"Yea," I grunt at Lee. He's the youngest Thomas brother and a shit-stirrer. He's the kind of guy to push your buttons until you crash out on him and then act oblivious when you go off—like you're the one out of line.

If there's anyone you should ignore, it's him. Don't know how Malaya deals with it.

"Leave him alone, babe," Malaya says, poking Lee in the chest. "They've been over for months now. You're just pouring salt in the wound."

"There's no wound," I manage the lie through clenched teeth. Jillian had devastated me and the only one who really knew about that was Korra. She was livid for me. It was embarrassing to think that I have ever thought I loved the witch.

We knew the truth of her that few other people did.

Korra pats my arm, pulling me from my painful memories. I send a smile her way, as brittle as it is, and she's satisfied with the gesture. She starts loading up food onto a plate in front of her, saying something to Kasey that I don't hear.

*I need a beer.*

I take one from the iced bucket in the center of the bar table the brothers are sharing from. The top twists off easily from the long neck and I take a deep glug of it. Smacking my lips, I look down at the label. "What the hell's this?"

Zach winces, the motion guilty as he explains, "I don't really drink. You know that. I just ordered the special they had. It's no good?"

Korra giggles from beside me. "You didn't taste it?" She asks while sipping her own cocktail. She's taken the time to put some of the food on a plate in front of me from the platter of hot wings and fries at some point.

"This is piss," I state. "Who is Douglass Moore? Why would he think this is good beer?"

"Beats me. But it's on Zach's tab, so I'm not complainin'," Lee says. He raises the bottle to his brother with a wink that Zach ignores.

Something like a dark cloud approaches us when several people climb the stairs to the lounge area we're in. It's my ex and her friends. Korra notices too. She nods over to Kasey and a wicked grin stretches her lips.

I don't know what they're planning, but if they're on the same page — it's probably not good.

Shaking my head, I try my best to ward whatever this plan is from Korra's mind. She only smiles in a similar manner to her sister when Jillian passes by our table. I stiffen and come to the realization that tonight I was meant to lose my shit.

"Hi, Zach," she greets with too much of that false sweetness. He gives her a careful nod back because he's respectful but otherwise doesn't care. "Bryce. It's good to see you," she says, pointedly not addressing anyone else at the table.

"The feeling is not mutual," I say under my breath. Korra hears me, but Jillian doesn't. She's standing there with her new guy like her and I ended on amicable terms and she has a right to conversation with me. I swig the god-awful beer in the hopes that it will eventually begin to do some of that numbing alcohol is supposed to. Or that she'll just go away.

"It's good to see you, too, Jillian." With her smile still in place, Korra leans around me so that Jillian can see her when she says, "We haven't seen you around lately. Could it be that fungal infection you got?"

I cough at the beer getting caught in my throat.

There's a look of absolute horror on Jillian's face as she's completely taken back by what Korra's said.

Looking at my friend, I try to determine exactly what she's playing at. I don't know if what she's saying is true, but one thing the Thomas family has perfected—having each other's back.

Korra looks to her sister for the assist. "Weren't we just talking about how we were so sorry to hear about that. Are the creams working?"

"I-I don't know what you're talking about." My ex's pale cheeks flame red, showing even more contrast with the melanin at our table.

Zach, Kasey and Korra all have the sable brown skin that Dr. Thomas has, where Lee and I are more ochre brown. Even the youngest sister, Nia has the deeper skin tone their dad has. A fact that I know Lee used to be teased about since he's the only one who doesn't look like the rest of his siblings.

"You have to be diligent with the application, you know? Really make sure you get it between the cheeks so it doesn't spread." Kasey says with her usual deadpan.

My eyes damn near bulge out of my head. Neither of the twins break character and I'm just sitting there not sure what in the hell is going on.

Jillian looks at her date, or whoever he is, shaking her head. "There is no—"

"It's okay. We won't tell a soul," Korra says and she makes an embarrassed face. "Well, Lee and Zach already know." The two brothers nod like it's a fact. Each with their own expressions of discomfort at the idea. "There's nothing to be ashamed of. Two weeks and that'll clear right up."

Terry swallows but makes a bit more space between the two of them. "You have an infection where?"

Jillian's brown hair flies around as she spins to face him fully. "I don't. They're just—"

"Look, I feel like you really should have told me that, before..." He looks over toward our table and moves her to the side by the arm. Obviously looking for privacy but there is not much space for him to get too far from the table in this lounge. His eyebrows rise with meaning before saying to her in a lower tone, "You know..." His shoulders rise like she should know what he's talking about.

We all know now that she's sleeping with this guy.

*Ugh. I don't need this.*

"It's the least you could have done. I get you, man." I grab a piss beer from the basket and offer it to him. "That's likely the least of your worries."

Jillian stomps off and Terry follows after telling Korra, "Thanks."

"No problem," she calls after him.

Korra and Kasey are cackling their asses off as they watch the two of them leave. "Oh, did you see her face?" My best friend asks no one in particular.

"That's a little evil. I didn't think you had that in you." I say, finally taking a bite from a chicken wing. The spice hits me quick, just the way I like it. How long has it been since I had wings?

Korra high-fives her sister in victory. Tipsy expression pleased with herself. "She deserves worse for what she did to you. I'm always gonna have your back," she hiccups.

"Did you make that up?" I ask.

She shrugs and with a deadpan to rival Kasey's says, "Guess we'll see when her tests come back..."

The table erupts with laughter.

The twins stay in Harmony Flats on the other side of town. It's not far from the club especially in comparison to the drive I'm going to be making back into Denver tonight.

Kasey busies herself on her phone in the backseat of my Mercedes sedan while Korra is knocked out in the passenger seat beside me.

I barely managed a third of the beer that Douglass Moore regrettably makes. By the time the dancing and celebrating came to an end, I was the most sober of everyone at the table. Though Zach was a close second. He managed to finish that ale, even with it likely being warm after how long he nursed it.

Passing through the town always hits me with nostalgia for a more carefree time. When my dad was still alive and my mother still knew joy. Before I found out that being the scholarship kid is a brand that will humble in ways you can't expect. Each street tells a different story as we found ways to entertain ourselves with nothing much to do. Especially through Main Street.

Arriving at the single building with three floors, it's easy to find somewhere to park in the single lot. In contrast, my apartment building has two layers of security to get to the garage before you get to the building with all the residences.

A twinge of something uncomfortable passes over me when I think about how unsafe their situation is. Like it always does.

*Nothing ever happens in small towns though.*

I park in the closest spot and Kasey gets out to help her sister. "Nah, don't worry about it," I say. "Go get the door open." She doesn't argue with me, likely uninterested in hefting her sister up the three floors of stairs.

Opening the passenger door, I look down at my friend. Her green dress is all rumpled around her and her hair is covering her face completely. Laughing, I tilt my head to try and see if she's awake under all those curls. "Time to get up, Kor," I coax.

She murmurs something and turns over in the seat.

"Got a long drive home. I'll give you to the count of three before you're going over my shoulder like a sack of potatoes." I wait a moment and offer, "Or you can walk by yourself and save yourself the nausea..."

"I'm potatoes," she slurs, swatting at me again when I pull her hand.

I chuckle. "C'mon," unbuckling her and helping her onto the pin-needle heels she came in. Once I've got her out of the car I reach back inside, grabbing the bag with her present in it. We're unsteady for a while in the grass until we reach the pavement leading to the stairwell.

"You deserve better than that, you know?" Korra says when we get to the first stair landing. She hasn't been as chatty as usual when she's had this many rum and pineapples.

Our eyes meet and the emotion there is clear though the inebriation is too.

"You didn't have to say that to her. I'll be okay."

"I know," she says, not letting me have any room to look away with how her eyes hold me. "But I need her to know she can't hurt you anymore. I'll make sure of it."

I swallow, catching my bottom lip with my teeth. "She's not," I assert. But she holds my gaze. "She won't," I amend.

Korra seems satisfied with that response. It's wobbly, but we make it up the stairs to the balcony that surrounds the third floor. The green Brillo pad floor covering greets us. It catches on her thin heels the whole way to their apartment on the opposite side of the stairwell.

"And what about Palmer? You ever going to let that guy go?"

"For what?" she asks.

My mouth hangs open for a moment before I plainly state, "He's trash. The worst. Why isn't *he* here? This isn't the first time he's let you down."

I know where we're going, but even if I didn't the plethora of planters and hanging pots would be my sign that I made it to their place.

"It's not even a big deal. I'll see him tomorrow."

The door to her apartment is wide open for us when we get there. I need to remind them about safety for women who live alone. Even in small towns.

"I wouldn't count on that," I grumble. "He can't even get the big events that matter right."

"Oof," Kor grunts, flopping onto her modular couch and kicking her shoes off. They hit the front door with a thud only moments after I closed it. "I don't want to talk about Palmer anymore."

I let her drop the subject since it'll do no good at this point anyway. "Were you waiting for me to close that just to kick your shoes off?"

"Nah," she yawns.

"Hey! No sleeping on the couch, at least get to bed."

"Can't. In outside clothes," she mumbles into a Monstera plant pillow.

"Can," I say, hoisting her up. "Give me three steps." She's no help, but I manage to get her into the room.

I look around the space and find the scarf for her hair first. With movements quicker than I could expect, she has her hair into some curly poof on the top of her head.

Crossing my arms, "Okay, ninja. Step one done. Think you can get your jewelry off next?"

"Ha ha," she snarks, swaying slightly but leaning onto the foot board of her bed for support. She yanks at her ears, wrists and finally her neck, dropping the cluster of metal and crystals into my open palm.

"Step two done, too. What are you sleeping in?" I ask, scratching at the side of my nose with my thumb.

I turn around, looking in the room for something like pajamas. There are more plants than anything else in the space. They trail down her dresser, and hang from the ceiling. There are large pots of them in the corners and even more in the bathroom. So much green and varying pops of colors. When I turn back around, Kor has slid down the foot board to the floor like a crumpled little doll.

Setting the gift bag on her nightstand, I ask "What about a t-shirt? That's better than nothing. I can see you fading fast."

"Top drawer," she says pointing from the floor to the cedar dresser across from her bed and us.

I hesitate in opening the top drawer because I mean... What else will be in there besides what you would expect? "Help me out here, Kor. Where in the top drawer?"

I hear her thump to the ground, "I'm potatoes," she murmurs from the floor she's laying prone on now. "Hurry," she rushes.

Gotta get back on task though it is pretty hilarious that she got so lit. I snap a picture and send the photo to her phone before returning to finding pajamas. The drawer is stuffed full with all kinds of clothes. It basically explodes and I start shoving things back inside without paying too much attention to what anything is. Still the red lace catches my attention.

*She's wearing that?*

My hand is moving before my brain is, catching the lace with my index finger.

"What are you doing?" she asks from behind me.

*When the hell did she get up?*

I drop the fabric, caught off guard by her sudden nearness and it falls to the floor. What it is made more clear by how it's landed on the grey carpet at our feet, mine in black socks and hers with bright yellow painted toes.

A red thong with many lace straps that tiny gold charms hang from where the hips would go.

Where her hips would go.

*Damn.*

Laughing, she scoops up the fabric and stuffs it into the drawer. "Are you done gawking, Bryce?" She grabs an oversized shirt and walks over to her bathroom, closing the door behind her.

I don't manage a response. My brain is still stuck picturing my best friend in those red lace panties.

# CHAPTER 3

## Korra

"No need to growl at me, I'm not the one sticking you today."

Bethany Prowder and her tiny terror stand at my desk waiting for me to check them in.

Small growls continue to come from the carrier in front of me. Little Bella already knows what's coming her way.

"Mrs. Prowder, I've got you checked in. Would you like to wait in the lobby or take Bella to the play room?"

"It took me an age to get her in this thing," she sighs, hoisting the strap onto her shoulder. "I'll break a hip tripping on one of those balls in there trying to get her back in. I'll wait here."

"Okay, it'll be just a moment." I page my brother to come grab his next patient and I can practically hear his grumbles from my desk.

For the past two years, my dad has off-loaded Bella's yearly wellness check onto him, saying, "It takes speed I don't have anymore. You're young, spry. You'll be better than me."

Where my dad isn't wrong, I have yet to see Lee come out of the appointment without a bandage—or two.

Bella is fearsome to be so small, only when it comes to needles and her deworming pills.

In his blue scrubs that match mine with the company logo embroidered on the chest, Lee walks to the half-gate calling for the two of them to come back with him. He wears a cap over his curls and I don't have it in me to tell him that it's askew. Annoyance is coming off him in waves that I can tell he's suppressing for the appointment. He looks like someone *trying* to be cool instead of the man who is just in need of a haircut and shave. Bella won't care either way.

Bethany and Bella are through the door when I call quietly after him. "Remember your speed, Lee!"

He rolls his eyes, letting the gate slam behind him.

My phone buzzes on the table with a text and I chance a look at it.

**Bryce: {picture msg}**

A stack of folders and loose papers sits at least two feet high on my friend's pristine desk protector. The single pen, highlighter and pack of flags are in a neat row beside the stack. I know that his extremely organized nature never lets up. Considering every time I've been to his house, the bed is made and not a single dirty dish exists—I'd confirm so.

The man is a picture fanatic. And by that, I mean he is the first to take them and I'm sure he has them just as meticulously organized on his phone by subject and whether or not they can be used for blackmail, I'm sure. I did not appreciate the one he got of me laid out on my floor the other night even if I did look like a sack of potatoes. He got a laugh from me, which hurt my hangover headache. Though I have changed all my profile pictures to the one he took of me with Rupert—that's what I've named the Taryn's Pottery laughing cat pot he got me.

**Bryce: And just when I thought I was wrapping this one up…**

**Me: Does skimming apply here? Ive done it for many contracts and I think it turned out okay *HANDS OUT EMOJI* Juuust sayin**

**Bryce: What?**

Bryce: You're joking right?

Bryce: Tell me you're joking

Me: *ZIPPED LIPS EMOJI* *LAUGHING EMOJI*

Bryce: No laughing! You should be reading all of those. Entirely.

The giggle escapes me before I can stop it. It's hard to not press his buttons. The man is so seriou

s. He needs a little bit of a palpitation every now and again to spice his life up.

Me: Is this your professional legal opinion?

Bryce: All my opinions are legal opinions. *LINE EYES EMOJI*

Bryce: And the professional is implied with legal even if you don't say it.

Me: *EYEROLL EMOJI* Well… in my administrative opinion, you need to take a lunch and a nap. That pile will still be there when you get back.

Bryce: Can't. Sleep is for prosecution.

Me: …

Me: You don't sleep enough regardless.

Bryce: …

Me: This would not hold up in court.

The front door chimes and I'm graced with a sight for sore eyes. Setting my phone back into my drawer, I exclaim, "Oh, look at you!" I hop up from my chair to squeeze my friend. "When did you get back in town?"

Zadie McLane pushes long red curls back behind her shoulders when we release each other. She wears a cream dress with a navy abstract print that contrasts her golden-bronze skin. A gold nose ring glints under the clinic's lighting, "You know," she says as she looks around the front waiting area and then finishes, "Today."

My head tilts to the side examining her more closely. "What are you doing here? I'd love to catch up." I look down at my desk. "I mean... I'm working right now, but I could always quit this job."

She laughs in her deeper tone that always makes me smile in turn. "You think your Dad would just let you quit in the middle of a shift?"

My lips twist to the side and I tap my pen against my cheek when I return to my ergonomic chair. "Probably not. I barely got this job," I joke. I've been working the front desk at Thomas & Friends Veterinary Clinic since I was nineteen.

I love my job and there's honestly never a dull moment up here. It's a dependable and stress-free way to spend my days. Plus, there's cute animals all the time.

"Yea, right," she says. "I'm not here to catch up—though we absolutely need to! I'm applying." Zadie points to the sign on the corner of my desk.

"You're gonna work here?" I pop up from my chair again. "You're hired!" I exclaim, coming around the desk to squeeze her arms. "I'm so excited that you'll be here everyday."

"Who's hired?" Lee says, obviously having taken my speed advice to heart.

Zadie glares behind me. "Considering he hired *you*, I'd say the job is as good as mine. Cleaning up your failures is my strong suit."

Lee unlocks the patient door, where Mrs. Prowder and her shih tzu, with two yellow bows clipped in, trot out. I hadn't seen Bella before now. I know she likely gave Lee hell but, my goodness, is she adorable.

To my brother, Bethany says, "Thank you so much for getting Bella her shots today. You're always so quick and efficient." She picks up the small dog who licks her hand immediately. "I don't think she felt a thing," she adds.

Lee pointedly runs a hand over his new bandage-wrapped finger. He might have wanted to say something snarky in response but he doesn't get the chance.

"He learned from the best," my Dad says, following her out of the patient door, tossing his gloves in the waste receptacle on the other side.

He's wearing a cardigan over his scrubs since he is only doing consultations today and likely won't be getting dirty. I make a note to check where he leaves that sweater. I think it'll go well with the skirt I just got online last night. I've been on a corduroy kick.

*Dads get the best cardigans. It's probably real wool.*

He catches me eyeing his garment, leaning his head towards the counter where Mrs. Prowder is waiting to leave.

Scurrying back behind the desk, I finish processing Mrs. Prowder's visit on my computer. After the deductible and final signature is taken, she leaves for me to get back to the action happening in my lobby.

My Dad makes small talk with another patient while Lee and Zadie stare daggers at each other. It's been too long since I've seen them go head-to-head. If I thought I got under his skin, Zadie wrote the book on it.

"Look what the cat dragged in," he says to her, lifting a curl with his company pen and she snatches it from him.

"You've been here for how many years and that's the best you could do?" She scoffs. "Count your days, *Bent.*"

"Lee," he corrects her. "We're hiring additional staff, not replacements. Don't get cocky."

"Is that another animal pun, *Broken?*" She rolls her eyes. "Pathetic. Are you coming from a throwback concert or something? Why is your hat tilted to the side like that?"

Well, I figured that hat was doing a bit much. It was an open target for my girl. A big sister loves nothing more than a good roast of her annoying little brother. *Gonna have to tell Kase when I get home.* I grab my can of mixed nuts from my crowded desk drawer to watch the action with a snack. They aren't going to let up anytime soon. Dad is none the wiser as he makes his rounds in the waiting room.

He adjusts the hat that became more askew after wrestling with Bella. "Lee," he corrects her again through clenched teeth. "The clients love it. I could teach you a thing or two about how to put your patients at ease. You need some work."

Zadie is about to reply, but my Dad comes back to the desk. "Are you ready?"

She adjusts the sleeves of her dress over her wrists and nods once. "Of course, sir," she says, patting her bag. "I brought my references and accreditations. I've been looking forward to this day."

*Sir*, Lee mouths toward me but I shrug, still enjoying my show.

"Please, call me Wayne. You practically grew up in my house." My Dad smiles, waving her formalities away. "I've looked over all of those. Let's talk in my office."

She follows behind my Dad, turning over her shoulder to wave at me but pointedly glaring at Lee.

"What is wrong with you?" I ask him when they leave.

His brown eyes grow large. "Me? Did you hear what she said to me?"

"You will not scare my friend off with your petty feud, Bentley Thomas."

He looks insulted, backing away from me with a hand on his chest. "You're choosing her over your own brother?"

I laugh at his ridiculousness. "Oh, hush. Take Mr. Sullivan and Haversham back for their appointment," I say, pointing over to the balding man and his turquoise cat carrier with my fake rose taped onto my pen.

He does what I asked and leaves with the next patient.

My phone buzzes in my drawer again, but it's not Bryce.

**Palmer: Lunch today?**

I don't reply as I attempt to calm my irritation. With his promise to do something Saturday night completely out of the window, I haven't seen him in a week. He was *too tired* after work to go anywhere and I have family dinner on Sundays. It's not like he had any real plans. I chose to ignore the calls yesterday and I'm going to be ignoring this text, too.

**Palmer: Come on. I'll bring it to you. *SUSHI EMOJI* You love sushi.**

Rolling my eyes, I put my phone away and get back to work.

What's more embarrassing than your boyfriend forgetting the literal single day that is supposed to be about you?

*Him not doing anything to actually make it any better.*

I don't ask for much. I have to share the day with my sister, which I actually love, but to compromise on this is not the issue I want to have with a partner.

Dating might just be a throwaway idea at this point.

I want too much and that's my fault.

High maintenance is not something I would describe myself as, but I have to draw a line somewhere. I want more from a relationship and my track record has shown me that it's too much to expect.

I want too much.

"Korra will show you where to get everything and they're pretty quick."

"I will?" I ask my Dad who is leaning over my desk with Zadie opening her bag to get her credit card out. "What am I showing her?"

"Zadie is joining the team. What do you think about that?" He asks.

"Time to celebrate!" I squeeze her hand. "We have navy blue or navy blue for you to choose from on the scrubs." I take the catalogue out anyway and turn to the page that has been flagged for our orders. "Size chart is in there."

She takes the catalogue and picks a size for me to order.

When I finish getting the order submitted, I turn to her, "Looks like it's time for my lunch. Wanna come with?"

Zadie smirks, "Well, I've got the day open now that I've got this in the bag." It'll be so nice to have her at the office all the time. She's been traveling so much that it's been years since she was even a resident of Harmony Hill. We really do have so much to catch up on.

The half gate opens, drawing our attention. "What do you have in the bag?" Lee asks, having finished Haversham's exams.

Mr. Sullivan comes over to the counter to be checked out.

"The lead tech position. It's mine," she grins. It's smug and instantly sets Lee off.

"Can I talk to you, Dad?" Lee sneers and Dad ignores him.

"Take your lunch, Korra. I'll stay up front."

He doesn't have to tell me twice. I grab my purse and phone while walking around to meet Zadie on the other side of my desk. "Want anything?"

My brother begins but Dad talks over him, "Whatever you bring back is fine."

# CHAPTER 4

## Bryce

"You would think that he'd figure out that running is not an option, right?"

It's me and Korra on her couch, tangled in a soft blanket, watching one of those two-thousand's action movies she repeatedly mocks but secretly loves. She's laughing with her mouth open and head tilted back.

God, that smile could kill a man.

Then... things shift.

The couch becomes softer, wider. A bed, maybe? But I don't question it. She's still there next to me. Closer than usual. Her leg brushes mine and doesn't move away. My hand is under the blanket, fingertips grazing warm skin.

Then, Korra's on my lap.

*Not by accident.*

I don't remember how we got here, but I know I don't want her to move from her spot.

She was wearing an oversized brown sweater, sleeves falling past her hands—but beneath it, red lace peeks out where the hem rises up over her thighs.

My breath catches in my throat. Korra doesn't wear things like this.

Not around me.

Not ever.

She's never this *exposed*. Why would she be?

Now, she shifts in my lap intentionally and that tiny movement sends a current up my spine like lightning searching for ground.

"Bryce," she says softly, voice heavier than simple teasing. She knows exactly what she's doing. "You're staring."

I should've looked away. I don't as more and more of the lace gets exposed on her hips.

"I didn't know you owned…" I gestured vaguely, voice cracking like a teenager. The word sticks. I clear my throat and try again. "That."

She grins, slow and alluring. "You never asked…" Then she moves closer, moving on my lap like it is the most natural thing in the world. "Is it a problem?" Her thighs bracketing me, that sweater hiked high enough that the lace shimmers in the low light. My heart's hammering. My hands tighten at her hips, anchoring me to something solid, something that makes sense… But nothing about this makes sense.

It's both familiar and new. The warmth of her on my lap, the smell of her hair, the tease of her giggle is all too much.

"Korra…" I whisper, a warning or a prayer, I can't be sure.

Her fingers trail down my nape light enough to make my heart stumble. "You think about this," she murmurs, her full lips a breath away from mine. "Don't lie."

My voice is gone.

All I can do is nod, and that feels like a confession.

"I think about you," she says. "Like this. More than I should."

I feel every word sinking under my skin, curling around something deep inside me. Her thighs tighten around mine and when she kisses me soft, then deeper, my chest cracks open.

Her lips brush my ear. "You're not just my best friend anymore, Bryce."

I believe her with everything I have, meeting her kiss with enthusiasm.

And then, just as my hands slide beneath the sweater, finding the smooth dip of her lower back where the top of the panties meet that sweet curve of her ass—

I wake up alone. Sheets twisted in a haphazard mess around me. Breath puffing out of me in ragged pants. Boxers stuck to my body from how turned on I was.

Shaking my head, I hop out of bed and splash water on my face in the bathroom before ultimately deciding to take a cold shower instead.

Good sleep often evades me, but this is the first time I'm waking up restless because of a wet dream. What am I? Twelve? And about Korra? Not ever.

That's not us.

We've always been friends. She's my lifeline to humanity if I'm being honest with myself. Without her, I'd forget that I was a person behind my career aspirations. Being able to talk to her and visit her and the Thomases is how I stay sane most weeks.

We've always been that for each other.

But in that dream... I don't know. Something felt too real about it and it's messing with my head.

I stare at my reflection for a minute, grateful my under eyes aren't too puffy from exhaustion. My mind may be haggard but I can't look like it at the office.

My dick still throbs and the worst part is I couldn't stop seeing the red lace when I closed my eyes.

It's not until after I get through the traffic and sit at my desk that I'm able to stop thinking about Korra's ass in my hands or the feel of her snug over me.

If there is anything that could deflate a stiffy, it's the pile of documents I'm currently staring at on my desk.

That and the fact that Korra is still the same.

Nothing has changed between us.

So when I text her, my brain begins to right itself and the dream I had fades into a distant point in the back of my mind.

Bryce: I plead the fifth

She doesn't respond to me right away, but it probably got busy at the clinic. I put my phone down and decide to actually get back to working. If I plan to make any headway on this case, I've got a lot of reading to do.

I've been at Warren, Keesley & Mozier for three years now. It's not by luck that I ended up in this office or that I've been getting the kind of work I only dreamed of back when I was just a scholarship kid.

*So why is it that I feel so unfulfilled?* I've come so far already. By all accounts, I'm doing well in life. Missing a few things but I'm still young. Those other *things* will come.

Seeing Jillian the other night was a kick to the gut I didn't need.

I shake my head, thinking about what Korra said to her. She usually doesn't have a mean bone in her body. Especially compared to any of the other Thomas siblings. I think she takes after Zach in that way. He's the nicest guy I've ever met and I'd say she's pretty close behind him in that department.

I've never been... nice. Not in the way that would make people think of me when they're thinking of "nice guys".

I'm more objective and less on one side or the other.

Something about her doing that just hits me differently. I sat in my bed staring at the ceiling for far too long thinking about that interaction last weekend.

And then thinking about the glaring red fabric that never actually left my mind or thoughts.

Hence that dream last night.

*God, it had been too long since I had slept with anyone.* That's all it is. Just hitting a bit of a dry spell since things ended badly with Jillian. I'd been foolish to let her think we could still hook up from time to time after but I had to let it go. For my own sanity. She was a poison, it didn't take much for her to get into your system but once she did, you were in too deep.

I couldn't think about Korra that way. My mind is just playing tricks on me.

Phil Mozier walks into my office looking at the stack of documents on my desk. His suit is pressed, his tie tied neatly in place. The hair that once was mostly black with a few grays peppered throughout is leaning more gray these days, especially with how short it's cut. He must be going to court today.

"Is this for the Forell case?" He asks.

Focusing on getting ahead is where my mind should be. The Forell case was supposed to be cut and dry, simple litigation, but it will be more than that by the look of this stack.

If I want to make senior partner at this firm, I've got to put in extra time and effort. I'm not the only one who is aiming for the position or recognition.

My mentor, the man standing in front of me, is as close to having it all as I've ever seen. He has a beautiful family and is a named partner here. It's no wonder that he lives and breathes this firm.

"Yes, sir," I say, opening the first folder with records I chose to start with. "I'll get through them before Wednesday with my notes for you to review." I'll be able to if I stay late the next couple of days and take a few of these folders home. It's a good thing I don't have anyone waiting for me.

When you're working the kind of hours I do now, there is no time for *it all*. Having it all is just a myth.

You can't have a relationship. Not one that wasn't already in the making before. It's a wash from the beginning otherwise. You can only make due with a couple of dinners a week—and I really do mean two. Possibly some time fucking but at the level of energy I currently have, I'd take the nap Korra suggested instead of making conversation and getting to know someone new.

You can't have a family when you're hardly there. You're not any sort of partner or father to your kids. Not from what I've seen. I wouldn't want to be a negligent parent. The idea disgusts me. I've got time to figure out the whole kids thing.

I'm barely hanging on to the friendships I have. Korra only lasted because she's ever optimistic and probably too forgiving when I can't be there. I show up for the things that matter and know I'm there for her when it counts. It's what she deserves.

At best you can aim for two out of the three. Family, career or friends. One is bound to get lost in the pursuit of any of them. The closest I've seen to having it all is Phil.

And still, I know Phil has no life outside of his family and career. But his third is philanthropic in nature, rather than friendship. He deserves a sainthood for how much he gives back. I admire the man for many reasons, but his generosity is probably the thing that I respect the most. He never let this job turn him into someone he is not. A feat that most couldn't say they have conquered.

The other senior partners at the firm rely on his hard work or, mostly, the work of associate lawyers like me to carry the load while they get to gallivant to golf on the weekdays and trips every quarter to destinations I've only dreamed of.

I could afford to take those trips, but I could not afford to miss this time.

Phil went to my Ivy League school. Like me, Phil was a scholarship kid too—not a legacy of some powerful family. He went off the strength of his own mind and dedication to succeeding. It's because of him that I never lost hope. He gives back to the school by providing aid to students who show promise. I gained his favor because he saw a lot of himself in me. To me, that was the highest compliment that I could have received.

He's everything I wanted to be in life.

A successful Black lawyer who uplifted other young Black men who want to make it in this field.

If my dad were still around, I know he'd be proud. I didn't follow in his footsteps to be a cop, but I still work with the law and uphold it in every way I know how.

Corporate litigation is important. It keeps people safe and businesses within their rights. Mergers and safety concerns affect not only the CEOs and millionaires who own them but all the people who work underneath them too. It's seeing that bigger picture and keeping those ideals in mind that give me a unique view when it comes to helping my clients.

"Good, good," he says, absently looking around my desk. I don't have much on it besides the laptop that lives by my side and other supplies to do my job. The only exception are two picture frames.

One is of my mom, Korra and I at my graduation from college. Green leather law degree in hand. It was one of the happiest days of my life.

The other photo is a souvenir photo from a Water World rollercoaster years ago. The Thomases all went together for Lee's twentieth birthday. The whole cart was just their family and me. Korra and I are in the middle row with the wind blowing our faces back but the smiles are unmistakable. I'm pretty sure we all ended up with our heads in a toilet as the combination of chili dogs and slushes don't mix well with rollercoaster rides. But, I'm choosing to suppress that part and just reminisce on the fun.

"Did you need something from me before court today?" I ask. I don't want to rush him out of my office, but I do have a lot to do if I expect to meet that Wednesday deadline I gave him.

Phil rubs his chin, "You're a good kid," he says. I don't take offense since I am younger than his own children. "I brought you on because I admire your work ethic and you continue to surprise me. It's not my bias making me tell you this, so don't take it that way."

I nod my head. "I understand, sir. Thank you."

He straightens the photo of my mom, Korra and I so that it faces him more than me. "I'm getting old, you know? I'm ready to settle and retire." He meets my eyes with an intensity. "You see what I'm saying?"

My brows pinch. "I'm not sure I do, sir."

He doesn't qualify my statement with an answer, instead saying, "I want to know that you're not making the same mistakes I have in this field." I want to argue immediately but allow him to finish his thought. "There's a spot opening and I know you want it. But you're not the only one. Ultimately, it will be all the partners' decision on who will get it. And they'll be looking for someone who leads a well rounded life. Someone who shares the values they do."

*Well-rounded life? Values?*

"What does that mean?"

He points to the photo he was arranging. "Someone who can show commitment. Not just to Warren, Keesley & Mozier but understands what we stand for. Not a young buck who wants to show he has the biggest horns."

"I am committed. I—"

"Son, I know that. You don't have to convince me." He shakes his head, returning the picture frame and straightening his already centered tie. "You're the only single man on this floor. When we have company dinners, you show up alone. Listen, no one wants to invite the bachelor to a trip their wives and daughters are on. Especially when they look like you."

"I'm flattered, sir."

"You shouldn't be. Do you see what I'm saying?" He snaps a few times. "Well you used to bring the pale one, what was her name?"

Something feels wrong about Phil saying Jillian's name so I interject his pondering. "We're not together anymore, sir."

"I know it's not fair, but they take those things into account. Jackson just got engaged to his long time girl. You know how many pats on the back he received? I don't want you to lose the legacy I've set in place for you. But they will look at him as a stronger candidate for senior partner. They can take him on trips with their family and he'll have her to schmooze the women. The work is just one part of it. They want someone who will be able to come into the fold. You see what I'm saying?"

I try not to splutter over him saying he set a legacy in place for me. To step into his shoes would be a dream come true. "I do."

"It will be harder for you if you can't show them that you're serious. To Kyle and David especially, it will mean a family." Kyle Warren and David Keesley are the gallivanting partners who make becoming senior partner at a firm like this seem easy. All while picking someone like Jackson who is nowhere near as good an attorney as I am. No offense to Jackson, but it should take more than a fiancé to get that promotion. Mozier and I both know it.

"How am I supposed to come up with a family? It's not like I can just make a wife and kids appear out of thin air."

"Maybe not, but it's not too late to start giving the thought some merit." He taps my desk and leaves.

A family?

*Impossible.*

Where would I find a family anyway?

# CHAPTER 5

## Korra

"So what are you going to do about Palmer?" My sister asks from the living room.

Filling the sink with water, I pour a few drops of plant soap into my hand and under the faucet. Bubbles cover the surface as the water rises. Turning the faucet off, I swish the water around some more before getting my String of Rubies, aptly named Ruby, from her place in the living room. The hemp macramé design holding her pot should be fine to go for a swim as well.

People believe that just because succulents don't need to be watered often, that you should never water them.

The same could be said for many people. they often need more care than people acknowledge, silently withering away until their circumstances become dire.

*Myself included.*

It's absolutely untrue. This red lady loves her baths. The plant soap I'm using will keep her free of pests and dust as well as making her plump red leaves healthy. I don't believe she'll do any more flowering this year.

I use a soft cloth to clear some dust from Ruby's leaves as I inform my sister, "There is nothing to do. We had dinner last night and we're good."

My sister's eyes bulge out of her head from where she lounges on our couch. Today she has it organized in an L formation to better read on. Well, she was reading until she decided that she was going to interrogate me about my love life.

"You're good?" she questions in a flat tone that does not hide her astonishment.

"Yes, he apologized." I didn't want to keep dodging his calls. It was unlike me and I like phone calls. I don't understand why people are adverse to them. You can hear the other person's emotions in their voice which is completely different from a text. You have to rely on emojis and honestly, they do not communicate the full range of expression. Second best would be a voice memo.

I like those too.

But Palmer really did appear to be sorry to have missed my birthday. He'd gotten me a gift card to Planet Plant which I already spent the total of on mini succulents for my desk. After Dad banned me from any more flowering plants inside the building, I'd settled for fake ones to decorate the lobby. They're alright, I suppose. But who's allergic to succulents? I'll have ten of them arriving next week. I cannot wait to decorate their pots. Maybe I'll name them after some of our favorite furry patients.

That gives me an awesome idea for a contest of some sort for our regulars. I'll add it to the newsletter and—

"I really don't want to keep repeating what you're saying so here's where you tell me how you're still dating this man."

I grab my Burro's Tail, Malcolm, next and give it the same treatment as Ruby since it's been a while since I've given him a bath. This one I rescued from my Mom's studio. When Malcolm blooms, it makes the whole living room reflect the orange petals from the window his hook is next to. I think he might be done blooming this year too. Since I keep him inside, I'll still keep an eye on his soil moisture. I've started stretching the time between his baths as it is.

"Palmer is a good guy, Kase. Why would I not be dating him?"

"You weren't that drunk to forget that he was not at your only birthday of the year, right?"

"That was just one day. People make mistakes. Forget stuff, you know? He feels really bad about it." Her eyes roll until the whites show in a grand exaggeration of how displeased she is. "My goodness, would you stop? You know I hate when you do that."

"But you don't hate when your boyfriend forgets about you." She taps her e-reader harshly to go to the next page. No way she's reading while getting on my nerves right now, but she continues this farce. "I think your priorities are completely out of whack."

"My priorities are just fine. Thank you." With a bounce in my step, I ignore my sister's droll pestering and head for my room while my succulents drink up in the kitchen.

It's Saturday, my free day to take care of all my plants indoors. My planters outside of our flat get their loving on Sundays.

Like with any hobby, it takes time to find what parts of it you love. My Mom taught all of us that. I have loved flowers and plants since I was a little girl. She would ask me to help her in the garden outside our home on the weekends. It was my favorite thing to look forward to after being stuck in a class room all week. Kasey hated being outside, especially in the spring and summer. She preferred to stay inside with a book or read to our little sister Nia under the tree in the yard until Nia found her own things to do.

Mom used to call me on the weekends and we'd talk while she was tending our garden back home and I'd be tending mine here. It's days like today where I wish I could call her instead of having Kasey in my ear.

*I wonder what she would think about all this.*

She had such a light. Everyone would greet her wherever we went and she participated in all the community events. She loved a good hobby and of all her kids, I'm probably the only one who took after her in that department.

I miss her, but her love lives on through me. *In all of us.* I'd like to think it's through me the most since she was one of my best friends. We spent the most time together. I knew her better than any of my brothers or sisters.

My watering pot with blue and gold foil roses sends light in every direction when I set it beside me. I look into the reflection of my dresser mirror, trying to find the features that I shared with my Mom.

Kasey and I both have her thick curly hair and almond shaped eyes. Mine are just a little smaller and more upturned than hers. I let the shorter curls at the front hang like bangs over my eyebrows with the bulk of it clipped high on my head and out of the way.

My nose is definitely Mom's, it's smaller shape and defined nostrils are a dead give away. But the feature I love the most are my lips. Large by any standard and something that took time to love. My mom always said a bigger mouth is a gift you can share. "A bigger smile," she'd say, tapping my nose which made me giggle.

The memory makes me smile even now. In my reflection, I see the woman she was and the woman I am because of her.

She sought joy and was content in making her own if she couldn't find it.

I'd like to think I'm the same.

In a tiled planter, my Maranta, Maggie, sits beautifully on my dresser. I rub her rounded green striped leaves before giving her some water. She's been loving her new spot at the front where she can get some indirect sunlight in the autumn months. Maggie was a housewarming gift from Mom and she has lived in my room since the beginning.

As I inspect Maggie's leaves for pests, I think back to Kasey's words. I didn't care that Palmer missed my birthday, when it came down to it. I *meant that*. People make mistakes. I won't hold that against him. But the first birthday without my Mom is where everything really soaked in. My emotions were high and I behaved in ways I normally wouldn't. As someone who does not drink often, the plethora of rum did not benefit my behavior that night.

My Brazilian Snow plant, Andy, tries his best to out shine Maggie, but I've kept them far enough apart separated by my jewelry box. With his striped leaves less striated than hers, it's easy to see why he might be jealous.

It's an emotion I know all too well. Those things I said to Jillian were all because of a deep jealousy I've had towards her. One that I normally never voice... But how dare she bring Terry out and be happy? The green monster took over and while I have no regrets in what I said to her, I do regret that I did it so publicly. Especially when Bryce asked me to keep what happened between them a secret. That meant I couldn't go off on her whether she deserved it or not! But seriously, I wanted to trip her down when I saw how her presence was affecting him even months later. With a sigh, I give Andy some water and move to the next plant with my watering pot.

Sitting directly by my window, is a small foot stool I got from the flea market a few years back. My Calamondin orange tree is thriving with its white flowers all stretching toward the light filtering through the window. It's fragrant with sweet citrus notes. I press my nose into the blooming flowers. I'll get some fruit next year. I'm sure of it.

Moving into the bathroom, I open the curtain a little wider on the window above my bathtub. The Ellen Danica plant that crawls down over my bathroom organizer drawers will thank me for that later. I love how Cissus aren't fussy and this little lady has gotten so big. Her vines sprawling over the front of the door, nearly hiding the whole furniture piece. I give her a little water and add some to the Eucalyptus hanging over my sink as well.

My Ivies are last for now and they're hanging all over the house. I water them more often so they aren't in dire need of my love, but I like finishing off the day with them.

I've got to get Ruby and Malcolm out of the sink before they get upset with me. Leaving my room with an empty watering can, I'm met with more commentary from my sister.

"You know you baby that man just as much as you baby all these plants? It's a thing you do."

"Who?"

"Palmer." *Right.*

I dust my hands off on my linen jumpsuit while I wait on the water to drain from the sink. "I do not baby him."

"It's a fact, Korra. You baby him and that is why he thought it'd be okay to skip out the other night."

Setting my watering can down on the kitchen counter, I inhale and exhale before responding. Kasey is testing my patience. "He didn't *skip out*. He forgot."

"What is the difference? Is that any better? This is supposed to be your life partner and he can't remember one date?"

My brows furrow in frustration and confusion. "Life partner? What are you talking about?"

A sound of exasperation comes from my sister. "Why are you dating him if you don't see yourself spending your life with him?"

"I—" My response never comes. I don't know what to say. *I don't see myself spending my life with Palmer.* There are few people who I ever had. One of which, I can't have. And though I'm very close to the age I wanted to start a family at, I can't lie and say that I pictured starting a family with Palmer Richardson.

I chose to focus on drying Ruby's pot and getting her hung on her hook in the living room again.

"Exactly," Kasey declares. "I bet Bryce would agree with me."

"What does that have to do with anything?" I question when she begins swiping around on her phone. I get Malcolm hung up by the window so he can soak up some of this fall sunshine.

"I'm already calling him," she announces, lying back on the couch with her phone.

"Great," I mutter sarcastically, finally filling my watering can now that the sink is empty of plants for the time being. I'm sure I won't win a discussion about Palmer with the president and vice-president of the Palmer haters club. I'm lucky Malaya isn't here. I'm already outnumbered.

Grunts come from the phone as soon as it connects. Kasey leans up from the couch to look at me but I widen my eyes at her. "Bryce... What are you doing?" She asks with wide eyes of her own.

"Well, it's noon on a Saturday, so I'm working out." More heated grunts come from the phone. It's borderline obscene, but I'm used to it.

I'll admit that in my mother's absence, I have taken to calling friends when I'm feeling a little bit lonely while doing my plant maintenance. That friend is often Bryce, even when it's just me humming to music and the background noise of the gym as he goes through his reps. My sister is *usually* not out of her room interrogating me and doing a grand inquisition of my life. She's *usually* locked up, writing. But I guess since she's in between stories right now—she's got plenty of time to focus on my life.

*Great.*

"Could've told you that," I tell her, making my way to the first Ivy in our living room.

Kasey rolls her eyes at me. "Well, we won't hold you. I just had a bit of an inquiry, if you will…"

The clanking of weights dropping into place rattles onto the line. Then Bryce says, "I'm listening…"

Kasey carries on with a tone that mimics one that you might hear in a courtroom. I know she's putting it on to appeal to Bryce's professional opinion. At this point, I'm not looking for any more opinions from anyone. And I definitely don't need hers to appeal to him anymore than I already suspect it will. "Would you say that Korra is a babier?"

There's a pause where my friend is likely trying to figure out what the hell Kasey is talking about. "Come again?"

"Korra is a babier. She coddles everything she cares about. Specifically her plants, but in this instance, we're talking about Palmer."

A rich guffaw comes from my best friend as he registers exactly what Kasey is spelling out for him. *I don't like it.* I know that they're not laughing at me. This whole predicament comes from a place of concern. I can't help but wonder why it is that both of them can get on the same page about Palmer so quickly when they cannot agree on literally anything else.

"When you put it like that— absolutely. You'd think Palmer was some rare plant species that she had to have imported from another country and it's the last one of this lifetime. And she's the only one tasked with its survival." He chuckles, the stubble of his weekend beard growth rubbing against the phone. "If we're going with that metaphor, I would say that he is more like a dandelion weed."

"Okay, that's not funny!" I interject when Kasey is equally amused. "It's kind of mean. He's not a weed."

"He is," they both say in unison.

"I'll have you know that the world greatly benefits from dandelions. Pollinators rely on them in this country and several bird species use them for warmth in their nests." I cross my arms over my chest. "They're also delicious with many health benefits."

Then Kasey says, "That's all I need today, counselor, but if you have any further evidence to present to the court, I'll be more than happy to hear it," in her typical monotone.

"Any evidence I can present against the defendant will be arriving at your desk shortly."

"Both of you—stop sounding so smug." Turning to my sister, I point the watering can I just picked up at her. "You are no judge and this is not a court case, okay?"

She scratches her chin, fully upright now. "But isn't it? If anyone is gonna be able to get through to you and help you choose the better decision for your life then it's us two. We know you better than everyone else in this world."

I narrow my eyes at the Ivy by our front door, inspecting the leaves that occasionally get closed in the jamb. "I'm not breaking up with my boyfriend."

"No one said that..." Her shoulders rise with her hands in a placating gesture. Then her head tilts to one side, "You could stand to take a break, just to see if your life is any different with or without this baby."

"Stop calling him a baby! I do not coddle him. I feel like you two are making rash decisions that are extreme. People deserve grace."

Bryce scoffs. "Did you not hear the evidence that was presented just now?"

"Get back to your workout," I say, pressing the *end* button on my way to water the last ivy in Kasey's room.

"You gonna call Palmer then? Maybe you should stay the night there."

I bite my lip. I don't want to tell my sister the truth with her already on my ass. I huff out a breath before admitting, "No, I'm not. He's working again. I may stay over on Wednesday."

"Wednesday?" Her jaw hangs and I can't even be mad now. "What the hell happened to Sunday? The dentist office is not open tomorrow. How is he busy then?"

"He said he was really tired. He just wants to chill at the house."

"Without you?"

My shoulders rise and I readjust the clip in my hair. "Yea... I can be a lot, you know?"

"Tell me you're joking, Korra." She studies me and then throws her phone to the couch. "You have to be joking! Come on, I'm trying my best to understand."

"We have to respect people's boundaries. And if he wants some time to relax, then who am I to demand otherwise?"

"Korra," she stretches the sound of my name out to two exaggerated syllables that grate against my nerves. I wince at the whine in her tone. She's not done though. "Could you at least try not to prove me right? Between the two of us, I have to consider myself the expert."

"Writing about people having all the sex you aren't having does not make you the expert here," I snap.

Undeterred, she responds, "Considering I have created far more happily-ever-afters than you have, it absolutely does. Listen to the experts." She places her hands on my shoulders and walks me over to the far end of the couch. Removing the watering can from my hand and setting it on our coffee table next to her large iced coffee in its bright orange Thunderbolts thermos.

"Okay, expert." I say with as much sarcasm as I can muster. "You made your point earlier. You don't like Palmer."

"Yes, I need you to know that with certainty. *He is the worst.* But I have a more serious question to ask you. Questions, really."

"Kasey, I really don't—"

"What is it that you like about this man?" She holds a finger up to my mouth. "I don't want to know. It will likely piss me off." I take a snap at her finger, but she moves it before I can bite down.

"This has to be something you answer for yourself. If he doesn't spend time with you and finds that being with you isn't something he's desperate to do, what is the point in being in a relationship? Cross out the life partner thing I said before. Shouldn't you be excited to see your girlfriend? Shouldn't you *make* time to chill with her? And more interestingly, why is the answer he has to these questions the wrong one?"

"It's not like that. We're just having fun." The excuse rings frail and flimsy to my own ears but Kasey is on a mission.

"Are you? Having fun?"

We both know the answer, but she stops pressing me. Flopping back onto the couch, she's reading again.

I go back to tending to my plants but the questions loop through my mind on repeat.

# CHAPTER 6

## Bryce

*Was I being too harsh with Korra today?*

The thought nags at me for the entire drive back to my place. Even on a Saturday, the traffic is thick and I have no choice but to sit with my words.

When I finally park and get out of the car, I can't help but stop to notice whats around me. Wind rustles in a low rattle that fills the air with peace that is unique only to this time of year. First one leaf falls before several more join the first, floating through the air before finding a place on the ground among others who have met the same autumnal fate. A squirrels scurries among them to find buried treasures to take back to its tree.

When people say that autumn is the season of change I know they have to be on to something. It does feel like something is in the very air I'm breathing that makes me want more.

I wish that Korra understood that she deserves more than what that guy has given her. They have been together for several months and fuck that — he is a goddamn baby. What man in his right mind forgets something as universally important as their girlfriend's birthday?

From memory, he's forgotten that she's allergic to peaches and cashews, more than once. *She had to go to urgent care.* All because he couldn't remember simple facts about her.

There are many others I haven't listed.

Having met Palmer after the passing of her mother, you would think the guy would have more empathy for how she's coping without hers. Delanna Thomas was a pillar of Harmony Hill but also the heart of the family.

He insisted on introducing her to his own mother after only dating for a couple of weeks. From what I heard of the meeting, his mother is as clueless as he is.

Understandably, you can't expect everyone to cry a river of your own loss but is it not insensitive to rub what you have in the face of someone who is forced to go without?

'Til this day, I don't know how Korra is making it look so easy.

I lost my dad when we were teens. Korra was by my side, gave me something to care about when I couldn't be pressed to care about anything anymore. I'd be by her side at the Thomas house helping her weed their garden or just watching movies. Some days I'd be in a better mood but most days, I was just a shell of myself. That was after meeting a few weeks prior, not years long friendship.

She showed up anyway. Let me be there in silence or encourage conversation when I was a little less sad.

Her heart, it's something else.

This man doesn't deserve the consideration she's giving to him when he gives nothing to earn it.

I empty my gym bag into the washer upon entering my apartment and immediately go to my fridge for a protein shake. There are a few I've collected to choose from, but I decide on the premade one and chug it back as quickly as I can before hopping in the shower. Working out became a part of my routine in college since I spent so much time hunched over my books. My mental stregth was improving while my physical one was declining. I made the decision to take care of my body as best as I could and I'm grateful it stuck since I'm able to maintain the body that I have now. Even if I'm not sharing it with anyone else as of late.

With a towel around my waist, I grab some shorts from my closet to lounge in and check my phone.

**Bryce: I'm sorry about earlier. Dinner on me?**

A text is a cop out. *I know it.* But when it comes to this guy in particular, I won't be able to stop from ranting. Calling her is not an option right now.

Her response is quick. Should have known that she wouldn't hold any animosity towards me.

**Korra: {picture msg}**

She sent me a picture of some sort of red sauce bubbling away on her stove.

**Korra: Spaghetti's on. Want some?**

**Korra: It'll be better than your cardboard *LAUGHING WITH TEARY EYES EMOJI***

As she's sent that, my doorbell rings. I open the door to the extra large temperature controlled box. Hefting it over my shoulder I deposit it onto my countertop. It's this week's meals from a private chef company I've been trying out. These companies are popping up more and more frequently in Denver. Single portion meals with all kinds of dietary preferences to choose from.

My high protein, low carb meals are planned out for every course, so I don't have to worry about taking the time to make them myself. I open one, and though this company is more flavorful than the others I've subscribed to in the past, they are as Korra put it — cardboard.

I put them away in their designated spot in my fridge and start one in the microwave.

When it's finished, I send a picture back to Korra.

**Bryce: {picture msg}**

**Bryce: It's about muscle tone. I'm eating for nutrients and that's it.**

I could eat at the small table I got for the dining area, but I opt to stand over my countertop instead. It's not as if I will be savoring every bite. I stab the chunk of beef and swirl it into the mashed parsnips, taking a bite and looking around my space. Outside of a few pieces I've collected over the years, it's too bare in here.

*Cold.*

Not talking about the temperature either. In comparison to the twin's flat, I might as well be living in a model home. There's all the furniture and decorations but there's no life. Anyone would think it's for viewing only.

I'll admit that I spend more time at the firm or at the home office down the hall, but the absence of life here crawls up my spine like goosebumps before I can finish my dinner.

**Korra: {picture msg}**

**Korra: You could be having spaghetti bolognese with fresh garlic knots. There might even be protein pasta *SHOCKED FACE EMOJI* You're not the only one with GAINZ *FLEXED ARM EMOJI***

**Bryce: Damn. Express me some *SAD EYES EMOJI***

**Korra: Get it yourself *HELPFUL LADY EMOJI***

**Korra: Just kidding. I put a bowl in the fridge for you. But you still have to come get it.**

**Korra: I'm just a girl and Denver traffic is the worst.**

As tempting as eating what she's made is, I still have a stack of depositions to get through. I make time to see her at least twice a month for my sanity, but also because I know I'll miss that time without her. Though we talk everyday, I don't think that would suffice seeing her in real life. Wrapping up the Fornell case was a weight off my shoulders. That doesn't mean my work is done. No free time is forthcoming. I've taken on a merger that might make my head spin if I don't get on top of it.

Speaking of my head spinning, the not so formal heads-up that I got from Mozier about there being an opening with him wanting to retire is floating around my mind too.

*That was as much of a vote from him as I could get, right?* If I didn't know any better, I'd say that he was definitely gunning for me to take his place. *I'm not aiming for something completely unattainable anymore.* After all, this is what I've been working toward since I applied for his scholarship and, hell, the law school in general.

Becoming a senior partner is my dream come true.

I don't have the well-rounded life he described. It's the one thing I haven't considered in this uphill battle that gets longer and more rigorous as I fight for it.

There is no wife and not one kid. Something I was... not proud of—that's not the thought—but I was sure that it was the better choice in fairness to those non-existent wife and kids.

> **Bryce: Want to but can't *SLANT MOUTH EMOJI* Gotta catch up on work**

Three dots appear in her response and then go away and appear again.

> **Korra: You're always working. You do know the weekend is supposed to be for relaxing right?**

> **Bryce: If you love what you do, you'll never work a day in your life *SMILING EMOJI***

> **Korra: At what point do you think I'll fall for that line?**

> **Bryce: ...**

> **Bryce: This point? *SMILING EMOJI***

> **Korra: WRONG!**

**Korra: Promise me, you'll take tomorrow off**

**Bryce: ...**

**Korra: I'm looking for a yes here, counselor**

I chuckle at her persistence. She might be watching too many TV legal dramas. I'm gonna have to figure out if her and Kasey are binging one right now. The counselor title is new but not at all unwelcome. I like having some respect on my name.

Though Attorney Bryce Hampton always sounds good.

**Bryce: What am I supposed to do with my time then?**

**Korra: Botanical Gardens? They've got a fall extravaganza *PUMPKIN EMOJI***

**Bryce: Should have known it'd be plant related**

**Korra: *HEARTS WITH SMILE EMOJI***

**Korra: There will be obligatory pumpkin spice lattes...**

Laughing, I reply to her less than enticing message. I'm positive that she doesn't even drink them.

**Bryce: Well why didn't you lead with that? I am a fan of these high calorie sugar bombs. Count me in *LINE EYES EMOJI***

**Korra: I knew that'd be the one**

**Bryce: You're cute when you think you've won**

She and I both know that I'll cave now. There is a little lingering guilt I have for siding with her sister earlier, even if it is for her own good.

I'll never be on Palmer's side, but I'll always be on Korra's. As her friend, I should be on the side of what makes her happy. *I just find it hard to believe that this guy does.*

If I get started working tonight, I should be fine for the next week. I can always stay at the office a little longer if need be...

My phone vibrates in my hand while I contemplate my schedule.

**Korra: Come scoop me at one *SMILING EMOJI* *PUMPKIN EMOJI***

**Bryce: I'll be there**

# Chapter 7

## Korra

"Look at us, all fall'd out," I say, gesturing to our outfits. "You're on theme and I'm a big fan!"

Bryce looks down at his cream cable-knit sweater and jeans. He rubs a hand down his broad chest over the widest of the cables. "You did say there would be pumpkin spice lattes…" His lips curve into a smile that's hard to look away from. "You went for green… no shock there. But what is this? Hunter?" He pinches the fabric of my green cardigan that slouches off of one shoulder. I loved the orange and yellow leaves stitched all around. It seemed appropriate, given the day's activities. The cool autumn breeze catches my exposed skin there. I rearrange my collar to cover it up again. Once we start walking around more I'm sure I'll be happy about the optional ventilation.

The leaves started turning their gemstone shades last month. Now that it's October most of the trees are leaning toward the deep russet and brown colors, if there are any leaves left. They litter the ground in an artful way making the gardens look more picturesque than normal. A fair few people turned up for this Fall Extravaganza. I didn't expect it to be empty, but the coffee line was curled around the entrance when we arrived. We walk through the xeriscaping portion of the gardens that has been arranged into several fall themes. Some of the colored stones are designed like leaves and pumpkins. It's not a bad way to wait out the crowd.

"No, no, no, my friend. This is emerald green. It will look fantastic against the pumpkins." The tan tank dress I chose wasn't quite fall enough and I thought the green would compliment it perfectly. "You should try adding some color to your wardrobe, it'll make you way happier. I think green would be the best choice."

"Oh really?" He chuckles, "You? You thought green should be the color I add more of to my wardrobe. No kidding?"

"Not one joke," I say, shaking my head on a giggle. "Look, the line has gotten much shorter now!" Grabbing Bryce's hand, I race over to the coffee truck as quickly as I can in suede booties.

The Botanical Gardens opened its loading parking lot to several vendors and food trucks. The smell of fall is rich in the air with not only pumpkin spice lattes, but there are a few other trucks we will not be missing out on.

With only two people in front of us now, we secure our drinks pretty quickly. The open top has whipped cream piled high. A signature pumpkin spice blend forms a pumpkin shape that is so on-theme, I smile at how perfectly the drink is fitting into my plan.

Upon first sip, the spices assault my senses. I sneeze and hold the drink away from me. He grabs my cup as another sneeze comes.

"You alright?" He asks after blessing me for the second time.

"Yea," I rub my nose with the back of my hand. "I just didn't expect it to be so..."

With a smirk, he questions, "Spiced?"

"Don't laugh at me. It's my first PSL."

"What?" He asks, taking a sip of his own drink. "This was your idea."

"Well, yea... I always see people talking about them. I don't really drink coffee. It's more Kasey's thing."

"It's still weird to me that you don't drink coffee." He sips his own drink, frowning at the sweetness no doubt. "So, yesterday when you were talking about pumpkin spice lattes, you thought it was something *I'd* like?"

"I don't know. I figured I would try something new and it was on the email. You make a good candidate to try it with."

"Because I'm so adventurous with my food…"

I consider him for a bit, "I don't know that adventurous is the word. More like… Ambitious." I think for a bit longer. "Yea. That's definitely the word. You're not afraid of a challenge."

"I'm failing to see how that amounts to trying a coffee drink you can get literally anywhere this time of year."

"The challenge is not in obtaining the drink, Bryce. *Think bigger.* That's where you excel."

"Help me out here, Kor."

I take my drink back from him. "What would be the reason that I'd pick you to come to the Gardens today?"

"Because you like the Botanical Gardens…" He motions around us. The other trucks look more appetizing after the PSL nearly took me out a few moments prior. Apple cider donuts might have been a better choice. They spin on a well-lit display in the next truck's display window.

Bryce notices how I'm eyeing them down and gets a few for us to try.

"True," I say, looking around us wistfully. "I do love them. But this is not about me." I gobble one of my donuts using the cream from my drink as a dip. Humming happily at the cozy feeling of walking through crunchy leaves with my bestie by my side and a sweet treat in hand.

He takes a photo of us, me mid-bite and him holding his coffee cup to the camera. With a napkin, he swipes some sugar from my cheek before asking, "It's about me?"

Nodding into my next donut, I reply, "It is."

"What do I have to do with this place?" He takes a bite of his own donut. This treat he likes better than the latte, going for another. *One point for Kor.*

"It's not about this place either," I tell him, finishing my last donut. Noticing that I have an empty hand, he puts his last donut there. These really are the best. Maybe I can figure out how to make them at home.

"Okay, you lost me again."

We walk a little longer, passing beautiful arrangements of perennials that range from spooky and haunting to warm and silly. I consider whether I should create a fall arrangement at the entryway with the empty raised plant bed I have outside the front door.

"If it's about you..." I hedge. "But not specifically about this place. And you're ambitious..."

Confusion crinkles his brow in an adorable way as tangible proof that he's really trying to understand why he's here. "Korra, please just spell it out for me."

"Look around you. What do you see?"

"People," he grumbles at the line we're in for mini potpies. "Food." The food is definitely a perk, but he's getting close. "Pumpkins," is his final observation. There *are* an abundance of pumpkins, but as soon as he was getting close to the point, he fell completely away from it.

"Yes... But what are those things?" With his blank face, I choose to give him the answer I'm looking for instead of trying to tease it out of him anymore. "It's life. Real life. You know? That thing you're missing out on as you become *attorney of the year*."

He sips from his drink, frowning at it again. *Too sweet.* "That's not a thing, Korra."

"Oh, but it is," I say before realizing what he was referring to. "Okay, maybe not the attorney of the year thing but the life thing. Let's go back to that. *This is real life.* Seeing, tasting, trying, and experiencing! It's the best part about being alive. You're missing that when you're holed up at your high-rise apartment or glass skyscraper just deposition-ing away with your highlighters and 'sign here' tabs."

He sucks his teeth. "I've been meaning to ask which TV series you and Kasey are watching recently. I fear that they paint an inaccurate picture of what I actually do."

"That's not important." I swipe his tangent away with a hand. "What's important is that you continue to experience real life while you are chasing these dreams. At what point are you going to say, 'Hey, I made it. Time to enjoy the fruits of my labor.' And actually experience what life is all about."

"Real life?"

"Mmmhmm," I hum. "Just look at that guy," I point to the far side of this area where several wooden buckets are filled to the brim with water. There are several people around them chanting. "He's going to get the most apples for his team." The man pops out of the water with an apple sunk between his teeth and spits it to the smaller bucket to his left. "He's going pretty fast. You think you could out bob him?" I raise an eyebrow.

He raises one back. "I'm not bobbing for apples."

I'm entranced by the ferocity that he attacks the floating fruit in the barrel. "That guy is literally grabbing life by the teeth."

"Yea... won't be grabbing life by the teeth then," he says dryly.

"Okay forget the metaphor. Let's look at the bigger picture again."

"The bigger picture being?"

It's our turn next and we both get a hand pie before looking for an area that isn't as crowded to eat. The steam rising out of the paper bag the pie is in means that it will be some time before we can safely bite into one. It's doing a great job of warming my fingers though.

We find the last of the picnic tables on the lot and sit. Trash from the previous family sitting here remains on one side, so we both pick the right bench.

I poke his chest. It's firm under my touch and it flexes when he crosses his arms. "You literally make thousands of dollars to make conclusions for a living. How are you so off topic?"

"Korra. You started with pumpkin spice lattes and now we're at bobbing for apples. What exactly is this picture?"

"Ha! So you were paying attention!" I tap his nose once with my finger and he swats my hand away. "That is the picture! The picture is the moments. The moments are what make life special. You're missing that in a courtroom or at your desk. You're supposed to work to live, not the other way around." He opens his mouth, no doubt to say his tired motto. "Ach, don't you dare say it!"

His shoulders rise, "Well I do love my job."

"And that's sad. Not that you love your job, but that you can't refute my claims."

"But my bank account isn't..." He makes a pouty face when I shake my head at him.

"We both know it's not about that."

His head tilts from one side to the next before his lips twist to the side. "It's kind of about that." He shrugs, "Mozier was saying something similar this week."

"Whaaaat?" I gasp with a hand over my mouth. "Something Phil and I agree on? What did he say?"

"Don't know. Something about a well-rounded life and values." Bryce basically hero-worships this man. I know he remembers verbatim what Phil told him. I don't know why he's trying to play it cool with me.

"Hmm," I say in response to his words. I tap my chin before chancing a bite of my hand pie. *It's delicious.* Tender chicken and soft vegetables all in a savory gravy. My goodness, I'm so glad we got these.

"What do you mean hmm?" He asks before biting into his own. His eyes crinkle at the sides and I know I've officially won today. It takes him no time to finish the pie. I found something he liked today.

Feeling pleased with myself, I say, "Big picture. I'm not the only one who sees this about you." I mime a gavel slamming with my fist on my left palm. "I rest my case."

He wipes his mouth with a napkin, finished with his pie. "Now, I'm confused. Are you the judge or the attorney?" Handing the rest of my pie to him, he takes it and finishes it too.

"I'm none of those things, I'm the friend who is getting the attorney out of his lawyer hole to experience something new. And we're doing it together."

He wiggles his eyebrows. "Speaking of doing it together..."

My eyes grow wide before I burst into laughter. "Worst segue ever."

That was something I loved about my best friend. He could be as serious as they come and then say something like this, taking me completely by surprise. He needed more opportunities like this one to let the silly dude in him out.

"I stand behind it," he smirks, but continues, "Thanksgiving is coming up. What are you doing for it?"

My mood sobers as I think about it. "It's the first big holiday without Mom, and I was hoping that you'd be there..."

Bryce's breath of relief blows out of him. "I'd love to... if you think it won't be a big deal. Tara is going to Singapore and I declined the trip. I'll just be at home otherwise. Probably order in." Tara, his mother, has been avoiding big holidays like this since his father passed. Now that Bryce doesn't live at their family home, she's been traveling more often. I know it makes her happy, but I don't think she realizes how it affects my friend.

"I can't guarantee that the food will be better since I don't know what we're having or who's cooking it. However, I can say that it will be food."

"I'll take it."

# CHAPTER 8

## Bryce

It just made sense to go to Thanksgiving dinner at the Thomas family house. With my mom gone I really didn't have anything else to do. Sure, I could have worked some more, but I was listening when Korra said her piece. Sitting around at my apartment alone would have been depressing as all hell. It would have helped no one.

I could be there for Korra with her having to face her favorite holiday without her mom, the person who had made it so. Most of her siblings had a fond affection for Christmas time. For many reasons, I knew Thanksgiving was the one that Korra loved best. I'd been to a few of them and from the food alone, you'd add it to the top of your list too.

Delanna was an incredible cook, probably because she put extra servings of love into everything she made. That was her way though. She loved everyone like they were her own.

Even me.

Somehow, after Phil brought it to my attention I'm seeing more and more where the holes are in my life. I had my head down, working hard...

And now I can't stop looking up and looking around.

Looking at my empty apartment.

Looking at my empty nights.

Looking at my empty weekends.

There is a lot of life I've been missing out on. I'm a single guy, but I know I want to be with someone. I've got things I *need*. Working out and my fist are only going to burn off so much of that need. They say the healthier you are, the hornier you are. I keep in shape so... you do the math.

Like I said before, I don't spend a lot of time trying to date or hook up.

Until lately, sexual release has been just a biological thing to get out of the way. A burden that was only in my way after I had to cut Jillian out of my life, especially.

But what if it could be more than that? Enjoying sex again...

What if I were able to find a way to make space for someone else in my life? Even if it's not all three things, couldn't having two of those three things be somewhat worth it? Sacrificing one for the other two is not an idea I want to consider right now. I couldn't stand to lose my friendships—especially with Korra.

She is the oldest friendship I've ever had. Our relationship is one I cherish. I couldn't let something get in the way of that.

Her voice cuts into my internal debate. "Did you hear what I said?"

Scratching my jaw, I admit, "No, sorry. I was thinking about something else."

Korra hands fling into the air. "So help me God, if you were thinking about a case or something after I just had the most beautifully laid out intervention set for you I will—"

"No, it's nothing like that." Though it would likely cost me a late night or two next week, I'm happy I came here with her. Fall had come and I'd basically missed all of it. The cozy theme of this event plus the scents surrounding us felt like I was getting all those comforting fall feelings in one go. *Like I was catching up on what I'd missed.* My smile is small when I answer her. "I was thinking about how I could help with Thanksgiving."

Walking through the grounds of the Gardens, I notice how happy everyone is around me. It might even be infectious. Several family groups happily participating in the event make me wonder what having kids would be like.

It's not that I never thought about having children before. I just thought maybe I'd be an old man, an older man. You know the one dad that's already gray in the pick-up line waiting for their young kids? That seems to be the way for many of the men in my office. *Though Phil did have his kids younger.* I still think that he was older than me when he had his oldest son.

I'm not saying that I'm envious of the guy who's dunking his head halfway into a barrel full of apples, but I am saying that he looks to be having a really great time doing it.

Korra's pleased with my response, looping my arm through hers as she sips her spiced coffee. "And in what way would that be? Are you some sort of chef I didn't know about?" She teases. "Have you been making Thanksgiving dinner behind my back and I didn't know?"

"Yea, no," I say with a straight face. "Nothing like that. It's probably best for everyone's sake that I don't cook anything."

There's cheering coming from another section of the Gardens that we both are caught off guard by. We follow the sounds to see that they've started doing a race of some sort. Thankfully, I'm a little taller than most of the people who are gathered around. I can see that there are ten people all in burlap sacks racing towards the end as people cheer them on from the sidelines.

Looks like two kids are racing head to head at the front of the contestants while some adults are trying their best to catch up to them. The boy with a short, black crop haircut has a look of complete determination as he uses all his might to hop towards the finish line. The girl next to him with brown hair billowing behind her also looks determined, but she's smoking this little guy.

"Savannah, Savannah, Savannah!" is being cheered the loudest as she completely overtakes the boy and crosses the finish line.

A man, who looks almost identical to her, scoops her up and spins her around as the rest of her family cheers along with the crowd about her win.

With a mic in hand, there's an announcer who says, "Congratulations Savannah! Please visit the front desk for your prize!" The other contestants remove their sacks, making a pile in a bucket on the side. "Anyone else want to compete for a chance to be the next sack race winner?"

I looked down at Korra, who's already bouncing on the tips of her toes. *No surprise there.* Korra may not like clubbing or big social events, preferring her cozy activities, usually plant related, but she is *extremely competitive*. Maybe it's a twin thing or maybe it's a *her* thing. Who's to say? All I know is that when she sets her mind on winning something, she cannot let it go.

"You know you want to..." she cajoles with her sweetest voice. Her eyes sparkle with excitement as she waits for my response.

"Okay, but don't be mad if I win," I wink.

"Yesss!" She says waving her hand in the air. She's quick to grab up a sack and go wait at the starting line where we wait for more people to join us.

"You know little kids are gonna be doing this right? You should probably let them win."

"Nope," She stretches her arms over head before bending at the waist to stretch her legs. "They've gotta learn fair and square that winners win and losers lose!" She says with her game-face in place."I'm betting you that I'll beat you and you'll have to let everyone know that you were the loser of this race. I might even make a sash or something."

"That's what you think." Rolling my eyes, I step into the sack. "You might be smaller, but I've got strength on my side."

"Oh, we'll see," she says. "Get ready to eat my dust!"

The announcer states the rules, which are pretty intuitive, but has to let everyone know regardless. All the while, I catch Korra gearing up for this race like there will be a ten-thousand dollar cash prize at the end. Her intensity is hilarious.

She holds onto the edge of the sack with an iron grip, and I'm watching her in fascination when the horn blows. She's moving at a pace I have never seen her move before.

She was fast on her way to get a pumpkin spice latte. But getting to this finish line, I think I did actually see dust kicking up behind her.

*Pretty impressive for a burlap sack and booties.*

She has zero remorse by the time she gets to the end and all the little kids are still struggling to hop their way along.

"We have a winner!" The announcer bellows. "What's your name?"

"I'm Korra..." her name trails off as she spins to look for me. I'm not right behind her like she probably suspected I was.

I stopped to see if I could help one little boy who had gotten all tangled up in his sack. His frustrated little grunts made me pause when I hopped along beside him. I untangle his legs and help him to his feet.

Korra turns to see that there's still more people coming along in the race and I am right behind the little boy who is giving it his very best.

Her face softens from confusion to admiration as she witnesses me helping him to the end when he trips once more, and I have to untangle his legs again.

We're the last two to finish and there is all manner of whoops and hollers for the little guy completing the race.

The announcer comes over to us and asks, "What's your name, little fella?"

"I'm Toby," he beams with three missing teeth adding to his adorable little smile.

"And how old are you, Toby?"

"I'm seven years and a half years old."

The crowd collectively *awws* at him and his mother comes over to help him out of the sack, brushing dried grass from his hair. "Thank you," she says to me. "He wouldn't let me help him in the race. I'm glad you were there to give him that extra push to finish."

The announcer pats Toby on the back. "We're all glad to see that Toby made it to the end. And for such a valiant effort, you may also claim a prize at the front desk with Miss Korra here."

"Gotta admit that I'm very surprised you picked the photo shoot instead of the year long membership." I say as we leave the office, headed toward her prize. "What happened to *winners win?*"

"Well Toby seemed to really enjoy this place and I was going to get a membership anyway. Now I've got a reason to get adorable photos to commemorate my win," she teases, poking me in the chest again. "And who better to hold my trophy than one of my favorite people in the whole world."

"There is no trophy." I say, drolly. "Well you've got lots of options to choose from." There's a sign that has arrows pointing in different directions to the various setups. Each arrow has a drawing and a name for each photographable display. "We've got the Leaf Wall to the left. Wonder how long it took them to put that together."

She thinks for a moment. "Very tempting. I do like fall leaf colors, but I might blend in with my sweater." We both look at her stitched leaves all over the sweater and decide against that one.

"Also got the Pumpkin Archways that seem extremely macabre." I suggest. "They've just speared all the Jack-o-lanterns through the middle? Who carved all those?"

"I think they're painted. I saw it in the promo email. Not a fan of that one either. Too spooky."

There are three different displays this way but I proclaim, "Oh no, this is the one you want." Taking her hand, I start heading north like the sign suggests.

"Which one?" she asks.

"Trust me?"

Narrowing her eyes, she says, "Well, yea..."

"Follow me, then."

A short woman sees us standing in front of the hay bale corral leading towards the set up and perks up. "Oh, wonderful! Hurry, hurry! We're getting into some beautiful lighting right now. Have you heard of golden hour?"

Leaning around me to see what I'm standing in front of, Korra says that she has. There are several hay bales that lead down a path to an old pick-up truck that's been reversed into this spot here. Pumpkins are stacked up all around the bed of the truck with the tailgate open. White, light orange and deep orange, they form a pyramid on one side and overflow into the bed of the truck on the other. It's very autumn coded and upon seeing it, I know that it is exactly what Korra would love.

Everything is cast in a gold shimmer as the sun sets behind the photographer. The way the light reflects in Korra's hair is reminiscent of the way it reflected in the club. I don't know what she puts into her curls, but they're glittering in this light as well as making her smooth sable brown skin glow from within.

She's energized anew as she hurries down the long path towards where the woman waits for us. "Hi. I'm Korra and this is Bryce. What's your name?" I give her a wave from where I stand looking over the set up more closely.

A large barrel full of apples sits in front of a small step stool, to camouflage it from the photos I suspect. In the truck bed, there's a large plaid wool blanket in front of the pumpkins. Either it's thick or they have plenty of other blankets beneath it because it's plush and comfortable when I press down on them.

Landing stretches to the east with pumpkins if all sizes fit the pick-your-own crowd. The low hum of a truck like this one with a modified cart for passengers chugs along. I should take Korra there next so she can get one. I'm sure we won't be able to take any of these with her.

"I'm Wuying. It's lovely to meet you both. Please sit. Find whatever position feels comfortable for you. The sun will only be doing this," she gestures to the general glimmer around us, "for the next twenty minutes. So, if there's any shots that you think of — we will be sure to get them."

"Oh, great," Korra says with a wink in my direction and hurriedly takes a position on the bed of the truck with the plaid blanket. I take a spot beside her, moving her closer into my body, so that there's not some awkward gap between us.

"Yes, that's perfect. Now, put your arm around her shoulders," Wuying says.

I do as she directs and Korra settles in next to me. She starts moving her hair, so that it's not assaulting my face. I chuckle at how she fusses. "Look at me," she says. "My hair sticking up all crazy?"

I look down at her, moving some hair from her face. The sun really is hitting her at the most perfect angle. I can see the tiny moles dotting her cheeks and a little bit of the shimmer from whatever she has on her face. *It's beautiful.* I have the urge to take this picture myself as I observe more details of her face in this lighting. Her eyes flick between mine as I'm stuck cataloguing the myriad of things that make Korra beautiful at golden hour.

I hear the camera click a few times and then I finally am snapped out of whatever that just was.

She chuckles nervously, no doubt feeling how the energy has changed between us on the back of this truck.

"That's good," Wuying says as she moves around in front of us to catch another angle. "This will be perfect for a fireplace or anything like that..." With a few more clicks she says, "You let me know and I can tell you where to get these developed. I can get a really good deal on stretch canvases or maybe you prefer a more traditional photo."

"Oh," Korra responds, sitting up a little straighter. "We aren't..." she trails off. "We don't live together... I mean we're not together."

"Mmh," Wuying hums, and takes a few more shots. "How about we try some leaning against the edge of the truck?"

We continue taking photos until the sun eventually sets completely. But, I'm stuck in yet another confusing moment with my best friend.

They appear to be racking up.

# CHAPTER 9

## Korra

"Okay, well... I'm voting for getting the turkey from some restaurant or something," my youngest brother says.

"There's no way we'll get one so last minute," I comment, striking a line through *turkey* on my list.

"We'll be lucky to find any at the grocery store," Kasey confirms. Of the two of us, she cooks the least. That's why she was always designated to help Mom do the groceries, especially around holiday time.

I had spent so much time pretending this holiday was not going to happen without Mom that I dropped the ball on actually preparing for it. *Guilty as charged.* Now I have to manage the preparation of it with my brothers and sisters, at the last minute, which is not the family bonding opportunity I thought it could be.

"Backup plan, we could roast some chickens instead. Do you think three will be enough?" Zack asks, as we all gather around the dining table in my childhood home. There was a time where this solid wood table seemed like the biggest I'd ever seen since it comfortably seats twelve people or twenty when the big holidays or celebrations come around.

Zach looks beyond tired, having just come off of a three day shift at the firehouse. Even with him being exhausted, he's the most accommodating at the table right now.

I sit with my notebook and try to dole out the tasks of getting this meal together. It's proving to be more difficult as none of us are really cut out for a marathon of cooking like Thanksgiving entails. I'm awed at how much my Mom really did accomplish with all of us being—well, all of us. Five kids and a husband are a lot of mouths to feed. I'm annoyed just having to feed Kasey and I on a daily basis. *How did she do it?*

"Well, the biggest thing here is not actually the meat." I point out. "It's all the sides. Mom used to be already cooking at this point. Who's gonna make all these sides?" I turn the paper I was writing on around to show them how long the list is. This table used to be filled with serving dishes of all our favorites with a massive turkey dressed up in the middle.

Lee kicks his feet up onto the empty chair next to him. "Honestly, I think we should probably buy those, too. I do not trust Kasey to make macaroni and cheese. I don't care how many videos she said she watched." He's still in his scrubs from work but I changed out of mine before coming over. I needed an oversized sweater with stretchy pants for this.

My sister sits at the dining table with her arms crossed over her chest. She leans onto the top of it to glare at our brother. Her hair, smoothed back into a high ponytail, makes her serious expression more severe. Our brother is completely unaffected by her deadly look. "What the fuck ever. I'm still gonna make it. You won't be getting any now, Lee."

"That's probably a blessing. How much longer do you think this is gonna take?" He asks.

Flopping back into my chair, I sigh long and loud. I swear I'm sick of them and the holiday hasn't even started yet.

Listen, I love my family. I love them! I do. Probably the most out of everyone here because I was the closest to Mom. I saw the best of my siblings because my Mom showed me how to see the best of my siblings. *She showed me how to see the best in anything.* But right now? My patience is being greatly tested. Because what the actual hell is this meal going to be?

"All right, I will take care of the food. I'll get everything together so we at least have something on the table for us to eat."

Lee pipes up again, "What about all the guests? Are we still gonna be expected to entertain all the people who come to visit? I mean anybody who would come by knows that she's not here. I imagine that they'll probably come with like those casseroles and shit that they had after she passed." Holding his hands in front of him he adds, "I'm not saying that I didn't love not having to cook for a while. But I don't know what I'm gonna do if there's gonna be all these people in the house, too."

"Everyone knows how big of a deal this was for her. It's the holiday to celebrate family," Zach says. "I think people will come, but maybe not with funeral casseroles."

"Well, I don't know if people are or are not coming. We'll have to wait for Dad to get home and see if anyone has said anything to him about it."

My Dad's been going to a grief counseling meeting for the past few months. I guess it's been a little over half a year at this point. It seems to have helped him in coping. Instead of doing it by himself, or with us fumbling our own grief as well as helping him with his, he's able to do it with the group. I think it's been really beneficial. It has made a marked difference in him since he started.

"Yea, let's wait for Dad. I mean he should be home in the next ten or fifteen right?"

"No, he's home now." My Dad says from the front door.

Oh good. I smile at the thought of getting to see my Dad today. Yes, I was a mama's girl but I still love my Daddy something fierce. When he enters the room, we all look to check on him.

My father has always been the biggest man in the room, especially when I was a young girl. My Mom loved our big Daddy more than anything else in this world. And that is saying something. He was a man who walked around like he had the abundance of love that she gave him in his spirit and that radiated off of him.

When she passed, we all felt the loss in different ways.

For my father, it was like someone turned the life off in his eyes. You could feel the hole that was in his spirit missing the love that once was. Over thirty years married to one person is hard to fathom. But spending that much time and then losing them? Unimaginable.

"All right. What's the family gathered 'round about?" he asks.

"Well, you know what holiday is tomorrow. We're trying to figure out how we can still try to make it look like... I don't know ..." Lee shrugs.

Understanding hits Daddy, instantly and he supplies, "How your mother did it?"

"Yea," we all reply in unison.

"It's interesting that you all are talking about this here because I was just talking about it there." There being his group session. "We talked about how traditions make us feel safe and happy. We continue to come back to them because it's something we can rely on. It's something that brings us comfort." He pulls his chair at the head of the table out and takes a seat. Emotion weary on his face. "I want to tell you that all this is not going to do what you think it's going to do. I hope you weren't doing this for me because it will only show me how much my wife is missing." He pauses for a bit, swallowing thickly before continuing again. "I appreciate the gesture, I do, but at this point I think we should really try to make new traditions. Honor the purpose of why she did what she did when she was alive."

"So, we just shouldn't celebrate the holiday?" I ask, placing a hand atop my father's on the table.

"Well... This one was really built on a massacre anyway, so we might as well do something else. Plus, I'd like to just watch the game in peace and have my family over. Hell, we can order a pizza. Or make frozen ones in the oven. It doesn't matter to me. The point of this time was for us to gather together as a family and celebrate that we have each other. We might be one less, but we are still a family."

"That's right," I say, looking at everyone gathered at the table. "I just wanted us to be together and for us to feel like the family we once were."

"But we aren't the family we once were. Mom was everything. She was the glue that held us all together. She's the reason why these holidays felt special." Kasey says across the table from me.

Agreeing, I suggest, "We have to figure out how we can be together and still make it feel special... And celebrate who we still have without ignoring the fact that someone who was so important to us, our Mother, is gone."

Kasey nods and sits back in her seat, satisfied with what I've said.

Zach is the first to speak again. His brows are pinched low with a frown when he asserts, "As the oldest, I think it should be my job to take care of you all. And I know with how work's been I haven't been able to be as present as I'd want to be." There are grumblings of disagreement around the table before he continues, "You all can say whatever you want to, but this is what I want. I wanna step up and help keep this family together no matter what. And the last thing I want is for her absence to mean that we grow apart or that we aren't as close as we were when she was here."

"Same, brother," I pat his hand and he gives me a gentle smile. He turns his hand over to squeeze mine. I love my big brother. I love all my siblings, but him wanting to step up and be there for us is no shock. His heart is the biggest out of everyone at the table.

"We will be sure to see guests here tomorrow, whether I invited them or not. My wife left a lasting impression on the folks in this town. Pizza and the game are unlikely, though a pleasant thought," Dad says. "Nia is coming home tonight and she'll be staying at the house. Is anybody else staying at the house too?"

I'm not sure if I will stay the night since I would normally be going home to water my babies and adjust any lighting that may be too dim for my plants indoors that need them. They could go a day without my fussing but I'm only fifteen minutes from this house.

I'm sure Palmer has the time off for the holiday. Maybe we could spend some time together *as a couple* before the family time starts. I hate to think of him as the sole provider of orgasms. I can take care of my own needs, but it has been a while since I got what I was looking for from him. *Though he has not been missing any.*

We talked about how we would split the time between his parents house and mine earlier in the month but never came back to the idea. I decide to send him a text to confirm we're still starting here and then going to see his family later in the day.

> **Korra: What time do you think you'll be here tomorrow?**

While I wait for his reply, I say, "I think Kasey and I are gonna just drive up early in the morning. Right, Kase?"

She nods, tapping her fingers on the table.

"I'll probably stay the night at Malaya's spot. I think she's having late dinner tonight or something, but I'll be here tomorrow morning."

My father turns to his oldest son, "You staying?"

"Yea, I'm wiped out. Got my bag in the truck. If I go to sleep at my place, I'm likely not coming over until way later tomorrow night. At least if I'm here, one of you all will come and get me to come down for the game."

"Oh, I will," My dad assures him. "Thunderbolts are playing on Thanksgiving for the first time and I will not be missing it."

"Perfect. So that leaves Nia and Zack at the house." I scribble that down on my notepad. "Lee, Kasey, and I will be over tomorrow and... I don't know. We'll do something. It might not look like Mom's Thanksgiving dinner, but it will be a little better than frozen pizza."

"What about the guests?" Lee asks. "Ma always had the open-door thing. Are we supposed to be feeding and entertaining them?"

"They are your community, Bentley. We're not turning people away, but we're not feeding them either. I expect you to treat them with decorum. Act like you've got some sense," Dad says.

Lee scoffs, "I have sense. But I'm going to dip if any of them start crying."

"That's what Dad's talking about. You need to be respectful."

Pointing to himself, Lee argues, "I'm grown and so are they. I don't have to do shit. They'll get five minutes."

"Why are you like this?" Kasey glares at our brother again. "Mom would be ashamed."

He shakes his head. "Mom knew who I was and she wouldn't be surprised. Besides, the rest of you will be there to *polite* them to death."

Zach cuts in before her and Lee can go back and forth like this. "Agreed. Lee is not allowed around any guests. Is that all we have? I'm ready to sleep."

"I don't have anything else. Do you, Dad?" He gives a look that communicates he has nothing to add.

"Great. I think we're good then."

With a plan in place, I let everyone leave. My Dad kisses my forehead before leaving the room.

My phone vibrates on the table with a text. I need to get on the same page with Palmer before I get fully wrapped up in preparing for tomorrow.

**Palmer: We need to talk**

**Korra: I know. That's why I'm asking about dinner tmw**

**Palmer: No, not about that**

# CHAPTER 10

## Bryce

When I pull up to the Thomas family home I know it's about to be crazy.

Their driveway is already full. I see the twin's cars, Zach's truck and Lee's motorcycle. There's a smaller Volkswagen that means Nia's home, too. They're all blocked in by more cars parked along the side. I had to park down the street to find a space.

I figured that since their mom passed it wouldn't be as busy as I know it can be.

This is an unexpected turn of events seeing that it's just as busy, if not more busy than it was in past years...

Their house is one that I would think of when you're picturing a storybook house. It has forest-green siding and ivory trim with a distinctive turret at the front many of the homes in this neighborhood share. The wide wraparound porch is both warm and welcoming. It has large windows that let in lots of light to the space, but what sets it apart from the others in the area is its stunning landscaping. It was more intricate when Delanna was alive, but with the company that handles the work, it's still a standout feature of the property. It always looked very healthy.

As warm and inviting inside as it appears on the outside.

I didn't know how early to come since Korra told me to be here whenever I could. And I haven't really heard back from her all day. She must have her hands full with whatever is going on in this house.

I said I'd be a help to her. I didn't exactly know what that meant. The three sweet potato pies that wobble in my hands feel meager with how many people are here. It's definitely not enough. I know that for sure. I suspect she'll put me to work as soon as I get inside.

The sound of chatter and the football game compete with each other as soon as I open the door. It's completely unlocked—which is not unlike how you would normally find the house—but there's never this many people all here.

Something happens in the game, where the announcer is shouting, joined by most of the male voices in the house. By the explosive volume, it's clear that there are loads of people in this house. I hope my friend is not completely stressed out with the attendance, in addition to the holiday blues.

I find my way to the kitchen, which I'm hoping will be a little more quiet and absent of people as I look for Korra.

I run into Lee first. He's leaving the living room to, I'm guessing, get another beer since the one in his hand is empty.

"Hey, man." He claps my back. "Didn't expect to see you here."

I give him a look that conveys my confusion of him not expecting me here. Korra and I are close friends. This is the first holiday she's having to do without her mom. All of them should know how hard this would be on her.

*Of course, I'd be here.*

She's been playing it cool like she isn't feeling Delanna's absence, but it's in the way she talks about it. There's more pep in her voice like she's forcing extra happiness to mask her true feelings. She can't hide it in her eyes—they dim enough to be noticeable.

Choosing not to voice my opinions on the matter, I simply respond, "I'm here to help. Who are all these people?"

He shrugs. "Don't know. Dad invited some people from his support group and they might have brought people... Along with a few more that are here to *support* with Mom's absence," he says with derision.

I follow him into the kitchen, where he grabs another beer from the fridge. "The group's not anonymous?" I ask.

He laughs, twisting the top off his lager. "It's not AA, they're just sad."

Another crack of cheering hits us from the living room and I raise an eyebrow. "Seems like it."

"Really hoping nobody else comes," he looks around him, "but from what I hear dad still is expecting a few others. Hey, the Geiers are definitely gonna make an appearance." He claps my back again. "Maybe Korra will bring the claws out again."

"Bryce! Thank God you're here! Lee, get out!" Korra chides while shoving her brother out of the kitchen. There's a card table in the middle of the space which must be where the overflow of people will be sitting since there is no way the people in the living room will fit at their normal dining table. She must have been in their extra large pantry before now that she's sidling around the temporary table.

She looks as frazzled as I imagine she would be. All of her hair is swept up into some sort of clip on the top of her head and there's flour or something on her cheek. Her apron is completely trashed. Who knows what she even made today? It's not clear with the mess she's wearing.

"Where do you need me?" I ask to try and be helpful as I promised I would be. She's the only one in the kitchen though I know her siblings are in the building somewhere. "Why aren't they helping?"

She knows who the *they* I'm referring to it without further explanation, using a shoulder to brush a loose curl behind her ear and out of her face. "They were, but I kicked them out."

"What happened?"

"Zach means well but he's a micromanager and so am I. We just clashed. Nothing serious." She hurriedly presses some button on a timer that she sets back in place on the stove top. "He made his sides and went to watch the game."

"Only Zach helped?"

Taking the pies from my hands to sit by some other desserts, "Kasey made macaroni and cheese. It's in the oven. She was... Kasey. She had to go too."

I nod, "Fair enough." Looking around the kitchen, the counters hold dishes with lids on them so I still don't know what is going on the table but it smells good. "What do you need me to do?"

"Please just take those bags out of the kitchen. I haven't had a chance to and we need the space to walk around."

I spot the extra large trash bags that are full to the brim and walk them out.

On my way back inside, I see an all too familiar vehicle pulling up and parking.

*No, for the love of God, no!*

I thought I had more time. I quickly head back inside.

"The Geiers are here," I say in a hurry to get Korra more presentable. The animosity between Korra and Jillian goes back farther than I could say since they both grew up here. By the time I moved here when I was sixteen, they already hated each other.

Korra's mother taught most of the music classes in our school from grade three through twelve. Jillian was a decorated vocalist and in Korra's eyes, completely undeserving of her talent and her mother's affection or attention. It wasn't that Delanna loved Kor any less but the fact that the kind of praise Delanna gave Jillian was never something Korra would experience.

Jillian knew that and never let her forget it.

I know their feud had everything to do with the fact that Jillian was a favorite student of Delanna's. Because of this, Jillian's parents, Rick and Jenni Geier, were close with the Thomases. It is not surprising that they would be here today.

With a family as musically inclined as the Thomas family is, being the one sibling who can't carry a tune or keep rhythm is... difficult. Her competitive nature made the relationship between Jillian and Korra tense, to say the least.

One thing I know would upset her more than anything is for Jillian to see her looking like this.

"What?" She says, turning from the stove with her phone to her ear. "Hold on, Malaya."

"Call her back," I urge. Her head tilts to the side and she raises an eyebrow. "I understand you're busy but Jillian's parents are here and that means she is probably also here."

Realization dawns, "Feel better, okay? I gotta go," she says. "I know," she nods, though Malaya can't see her. "I'll call you later."

Once she finally gets off of the phone, I'm able to help her get cleaned up. She rips the apron off, throwing it onto a cabinet door and starts fluffing out her hair as she's walking towards the dinner table.

A large arrangement of warm toned blooms and small pumpkins give the table the festive feeling you'd expect from a fall dinner. "You did this? I ask, pointing to the arrangement.

"Yea," she says distractedly. "I was inspired by the extravaganza. Isn't it cozy?"

"You made it all fall'd out in here." I say and she throws a look at me with my teasing. She's wearing a fuzzy cream sweater with a deep green suede mini skirt that I'm impressed she didn't get any food on. "And you're still making dinner?" Pulling the sleeves down, she unzips her knee high boots to adjust her sheer tights. Korra is well put together beside what apparently couldn't be protected by the apron.

"Uh-huh." On the table she grabs her purse, and she begins taking products out of the bag. When she opens up the small mirror, she makes a gasp and looks to me in disgust, saying, "What the hell is on my face?"

"I don't know, but you've got like thirty seconds to get it off."

"By the way, Palmer broke up with me last night," she says, adjusting the green crystal necklace that's twisted around her neck.

*Record scratch.*

Brows slamming down, I demand, "He did what?!"

"He said that he *just really wanted his space* and that *he cared about me* but *he knows I was not the person for him.* And I just said okay. I had nothing else that I thought of. I'm surprised but maybe not. I know I'm too much to deal with for most people." The voice she uses to relay his words to me makes him sound like the absolute dolt that he is.

"That is the furthest thing from the truth. You are the good in everyone's life. Having you there is never too much to deal with." I hold her chin for her to look at me and pay attention to what I'm saying. "You have a big heart and patience. He's a moron but he did you a favor by leaving. You know that, right?"

She wipes at her face, getting the food off, and then puts something on her lips. "I guess. His timing is so shitty though. I didn't want to spend today alone. We had plans to go to his parents' place tonight."

"Well, I'm here so you won't be alone."

She sighs, not at me, but obviously at the situation. That's why she had been frazzled and not on her phone. Definitely avoiding whatever the hell Palmer is doing. She starts arranging her curls, still in thought. My hands are also in her hair, helping the curls that have gotten a little stuck in the back to fall a little more naturally.

"Oh, this is no surprise to me," is the first thing I hear from my ex's voice when she enters the room. "Korra taking my sloppy seconds."

With me covering Korra, my hands in her hair must look more salacious than it is. Especially with us in this room away from everyone else. The irritation at Jillian's voice and what she says, has Korra scowling and pursing her lips.

Removing my fingers from Korra's curls, I turn to see Jillian standing there in a tight top and jeans looking extremely casual. To my surprise, Terry is standing next to her. I would've thought that after what was suggested at the club by Korra that he would've ran for the hills. But I guess her claws are sunk deeper into him than I realized.

"I don't remember inviting you, Jillian." Korra says, stepping around my body. "How unfortunate to see you here where you aren't wanted."

Jillian smiles condescendingly at her, "No, sweetheart, you didn't. Your father invited my parents, you know, since they are good friends? And our mothers were best friends. It only seemed right that we come over like we do every year. Duh."

"Pardon me. Does doing the right thing actually register to you?" Korra sneers back at her.

"Don't bother," I say to Korra, hoping that she'll leave it be instead of a repeat of what happened at the club. She looks into my eyes, searching for something. I recognize the moment where she decides that she's satisfied with whatever she finds there.

"Ladies, let's not do this here. Where should I put this?" Terry asks, holding an aluminum tray of something. To be honest, I'd almost forgotten that he was standing there since he was so silent as the two women went back-and-forth.

Korra has calmed down and responds to Terry. "You can just set it onto the counter in the kitchen. The rest of the food is on a timer right now. We'll all sit down to eat soon."

He kisses Jillian on the forehead before walking out. She places a hand on his shoulder just before he leaves and it's then that a glint catches my eye.

On Jillian's left ring finger is a diamond band that could be nothing else than an engagement ring.

She notices me noticing and presses the hand to her chest. "We've already shared the news with your family, but I guess you should know, as well. Terry and I are getting married."

My brain stops working for a moment, and I can feel my heart pumping in my ears. My throat is thick with words that I can't say but recall from Jillian's own mouth.

*You never put me first.*

*I'm not important enough to you.*

Korra kills the silence in the room by saying "Unfortunate indeed. Does he know he has to be married to you?" I hear her words, but I'm frozen in place.

Jillian rolls her eyes, "I'm sorry, where is your boyfriend? Not here again?" She tosses the line at Korra before leaving the room and the two of us alone. Now, it's Mozier's words that swirl steadily through my head.

*They'll be looking for someone who leads a well rounded life.*

*Someone who can show commitment.*

"It's time to eat and I'm starving," Kasey says, completely oblivious to what's happening in the room when she enters. "The timer is going off. Let's go pull everything out."

People began piling into the room. And everyone adjusts based off of who can fit where. There is the extra table in the kitchen and the additional barstools, but this is too much for me right now as more and more bodies come into the large dining room. Conversation and shuffling filling the space and I'm still thinking about the words louder than it all in mind.

"You okay?" Korra asks, noticing my inaction. She places a hand on my arm. "Bryce?"

"I-I'm fine." I shake my head to clear my thoughts. "What do you need me to do?"

"Nothing right now. Just sit. We're gonna start bringing the food in."

I do what she says, taking a spot next to Zach who's talking to a man I've not met before. He's about the same height as Zach. I wonder if they work together at the station or what.

"Hey! I'm Gonzalo," he says, holding out his hand for me. "If you see a little girl that looks just like me but with lopsided puffs, that's Lucía."

The table is full now with some people pulling up chairs to the large table that normally seats twelve but holds almost twice as many people now. I can only imagine what the other table looks like.

"Nice to meet you," I say, taking his hand. "I'm Bryce." I don't see the little girl he mentioned. I'm not really looking since Korra is moving quickly in and out of the room with her sisters following suit with their hands full.

"I see," he says in a tone that suggests he's heard something about me. "It is nice to meet you. You're Korra's friend, right?"

"Right," I tell him, looking for my friend now that platters and bowls are starting to cover the table. It's a beautiful spread—though untraditional.

Lasagna rolls, salmon fillets, large mixed salads, a few dishes with the lid still covering them. A handful of whole roasted chickens and an even bigger bowl of mashed potatoes loaded up with toppings. More food is coming in, but I turn my focus to Gonzalo again.

"Oh, I see Lucía!" Zach says, hopping up from his chair and skirting around the edge of the table. He scoops up the little girl and brings her back to where Gonzalo is sitting. She giggles the whole way since Zach is basically carrying her by the foot. "Caught something that belongs to you, sir," he teases, depositing the giggling girl into Gonzalo's lap. As he said, she does have two lopsided puffs that show she's been having plenty of fun. With the combination of a blouse, sweatpants and cowboy boots, I'd say she dressed herself as well.

"Aye, mija. Necesitas comer un poco antes de poder volver a jugar." Gonzalo tells her as she wiggles to get out of his lap again.

The few open spots for the sisters remain and I'm anxious for Korra to finally sit. A thought has been forming after my brain had a hard reboot earlier. I don't know if she will think I'm crazy or just not care at all, but the longer I sit here as everyone chatters around the table the more affirmed I am in my brewing thoughts.

Nia is the first of the sisters to come and join the table. Then Kascy sits toward the end closer to my ex and her family, including her new fiancé. She gives me a look to inconspicuously draw my eye to Jillian's ring, mouthing *what is that?* I don't respond back to her, still looking for Korra.

Finally, she emerges with a few serving utensils that she puts with the dishes that still needed them. Taking the seat next to me, I angle my body so that I can whisper in her ear without anyone being able to read my lips behind her curls.

"I have to ask you a favor." I pause, "The favor of all favors."

"Sure, whatever. I got you." She says, taking a sip from the water in front of her. She waves across the table to someone before returning her attention back to me.

I stand from my seat. At this point there would be some sort of blessing to say over the food, but I'm not giving a prayer right now.

*I'm taking a huge leap.*

My mouth is moving before my brain can really figure out what my mouth is doing.

Clearing my throat, I hold my glass up and others at the table join me. Wayne is the first to raise his from the head of the table. "I wanted to let everyone know something important and I don't think it can wait any longer."

Korra suddenly stands beside me, not knowing what I'm doing, or that this makes my plan feel more believable. *How is it that she can support me even when she doesn't know how or why?* She places a hand on my arm, pulling me toward her to whisper in my ear. "What are you talking about?"

"Just go with it," I whisper back to her and meet the sepia of her irises. She nods though now with more trepidation.

"Everyone, I'm glad that so many of you are here today to make this news easier on us."

"Make what easier?" Wayne asks, now visibly unsure of my speech since it's clearly not a blessing or prayer like he probably thought I was going to do.

I look back to Korra. Her eyes search mine for meaning. And I have no explanation right now because my mouth is still moving much faster than my brain.

Usually, I'm thankful for that. I can talk my ass off about any given subject, especially when I need to stall or come up with something to say in front of a judge or to a client if I'm selling them on something. But right now, my brain is working triple-double overtime. *I can't make it stop.* I also can't make my brain say that this is a bad idea. I cannot do anything besides say what I'm thinking.

I don't know what this is.

But something just clicked for me and I can't let go of the idea.

I look down at my best friend and then at all the eyes who are waiting for what I have to make some big announcement for.

"I'm pleased to announce that Korra and I are engaged."

# CHAPTER 11

## Korra

Cheers and congratulations are still being thrown out as food is being passed around. I barely feel the hugs as each of my family members take their turn ending with my Dad.

But me? I'm reeling.

*What is Bryce doing?*

I mean... he's passing food around the table and accepting the well wishes from everyone around the table. He's putting food onto my plate and carrying on like that wasn't an off-the-wall random as hell declaration he just dropped here.

My family is watching us more closely than the other guests so my processing is extremely limited right now. Jillian's smug face catches my notice too often but I can't give her the satisfaction of my confusion or surprise.

Forget this meal! I've got to get to the bottom of this.

"Can I talk to you, in the other room real quick?" I smile at everyone in the room though my voice is tight with disbelief. Tugging Bryce's arm up from the table, I lead him upstairs to my childhood bedroom.

"Excuse me, but..." I take a deep inhale in for calm. Trying, trying so hard, to stay grounded before I continue. "WHAT THE HELL WAS THAT?" Is what I whisper-shout once the door is closed behind us.

He flinches at my ire. "Hear me out, okay?"

"No!" I point at him. "No! Not okay! Are you out of your mind?"

"Not out of my mind. I just think that this could solve both of our problems."

I narrow my eyes at him. "And what problem do I have?"

"Well, you have a Palmer problem. You've *been* having a Palmer problem. And this could help you with that," he says casually from where he sits on my full sized bed, still fitted with green lace linens.

"How exactly could *this* help me with the boyfriend that just broke up with me?" I press my fists into either hip. "If he wanted to be with me, we would not be broken up on *this holiday*, of all holidays."

Catching my reflection in the large mirror above my dresser, I jump to action. *Is that a piece of romaine in my curl?* I grab a spray bottle from the top to fill it with water and do something to resurrect the smushed and general haphazard way that my curls are behaving right now. *First, the piece of lettuce has to go.* I was in a tizzy to plate everything and now everyone is downstairs enjoying the food I made while I'm up here trying to understand what the hell Bryce was thinking.

At least, I hope they're enjoying the meal and not also thinking the same thing I am.

With that bomb and now our absence, it is probably a tense and awkward meal.

"Well..." he starts, "Now you don't have to tell your family that you broke up with Palmer. You can just say that you found someone better. Which is not a lie—I would say that I am leaps and bounds better than Palmer. Objectively speaking, of course."

I spray more water at the back of my head to rehydrate the curls there. "I don't think it's fair to compare the two. It's like apples and oranges between you two." Scrunching the hair with both hands to reactivate the product, I ask, "But I do want to know how you think that our families are not going to completely see through this lie?"

Of all the crazy things that could have come out of Bryce's mouth I did not think that this would be one. Who the hell just springs *engagement* on someone? My best friend apparently that's who.

*Best friend.*

We aren't even dating.

But I've got to admit that I'm curious about this...

He's been thinking over how he's going to respond, but I cut him off with another inquiry first. "Let's say for shits and giggles, that I go along with this. Why would you even do any of this?"

I can hear him scratching his chin. "It actually makes a lot of sense for me. My firm wants to see someone who's *committed* and who has a *well-rounded life.* I can't imagine that being engaged to you would not work in my favor with the senior partners. They know who you are already and it just makes sense that we could be more." He's parsing this out as he speaks.

My eyebrow rises, as I turn to face him. "That is ridiculous, you know that right? Friends and now we're suddenly engaged? That is not something people do." Responding with an unaffected sound, he's still thinking. He's lying on his back with an arm behind his head. Completely relaxed when he very well *should not* be. It's so reminiscent of when we were teens, except we both had way more acne. *How far we've come.*

Petulant about being put on the spot, I spray the bottle towards him a few times, disruping his peaceful contemplation. Before he can respond, I continue my questions to add another important one. "How long do you expect to keep this up? I can't just be lying to my family indefinitely about an engagement that *does not exist.*"

He remains deep in thought as he wipes a hand over his face to remove the water there. Looking up at the stars glued to my ceiling, he says, "People stay engaged for years... We don't have to be in any rush to do anything."

I kick his leg off the bed, so that he's forced to sit up with the momentum. "Have you considered that maybe... I don't want to be engaged-not-engaged to you for *literal years.* I do actually want to end up with someone." That someone can't be Bryce. That much has been made clear more than once in our friendship.

"And not me?" Bryce fake pouts, giving me puppy dog eyes. I narrow mine on him, reeling my leg back for another kick to the leg. He holds his hands out in front of him. "Okay, fine. Look, it does not have to be for years or indefinitely. I think for at least six months—max." He holds his hands even higher, wincing with one eye shut as I brandish my bottle at him again. "Until I get this promotion... And then we can break up, but still remain friends. People do that, right?"

"I have never seen that work out. Who stays friends after they break off an engagement? Nor do I have any intention of lying to my family for six months, Bryce."

"Please?" He begs. "Think about how much it would be helping me... How much easier it would be to avoid everyone on your back about Palmer... As the founding member of the Palmer hating club I think that this is—again—a great step up."

I huff out a breath, crossing my arms. "One month."

"Five?"

"No way. Two months."

"Four? Come on, Korra. I'm not a miracle worker. I only got a heads up that this promotion would be up for grabs soon. I don't know exactly when," he pleads.

"Three months. That's as much as I'm giving you. It'll see you through all the holidays. Final offer."

His smile stretches his cheeks and I have a feeling he knew what he was doing the whole time because of course the *attorney* did. I'm way out of my depth here. "Deal. You sure you didn't go to law school?"

"Your flattery will not get you on my good side." I plop down on the bed next to him. "If we go along with your plan, how is this going to work? We have been very much so *friends*—and I cannot stress the word *friends* enough—for this entire time. So... what? I've just been cheating on my boyfriend or what was going on there?"

"You can call it exactly how it is. I finally convinced you to break up with him because I wanted you all along."

I choke on air. Spluttering at the words. Unsure if they are true or if he's just saying that for this plan he's concocted.

When hc says the words, his face contorts in confusion. He's having a reboot of some sort. I don't really know what's going on there, but then he starts again. "We're a very believable couple. Of all the people in my life, you are the closest one to me. And I have tons of photos documenting us spending time together alone and getting close."

My voice is hushed when I say, "That could be said about any friends." Still thinking about his words and replaying many interactions between us.

"Yes, but we are *a man* and *a woman* who are friends." He emphasizes our genders by pointing his hands to the left and right. "People just expect friends like us to end up in some sort of romantic situation anyway."

I look at him with fresh eyes. "You feel good about lying to all of our closest friends and family just so that you can get ahead in your career?"

"No, I don't feel *good* but it's just a means to an end." He shrugs. "Don't forget—I'm also helping out a friend. A friend who does not want more people prying into her relationship problems. You can process the breakup without anyone meddling... Maybe me, just a little, but still better than all the Thomases combined."

"Well, it wouldn't be a problem. Except for you all made it a problem."

He shakes his head, still taking his presidency seriously. "It was a problem. And now—it's not. Because I'm here."

"Mmmhmm." I tap his chest, "And this has nothing to do with the fact that Jillian has brand new jewelry?"

He squeezes his chin a few times before saying, "Nope," he rushes. "Why would it?"

I don't believe it for a second. I'm the first to say that she is the worst. I will always be that person. What she did is inexcusable and I don't want her to ever have happiness after how she manipulated Bryce. However, I don't want to be caught up in something that feels like tit-for-tat between those two, no matter how much I hate her.

"Right. We need to wrap this up. Gotta get downstairs before they think we're doing something up here."

His eyebrows wiggle. "Was that not the point?"

I laugh at his silliness, flopping back onto my bed and then sitting back up. No need to ruin my hair after all that work I just did. "So you know, I don't think we're gonna be able to pull this off."

"I think we can. Plus, I've got something that I have not shared with you yet."

"You mean besides the fact that we're apparently engaged?"

He continues, ignoring my snark, "A secret weapon if you will."

I put my hands over my eyes and peek at him through two fingers. I'm scared to ask, "What did you get?"

"Just look," he says, turning his phone so that I can see it.

I don't believe my eyes.

If I didn't already have the idea in my mind, it would be so hard to miss.

On his phone is the most beautiful photo of him and I looking into each other's eyes. With his hand on my jaw and the sun setting perfectly around this extremely picturesque fall scene.

This could be our real engagement photos.

"They look like ..." my words trail off, but he has no problem finishing my sentence.

"Engagement photos, I know," he beams. "At first I thought *that's kind of silly.* You know? Like when friends go to the mall and get photos taken at the department store? I was thinking our photos would be that hilarious but this looks like a believable set plan—a proposal kind of thing."

"There's just one thing missing," I point out.

He swipes through more of our photos and they are, admittedly, adorable. Him fussing over me. Some of the sillier poses and candids. Or the way Wuying captured me laughing at him...

I went to the shoot mostly thinking it'd be fun. A way to commemorate how I beat him so epically at our sack race. A bragging right and nothing more. Bryce was the one to give his information for the photos once they were edited. He loves collecting them so it wasn't abnormal or exceptionally meaningful in any way.

"And what's that?" Bryce finally asks.

I blink at him owlishly but he doesn't get the hint. "A ring? Hello? Anyone in there?" I ask, tapping his forehead.

"Oh yea, we can do that anytime. There's plenty of time for it. Besides, it's the sentiment that counts right? *Emotion just took over and I needed to ask you in this perfect moment.*"

"What is that voice?" I tease. Taking a serious tone, I state, "For my fake engagement, I want a ring if I'm going to do this. I would not be the kind of girl to go without."

When I got that text from Palmer, I felt so betrayed. *I had defended him—to everyone.* I had tried to make sense of why I could not be enough for him to care about us, or this relationship, or me.

My mind was looping through all the ways I went wrong last night.

I tossed and turned.

Then showed up here to my Father's house, completely flustered. On top of the fact that it was a nightmare to see so many people in the house before I even got started on this piece-meal dinner.

I'm not hating the idea of looking like a prize to be won—to show up and throw that in my ex's face.

Palmer is not the kind of guy to remove me from any of his social media or something like that. He'll have to see my news. I don't know if there's someone else for him and I really don't want to know. I had thought that this man was someone that I could make space for in my life. I changed so many things for him. *Lowered my standards.* And if I'm going to *show him what he's missing*, then I need to look like someone who deserves a thoughtful engagement. The photos aren't enough.

"You don't have to drop a mortgage on it, but I would like for it to at least seem like you care about me. And showing people you care for me too. I've had enough of the *half-assed relationship situation* to last a lifetime."

"Done and done. I can easily make that happen," Bryce assures me.

"What are you going to tell the family now? They're going to have exactly one million questions when this meal is over. You know that the inquisition is about to start?"

He rubs a hand over his face. "Yea, I should probably talk to your dad first..."

"Oh my god. I'm the first daughter to get engaged. *The first child, really.* This is not gonna go well for you."

"Your dad loves me. Why wouldn't it go well? "

"I didn't mean it was going to be bad or he was gonna be mean to you or something. He's an emotional man. Probably even more emotional now that he's been seeing a therapist and talking about his feelings more openly. You are going to get cried on. That much I can be certain of."

Standing, he waves that idea away. "I think I can handle it."

"Fine, that's all you, buddy. Three months and then we are rectifying and turning things back the way they should go."

"I only have one thing to ask."

Pressing my fingers to my forehead, I ask, "Am I gonna hate this?"

"No," he shakes his head. "The only thing that I'm asking is that we don't let anything that happens in this fake engagement stop us from being friends at the end. You're the only real one that I've got. I don't know how I would function if I lost you. You're the only one who actually knows me and cares about me. I really don't know what my life would look like if I didn't have you in it. So if it ever comes to that, then we need to end whatever this is."

His words hit me right in the gut.

There's more emotion in this request than I was expecting. I thought for sure that he was going to say something else outrageous. Or more likely to have another bizarre request.

He's still my best friend and I should have known that he was going to say something like that.

"I won't let anything come between our friendship. I can't imagine anybody that I'd rather be faking being engaged to than you."

# CHAPTER 12

## Korra

"Engaged, huh?"

Kasey's straight facial expression is a lot more upset than it usually is. I think that anyone looking at her would suspect that she's not pleased by the turn of events. But I think more than anyone else I can actually feel how upset she is. It's not in what she says, but what she's not saying. Always leading with her probing questions.

I match her with a question of my own. "You're not happy for me? I thought this would definitely make you at least crack a smile." I say with as cheery a voice as I can manage.

I don't know that I expected her to just accept what Bryce and I had decided. But I did expect her to at least be a little happy that I'm not with Palmer anymore.

After all, it was her and him who were so anxious for me to get rid of my ex. And now that Palmer kicked me to the side, I'm simply trying to figure out what I should do next.

Yes, getting fake engaged to my best friend is probably not the better option of recovering from a break-up — but what am I supposed to do if this could potentially help Bryce out.

I'm a good friend. And my friend thinks that this will help him. I'd do anything to help him. He'd do the same for me.

Unfortunately, I kind of enjoy the fact that this is upstaging Jillian as well.

"No, Korra. I'm *not* happy that my twin sister got engaged to someone without even telling me that engagement was something she had thought about. To *Bryce*? Someone that we both know. How long has this been going on? Is this why you didn't care about Palmer?"

I bristle with her last question. "I did care about Palmer!" I take a deep inhale and exhale before I say, "I do care about Palmer. But we're not together anymore. I'm moving on."

"Moving on with your best friend? You can't just use him as a rebound. Don't you think that Bryce deserves better than that?"

My eyebrows shoot to my hairline. This was Bryce's idea. *How is it that I am looking like the bad guy here?* "You think that I don't deserve Bryce?"

She makes a sound of frustration. "That's not what I said, Korra. And you know that's not what I mean." She runs a hand over her ponytail and collects her words. "I just think that this is a little fast. And I don't understand why you didn't talk to me about it. If you were having feelings for Bryce, you know I would've listened. You know that I'm here for you for anything. But you don't talk to me about anything anymore."

"I do talk to you. I—"

"You *do not*. Ever since mom passed, it's like you have been living in this delusional little land, where nothing is wrong and nothing is of consequence. And I thought that maybe having Palmer around would make you happier and help you figure shit out. Because I don't know..." She picks at a cuticle getting visibly irritated talking about this. "I just thought that you were processing in some other way that you didn't need me for. But I've been here watching you do things that just don't make any sense. First, you and Palmer and that ridiculous situation that you called a relationship. Now you're jumping into another relationship with your best friend..."

The doubts that I had about pulling this off with Bryce are becoming more apparent as Kasey puts her brain to it. I chew on my bottom lip, not daring to say another word that could make this whole thing fall apart. I said I would try to make this work for Bryce's sake so I'm trying.

Under Kasey's scrutiny, I could crumble.

She thinks for a while longer and then asks, "So, that's what the whole birthday without Palmer thing was? And then going to the fall festival thing just the two of you? Then you've been holed up in your room more often. I mean everything is starting to come together."

Kasey is putting together a lot of things that I, personally, had not seen. There was nothing romantic about either of those occasions. Not intentionally, anyway. I can see how from the outside that actually works in our favor in making this feel more believable. If she's coming to that conclusion on her own, I can definitely use it to my advantage.

I did have fun with Bryce in both of those times she's recounting. And if it helps our case then I will start using it to strengthen our alibi. I'll have to let Bryce know that this is something else we can add. With the photos from the extravaganza that he showed me...

Everything does kind of seem like it was coming into place.

I don't like that I look like some sort of scummy cheater because of it though. That can't be helped at this point with the timing of everything, so there's nothing I can do as far as that goes. For the next few months, I'm going to have to make this look as believable as I can.

Nodding slowly, I let her romance-writing brain string together meaning from seemingly nowhere.

She continues, "Which I don't think is bad because I love Bryce. I think that you two could be good together. I just don't understand why you didn't say anything to me."

"Do I have to tell you about everything that I'm doing? There are some decisions I can make by myself. And what is all this? You say that I haven't been talking to you, but you clearly have emotions that you haven't been talking to me about either."

"I didn't want to push you, Korra. If you weren't ready to process, then I couldn't make you do that."

"But if you thought I was struggling, why didn't you say something? Instead of whatever this is," I ask, gesturing to the space between us that is apparently full of things neither of us have said to one another.

"I was blindsided. I did not see this coming at all. A couple of weeks ago, we were talking about you in a relationship with another man. And now you're saying you're engaged? What is going on here?" Her voice rises and rises as she tells me how she's seeing my life through her eyes. I had no idea that she was so upset about any of this.

Clearly there's something here that I had been missing this whole time. "This isn't about Bryce and me. This is about you."

"What?" she exclaims. "How is this about me?"

"How is it not? I announced that I'm getting engaged and you start talking about all these issues that you've had with me for months and you've never said anything. How is that fair to me? How was this not you making this about you?" I look at the face that mirrors mine and try to piece what exactly that could be.

"You know that's not what I'm saying. I would never try to take away your shine."

"It sure feels like it." Internally, I'm cringing about my words. I don't want to fight with Kasey. I don't want to make this a big deal. Bryce could not have picked a worse time to spring this on me.

"In what way, Korra? I just want to know what's going on with you because you aren't telling me."

"Nothing is going on with me. I'm in a new relationship. I'm figuring it out. I don't have everything planned and ready to go and perfect. *I'm not perfect.* I just want to figure out how to move forward without Mom and live my life. There's a huge hole where she is and all I can do is try to fill it with something that feels good to me."

"No, you don't have to do that. You could fill it with healing," She touches my arm softly. "You could heal the hole."

"Like you're doing? You never leave the house unless I'm the one making you. You certainly aren't trying to pursue any relationships of your own. You hide away with your computer, writing about other people finding love and happiness. *You aren't even doing that for yourself.* But you wanna accuse me of not *healing a hole.*"

We both stand in shock. Words I didn't know would escape me hanging heavy between us.

Her brows lower over concerned eyes when she says, "I'm not accusing you of anything. And we're not talking about me. You and mom had the closest relationship out of all of us. I just can't imagine that you're okay. *I know you're not okay.*"

"You don't know anything, Kasey. Just let me live my life and make the decisions that I think are best for me. I know you love me and I know that you've been trying to help me." I take a deep breath, "But I don't need it. I just want you to be happy with my decisions and stand beside me as my sister—as my twin, my other half."

Kasey crosses her arms. "Sure. I'll just keep my mouth shut and smile next to you when you're making crazy, wild choices."

"Thank you." I say, accepting her words, though I know they are sarcastic and facetious.

My sister scowls at me. For now I'm going to leave the conversation right where it's at. I really don't have any answers to give her. I'm upset by the fact that she has had these feelings that she hasn't shared with me either.

She says that I haven't talked to her.

*She hasn't talked to me either.*

We need to have a conversation and come to some sort of understanding about what has happened over the last year. *We aren't as aligned as we should be.*

Thanksgiving is over and all that remains are my family and Bryce. After the two of us returned to the room, Jillian and Terry's spots were empty which was probably for the best. Everyone else was excitedly congratulating us, including the Geiers. There were too many *about time* comments fluttering about for my taste. I didn't know what to do with all that praise over something that was undeniably fake.

Walking back into the dining room after talking with Kasey, where the rest of my family is still eating sweet potato pie—I start to feel a little bit guilty. My sister was right. I am lying to all of them. *It's just a helpless little one.* At the end of the day it's not going to be that big of a deal.

Right?

The talking continues around me as I take my seat next to Bryce. He's talking with Zack about the photos we took at the Botanical Gardens. He's been passing the phone around for everyone to see it. I want to be paying attention but my mind is still going over what Kasey said.

*Am I being delusional?*

*Have I been avoiding processing my Mom's passing?*

I've been doing the best that I can.

Trying to live my life without her and the only way I know how.

Kasey was right about one thing—I was the closest to Mom. I can do something to keep her memory alive. A way that we all could feel closer to her.

"I appreciate everybody coming for dinner today. I know she would have wanted it that way. I think we should do something to keep Mom's traditions going."

My dad reaches across the table to squeeze my hand. "What did you have in mind?" After what was a much shorter aside than I was expecting from my Dad, Bryce returned to dinner unscathed. And without tears soaking his bouclé jacket. I guess my Dad was happy about the engagement, but not overjoyed like I believed he might be.

"The scrapbook," I say. "She used to put all of our photos and biggest accomplishments in them. I can't believe it's been a year since we looked through them."

Lee agrees with me first. "I know. And they were good. She used to enter them into the contest the Brenford's hold every year. Obviously not last year, but maybe we could submit one of hers this year."

"I don't think it would be right to submit one she hasn't agreed to. Maybe we should do our own thing." I suggest.

"Let me look on the website. I'm sure there's rules or something we need to know. We might've missed registration or something," Zach says. My brother looks on his phone for a little while trying to find any information about the contest. I knew there was always some prize for them, but I never really paid that much attention to it.

When my mom was scrapbooking, I was often doing something else. She had collected so many different papers and stickers and all types of things. No one had gone through any of that stuff as her studio had remained untouched for the most part since she passed. None of us had the heart to go in there and change anything and we definitely hadn't packed it up. There was no point in doing that. No one expected her to walk in and be upset that we had touched her things, but it was nice to think that maybe that little piece of her could remain there.

Like maybe she would still be in that room if we walked in.

No music ever came out of it anymore.

No projects ever came out of it anymore.

It was like some untouched shrine for her.

"It says that it's open registration," Zach informs us after a while of looking.

"Well... that settles it then, we can definitely enter. What are the rules for this kind of thing?" I had this big idea, but I didn't actually know how I was going to be able to pull it off. It wasn't like I was some super experienced scrapbooking expert. All I knew was that she had her book, she took it up there, and they judged it. She never heard back about winning. I didn't know what the scale of this competition would look like, but it would be something that we all contributed to.

Zach flips his phone to show us some of the past winners. *We might be slightly out of our depth.* It's not likely that we'll win but it's about the process more than the prize right? "It says there can be up to five spreads. Ten total pages."

"Well what goes on the pages? And what are we gonna put it on?" Kasey asks, finally looking up from her own phone. It had taken her a little while longer after I came into the room to join us, but when she did—her eyes were glued to something on her screen.

"You leave that up to me. I'm going to figure it out since it was my idea. I don't want anyone to work on something for Mom out of guilt. If it's not your thing—I get it."

Bryce puts a hand over mine. "I think it's a great idea. I'll help you, if you want."

Turning to face him I say, "I'd love that."

One thing I could say about Bryce, he was always willing to help me, no matter what it was that I asked of him. It's why I agreed to help him so easily. Even if it was killing me to lie about it. He had my back, so I had to have his.

My youngest sister, Nia, speaks up. "I was really looking forward to Merry & Bright this year. It's been so long since I even sang anything. I think we should all do it together. I was in high school the last time we participated as a family." She meant Mom and the four of them, I was not included in that.

Around the table, my siblings all agree with Nia's proposal and I just have to sit there and take it.

Nia notices my silence and adds. "Oh, Korra. You can still be there..."

I can't help the straightening off my spine or how itchy I feel in my sweater now. "And do what? You all got that gene. I did not."

It's been a long time since I've actually felt that hurt of being the only one of us who can't sing. My Mom would always have us singing Christmas songs and carols together. *Everyone except me.*

I remember when she started to fall in love with the fact that a-cappella music had gotten popular.

It was a particularly strong memory for me.

All of them would be able to put together a song using only their voices. I was the beat or usually sound effects of some sort until I was  left out because I can't carry a tune to save my life, especially not in comparison to the rest of them.

I liked Thanksgiving much better. It usually involved a lot less singing and a lot more eating or floral arrangements or anything that I could actually do with my Mom and not be embarrassed to just be there.

Of the five of us, Nia has the nicest voice. It would not even be something she'd think about. But I was the odd one out when they would be harmonizing together. I would just be there... Being there.

"Don't worry about me, I will be fine on the sidelines for that. I'm sure she would be happy to see you all singing up there from heaven."

"Well, we all have something that we could be working on. I think that's what matters." Zach says to the table, breaking up the tension. "Nia, you can work on an arrangement for Merry & Bright. Korra, you can work on the scrapbook for now. The rest of us will get in where we fit in. Sound good?"

There are sounds of agreement around the table.

# CHAPTER 13

## Bryce

*Okay, easy.*

Get a ring, figure out why the fuck I opened my mouth, and hope that everything works out well so I don't completely destroy the best friendship I've had with one of the most decent women I've ever known.

*Ugh.*

Decent is not the appropriate or accurate word.

*I'm already fucking this up.*

There's only one jeweler in Harmony Hill, Stratton's Stones. And it's pretty obvious why a man my age would be walking into a jewelry store. If it hasn't already circled through the town, I'm sure there are whispers coming my way about the announcement of Korra's and my engagement.

When I walk into the store, I notice right away that it is abnormally bright inside. The lights have lights in this place. If there was any mistake about who I was walking in, there would be zero chance of mistaking who I was now that the lights are shining on my face. The brightness is making me hot under the collar, and I pull it away from my throat to get a little bit of relief.

It doesn't work.

*Why am I so nervous?*

The associate who comes to help me is someone who we went to school with. Micah Baird sees me and lights up immediately. *Pardon the pun.* I think I've been around the Thomases far too long.

It's Friday and though yesterday was tense, I think the engagement announcement went over well. I'd slept at Tara's place since she's in Singapore and the house is quiet. It also helped that I didn't have to figure out a sleeping arrangement with Korra at her place. Kasey stayed the night at their family house "to give us time alone." We did not take that time because we're not actually together. It'd been a while since I dreamed of lace but I bet you that my mind would try to fuck me over with recalling it when she was lying inches away from me.

*I could not have that.*

"Bryce," Micah says with a scandalized tone. Like I just said, there's only one reason why a man my age would be walking into a jewelry store. So it's not *that scandalous* to imagine what I'm here to do. "To what do I owe the pleasure?"

I'm sorry, at what point did I come to the store to visit him?

"I'm looking for something special," I state.

"You came to the right place. Do you have an idea of what it is you're looking for?"

"I need a ring. An engagement ring for my…" I stop myself before finishing the sentence. I don't actually know what the hell to say there. I should be saying *girlfriend* or *fiancée.* That should be the turmoil that I'm fighting with, but it was my first instinct to say *my best friend,* instead.

Thank God, Micah doesn't allow me to fumble around with my words anymore and fills in the gap for me. "Oh, I know it can be hard to make that transition to think of them from girlfriend to fiancée, but let me tell you— If you get a ring from here, you will have zero problems with her saying yes."

I wince, "She already said yes. So, I don't think that's going to be a problem either way."

"Oh," is all he says, eyebrows lifted to his platinum blonde hairline. "You proposed without a ring?" *Is it really that uncommon?*

"Yea, I did."

He places a hand to his heart, a look of disbelief on his face for a moment. "And she said yes?"

"She did. We've been friends for a long time. So the emotions were there... I didn't need the ring to prove to her that I was serious." Though that couldn't be further from the truth. I did have to prove that I was serious about our *fake* engagement. The feelings bit...

"Oh," he says again. "It's killing me not knowing who it is. Will you tell me?"

I scratch my neck, "Korra. Korra Thomas. She was in our–"

His eyebrows lift, not in disbelief, but with intrigue. "I know who she is," he responds. "Those must've been some pretty hefty words. You're gonna have to show me exactly what it was you said, and I can pass it along to other clients." He winks.

"It wouldn't work for them. Korra and I are a little bit different." An understatement for sure, but I think it does what it's supposed to because he begins to move around the room with the keys to the display cases in his hand.

"Well, let's try a few things that I think might be right. First, I've just got to ask you a few questions."

"All right." I say, standing a little taller. "What exactly do you want to know? I'm pretty sure her ring size is an eight."

He shakes his head, an amused chuckle coming from his lips. "Ring size is important, but fit is about more than the size of her finger."

"I'm not following..."

"Well, tell me about her and I can point you in the direction of a few options I think she'd enjoy."

"All right," I say again, hoping that these won't be too difficult and that I'll know how to answer.

The first display case we stand across from is filled with more jewelry than rings. Necklaces and watches are propped on velvet holders just below the glass. Our reflection gleaming back at the two of us. "Would you say that your fiancée is someone who gravitates towards traditional styles or something more unique?"

Without any hesitation, I respond, "She definitely likes something more unique... I can imagine her turning her nose up at something defined as *traditional.*"

"Okay, very good to know. We need to move from this shelving entirely." He picks up his tray and moves to a different counter on the other side of the store. "Do you think that Korra would prefer something with diamonds or would you be open to alternative gemstones?"

"You know? I think that alternative gemstones would be a good place to go... Maybe even crystals? I know she wears lots of them. I don't know what they mean, but I always see her with them on." It makes me recall that night and how I started seeing red in a whole new light.

My face heats as I tell him, "When I was taking her jewelry off the other night I just recognized that I always see her wearing crystals of some sort."

The night when I started having the very inconvenient dreams of her.

"That is very helpful... I know you say you don't know what they are, but would you remember what color they are?"

I wrack my brain trying to think of some of the colors of the crystals I've seen her in. "I've seen her with some green, some more clear-ish... She's had some red or black as well. She's got a lot of them around her house, too."

"Usually people who collect crystals have a strong connection to the meaning behind choosing them. I'm sure that you and her could have this conversation later on, but I think in terms of the ring let's think about the band for now. Do you think she'd like gold or white gold or..." He shows me a new tray with pink metal bands, "Rose gold—that's really popular right now."

"I always see her with gold. It goes really well with her skin tone too." The way the gold light hit her on the back of that truck or even with the yellow gold spotlight roaming over her at the club... She should always be in gold.

He nods several times, putting the tray of pink rings away. "Now, I'm getting a better picture. I think you're discovering that you know just a little bit more about her than maybe you thought before." He moves to a completely separate display that's in the back corner. It holds shelves with jewelry that look a lot closer to the style that I could see Korra wearing.

"This question really helps me decide exactly where I want to go with your recommendation. Would you say that she has a strong connection to nature or is inspired by natural elements? You know? Leaves, plants—that kind of thing?"

I chuckle. "How could I not say that? The woman's house is basically a forest. She's got plants everywhere. They're spilling out of her bathroom, in her bedroom, and they're all over the entryway. It's the main way that I know where her apartment is. She is very much so interested in *natural elements*."

He laughs for a moment and once he's gained his composure, unlocks the door to the display we're standing in front of. "I know exactly where to point you now!"

He pulls out a tray and I look it over for only two seconds. My eyes land on the ring that I know will be absolutely perfect for her.

Before I can stop myself, I reach for the ring that has caught my eye. It has the most delicate gold band that looks like stems with leaves all around. There's a collection of small green stones clustered all around a much larger crystal at the center. It's kind of clear but there's so much green leaking through it like vines. It's *absolutely stunning*. The gold that holds it in place mimics small leaves and even the prongs look like some sort of leaf holding the larger crystal in the center in place. It's so intricate and detailed but also still very whimsical and delicate.

"This is the one," we both say, marveling at the ring.

"Okay, perfect. I'll get this one set up for you. We'll get a beautiful box for you to present it to her with. Just because you proposed to her once without a ring there's no stopping you from proposing again—This time with something a little more sparkly."

"Right. I've got just one more thing to ask you about."

"What is it?"

"Do you have a green jewelry box?"

# CHAPTER 14

## Korra

It's been such a long time since I came into this room. Months if I really think about it. I usually avoid going anywhere in my childhood home outside of the main rooms downstairs and my old bedroom. Walking into my mom's studio feels like taking a step back in time.

I can feel her in this room so clearly.

It still smells like her.

A disarray of her latest project on the desk.

In the far corner, her grand piano is set up with the bench upholstered in bold rooster fabric. The last time I was here, I removed the plants that she had and took them to my own house. I couldn't bear the thought of them dying in here and attracting any sort of bugs or mold.

"I don't know where to start." I stand at her desk with my hands on the edge. My head hangs low between my shoulders, and I roll it around, trying to ease some of the tension building there.

"How about we just start with what you think we need," Bryce says from the doorway.

What I need is to talk about all the feelings that are too big inside me right now. But I know that's not really what he means.

Spinning in place, I choose to lean on the edge of the deck instead. "How are you so cool with this?"

I don't have to elaborate on what "this" I mean. He already knows. "Well, our *engagement* solves a lot of things for me." Then he shrugs away from the door to meet me at the desk. Long strides that eat up the distance between us in no time. "Maybe it hasn't hit what I've actually gotten us both into," he says with a chuckle.

Resting my forehead on his chest, I say, "You know, Kasey pulled me to the side to talk."

His deep voice rumbles through my mind when he asks, "How did that go?"

A heavy breath comes out with my exasperation. "Well, it didn't go pleasantly... She apparently had many ideas about this whole thing."

There's silence for a while as I wait for his response. Noticing that the silence is going on for too long I lean away from his body.

He looks down at me, skeptically, "Like what?"

"I don't know." I huff, "A lot of things."

Pushing off from the desk, I grab the box beside Mom's desk that's labeled *patterned paper*. When I sit on the floor, I start organizing some of the more fall themed papers around me. There are several cute little designs that I think would be amazing together. She's got some papers with leaves and some with buckets of apples. I could probably cut out this truck on another of them. Looks an awful lot like the one that we posed in front of at the extravaganza.

Bryce watches me patiently from Mom's desk chair. He doesn't push for an explanation, instead waiting for me to tell him what he knows I will eventually share.

Not looking up from my task, I continue, "She was saying that I am not processing Mom's passing. That I am living in some delusional world of my own making."

He raises a brow at me. "Are you?"

"I didn't think so. Do you think I am?" Looking into his eyes, I hope to find the honesty that I've come to know from him. He was never one to sugarcoat things or try to soften harsh truths.

"I think that you are just doing the best you can. It's hard losing a parent. And with how close the two of you were... I definitely thought that you would take it much harder."

Standing, I take a step away from him, then several more until I'm sitting on the bench in front of her piano. "Should I still be weeping about this every single day?" I flinched at how my words sound. "I am sad about her not being here. *I miss her all the freaking time.* Everything I do—she's there. So, I don't feel like it's a loss I should cry about all the time. I cried plenty. Should I still be hysterical now?"

I throw my hands in the air. "I don't understand how I'm supposed to behave. I'm just trying to freaking live. I don't know why that's not good enough for everyone else. I just want to remember my Mother the way that she was. Not as someone who's not here anymore."

"There is no right or wrong way to grieve." He stands and holds his arms open for me. I trudge across the low-pile rug with my boots, falling into a hug with him. He smells like he usually does, clean and crisp. And there is some comfort in being in his hug even being in this room. "If you take your time or do it all at once—it's your choice. What Kasey or I expect is irrelevant. Okay? We're here for you. She's likely just worried."

"I don't like how all her worry feels like an attack," I murmur into his chest.

His chuckle is warm against my body. "Kasey will be Kasey. She's a little rough around the edges, but it's all love. I know it."

I scoff and step out of his arms. "Come on, we've gotta make some sort of progress on this thing. I don't expect it to look as good as what Mom put together, but we can at least try."

"Well, I'm out of my depth here. I was thinking I'd be here more for moral support as opposed to actually doing anything creative." Bryce scratches the back of his neck, "As you can probably imagine, I wasn't born with the creative bug."

Patting his shoulder, I say, "Everyone has the ability to be creative. Yours is just maybe not in the same ways that mine are."

"Yea, we'll see about that," he mutters.

Gathering the papers I've already found from earlier, I begin looking through some of the other labeled storage boxes on her shelves. I find washy tape, stickers and several other papers that I could use for a fall themed spread. For whatever reason, this time of year has been speaking to me. I want to be a part of it and hope that the cold of winter will stay away for a little while longer. Puttering around the room, I get consumed with my task. Somewhere between the comfort of being in Mom's studio and Bryce's quiet agreement in whatever ideas I throw at him, a reprieve from my unease at Kasey's accusations comes to me.

Next, I look for some tools to put everything together. There's a double-sided tape roller on her desk along with a ruler and paper trimmer. The only other thing I need is an actual book to put everything in. She must have kept blank ones somewhere in here.

"Can you hand me that box from up there?" I point to the extra large one that sits on top of the storage shelves.

"Yea," he says, "See, this is the kind of help I can do. Getting the things done that you couldn't."

"Is this a short joke?" I question with a hand on my hip. "There is a step ladder in here, you know?"

"But could a step ladder look this good in a genuine Andean wool sweater?"

I knew that sweater felt soft. "Lemme see it real quick."

He sets the box in front of where I'm sitting on the floor. "No, no, no, my friend. I know that all sweaters in your possession will not be returned. Wayne warned me early."

"Allegedly," I giggle and point at him. "I won't be slandered in my own house."

"Yea, yea." He brushes off my claims before returning to where he was sitting. *I'll get the sweater, just you wait.*

Pulling at the top of the box, it doesn't come away like the others did. Turning it to the other side, I see that there is a latch on it. No lock on the latch. *Why would it have a latch anyway?*

Opening it anyway, I rummage around to find any unused scrapbooks, but I don't have much luck on that front.

Instead, it's mostly newspapers. Some whole and others that are just clippings. One from when she placed first in a choir competition. Some with her standing on stage with her mouth wide open and a microphone in her hand. She looks so young and beautiful. I decide to pull a few of them out to maybe use in the spread. I don't have a solid idea of what these two pages will look like, but I figure the more materials I have to work with, the easier it will be to put something together.

The last of the newspapers doesn't flop to the floor before Bryce asks, "What is that?"

I look back into the box and see what he's asking about. It's a lump of pale blue fabric. It's wrapped tightly around something that's hard in the middle. My fingers brush over its silky texture. "I think it might be a handkerchief or something."

Bryce moves the rest of the papers around to see if there is anything else unusual inside. "What's it doing in the box?"

"Dunno."

I start unfolding the fabric to see what's inside of it.

It's been tucked away for so long that the creases in the silk are hard pressed into place.

This is not a handkerchief as I first suspected.

It's *a necktie.*

The more I unfold the tie, the more I see speckles of brown.

"Is that blood or sauce?" Probably not my brightest idea, but I sniff the fabric. It doesn't smell like anything I can recognize.

Bryce looks at me before taking the necktie to look at it closer for himself. "Korra, that is definitely blood. I highly doubt that it's pasta sauce."

My worried eyes meet his skeptical ones. "Why would my Mom have a bloody necktie in a box latched on the top of her shelf?"

"I've got no idea, but she kept it for some reason. What was it wrapped around?"

I had almost forgotten about the card that fell to the ground. I pick it up and on one side of it is the Brenford Steel Mill logo but when I flip it to the other side, it's clearly an ID card for someone called Aiden Kindrick.

Bryce takes the card from my hand and looks at it. "This is not their logo anymore. This thing has got to be decades old. Look at the issue date. It's from the nineties."

"Okay, you're the lawyer here. I'm gonna need some conclusions or something cause right now I am having a lot of crazy thoughts." I fan my heating face with my speculations adding up rapidly.

"Thoughts like what?" He asks. "There's probably a really logical explanation for why Delanna kept this."

Looking at the face on the ID card there's something very familiar about it and I can't place it. It's on the tip of my tongue, but it evades me. "Who is this guy? Why would she be keeping it?"

"It's probably nothing. Who knows other than her? We're snooping through her things." Bryce brushes off my suspicions with ease.

I'm not so sure that I can.

"It just seems very weird that she would keep some bloody necktie from this random guy. It's not like blood-bath, slasher-film bloody but this does not seem like a regular amount of blood from like shaving your neck or a paper cut."

"I'm sure you're looking for something that's not there. We have no reason to suspect that this has any sort of significance or importance. I mean it's in a box with a bunch of newspapers about singing contests your mom entered when she was younger."

Picking up one of the newspapers, I start reading an article that highlights her win. "Look at this. These contests were put on by the Brenford family."

He shrugs, "So what? Almost everything in this town is put on by that family or they're a major sponsor. The only thing that they don't have a large hand in is the rodeo."

"I don't know." There's something here that I just can't place. It probably is nothing but what if it's not?

Bryce knows me too well. He sees through me. "The point of you coming in here was to feel closer to your Mom, not accuse her of something with no basis."

He's right, but I just have a feeling. My Mom was not a secretive person. She was an open book. She was honest and kind. Whatever thoughts I have are completely unfounded.

"Let's just try to make some headway on this spread because I still need to drive back to Denver tonight."

Straightening the hem of my plaid pleated skirt over my thighs, I suggest. "You know... You could stay at my place? With everyone thinking that we're engaged, it probably would make more sense for you to stay the night, anyway."

"But Kasey's gonna be at the apartment tonight."

"So, what? It wouldn't be the first time."

"You said she got on your ass. I don't want her to get on my ass, too." He says but with the way he's adjusting his collar, it looks like there's more to it than that.

"Well that's just not fair," I start laughing because he does have a point. "I think she feels bad for how she charged me up. If anything, she was supportive of us being together. Especially if it meant that I wasn't gonna be with Palmer anymore." I sort out the materials that I want to take with me to keep working on this and the ones that I'll be leaving here so we can get ready to go.

"See, my plan was the best plan. Now you don't have to worry about her giving you the third degree about Palmer. I think you know as well as I know what that relationship really was."

I scowl at him. "I thought you said that I was going to be free of this kind of conversation."

"From them," he uses a thumb to point out of the doorway. "Since I know what actually happened, I still have to be a good friend and let you know how much more you deserved."

"Yea, yea," I respond, putting my supplies into a box to take with me.

He rubs his belly before standing from the ground and stretching out his long limbs. "Since I'm gonna be staying the night, I guess I should go and get some leftovers from yesterday."

# CHAPTER 15

## Bryce

I hope the fall weather lasts just a bit longer. The leaves are barely hanging onto their branches. The sun still finds us through the large gaps in the tree cover. It's no problem since the cooler temperatures make it comfortable to walk up this trail. It must be global warming since I remember November very differently as a kid and even as a teen.

Korra pants from behind me, hanging onto my shoulder for dear life. "How much longer are we going to be hiking? You know I'm not seventeen anymore, right?"

Looking over my shoulder, I chuckle at her. "I told you not to wear a sweater."

"But look at how perfectly it matches the scene around us," she says with her fair-isle sweater pushed up her arms. The wool socks she has on, rolled down over her hiking boots, aren't helping her case.

"You're gonna overheat. At least take the sweater off."

She gives me a bizarre look, her eyes bugging out of her head. "I wore a heather grey tee under here."

"So...?" I ask, unsure of why that matters at all.

With her hands on her knees, she attempts to catch her breath. "I've got boob sweat and pit sweat. There is a guaranteed map of how hard this hike has been in this general area." She laughs but circles her mid-section with both hands.

I can't stop the one big laugh from escaping as I lean on a nearby tree. "It's only been two miles, Kor."

"Don't laugh," she says, laughing at herself again. She slides down the tree next to me. "I'm ready for a snack break... and to maybe roll downhill."

"We'll rest for a bit, but we're not too far from the spot I'm thinking of."

"There's more?" She whines, swiping the sweat from her forehead.

I nod and she groans. "Just take the sweater off. You'll feel much better."

She kicks at some leaves on the ground before conceding. "Fine." She struggles to get the sweater over her hair but I don't tell her that putting her curls up would cool her off even faster.

Korra wasn't kidding about her map of sweat. It's not localized how she thought but instead slicks the back of her tee to her body along with her stomach. It makes the slim cut top even tighter on her body.

I swallow when she lifts the hem of the shirt up to get some air to the skin underneath. The very edge of her sports bra exposed. Sweat rolls down her smooth stomach to the top of very tight leggings that highlight her shape.

Quickly redirecting my attention to my backpack to find the trail mix I packed is a far more useful activity to be engaging in. Definitely better than recalling the warm feel of her skin in my stupid dream.

Sleeping on her floor last night was nothing when I could have very well done something very unfriendly in her bed. The dream was back and I woke up with a very hard and very insistent morning wood. Why my mind was fucking with me is beyond me. *Is sleeping on the floor not bad enough?* Then I was forced to very quietly do something about the obvious tent before she woke up and saw me like that on her floor.

"Yes! This has chocolate in it," she snatches the trail mix from me, pouring some into her mouth.

Reaching for the bag, she moves it out of the way. "It's *supposed* to be for us to share."

"This is like a pound of oats. I'll share..." she stuffs some more into her mouth, "when my mouth gets too dry to chew anymore."

"Ha ha. Let me have some," I say, taking the bag back from her.

"How much farther?" She asks after finishing her mouthful of granola.

"I'd say about another mile—"

"Great."

"—and a half." She frowns. "I'm positive that it will be worth it. The sooner we get there the sooner you'll see."

She ties her sweater around her waist and fixes her shirt that's dried off a bit. The higher up we go, the cooler it'll be and she'll eventually be more comfortable.

On the way up, I ask her about the plants that were hanging in her bathroom. It's something to take her mind off the rest of our journey but I am curious since they were my only visual this morning while I took care of *business*.

She informs me about her Ellen Danica so thoroughly, I should consider myself a Cissus expert, as well.

"Now I think I might have to get one for my bathroom too."

"I could propagate a plant for you. I think a few would really liven your place up."

"Really? It's that easy?"

"It will take a little work on my end but they only need to watered every week or so once they get growing. In a bathroom is best since they're native to more tropical climates. You take enough showers to keep her healthy."

"Her?" I question.

She giggles. "Yea, *her*. She is an elegant lady. Wasn't that obvious?"

"No, no. It was very obvious," I say with my eyebrows high on my head.

When we get close, I take my backpack off, setting it against some large boulders. I catch the view first since Korra is still doing her best to get up the last rocks. *This is going to be perfect.* There's water rushing to our left and I know I'll need to get that in the shot.

I walk back over to Korra, holding out a hand for her to use in getting over the last rocks in her way.

The moment she sees the view her breath is stolen for a new reason. "Bryce," she gasps. "This is incredible!"

In the distance, the range is beautiful and clear. A valley dips between the tree line in all different colors of the season. It's the kind of view that Colorado is known for and today it's clear enough to see off into the distance for miles in the varied terrain below this lookout.

Taking my phone out of my pocket, I get a photo of the view and then one of a stunned Korra.

"Show me," she says when she's finally gotten her fill of the view. I turn it to show her and she smiles down at it. "Wow, even behind us is beautiful. Let's get one together."

I agree, getting prepared for the shot. She unties her sweater from her waist, throwing it on top of my bag.

"How far should we be? I don't want to fall over the edge." She adjusts her curls and swipes her hands over her face to get rid of the sweat, "Is here good?"

I set my phone to record and answer, "Yea, there is good. Are you ready?"

I jog to my backpack and place the phone down in such a way that we can remain in frame. She nods when I jog back.

"Are you recording?" She questions with a smirk, her mood more buoyant with the rewarding views from our hike up here.

"Yea, I am. I have something I want to ask you?" I didn't realize that my nerves would be getting to me as badly as they currently are. My heart is pumping double-time in my chest as I wait for her answer.

Korra is looking at me, perplexed now. I *don't blame her.*

I dig around my other pocket for the green box and try not to fumble it down the side of this cliff. I guess that's why they make these things out of velvet—so sweaty hands don't drop them as easily.

She looks down at my hand holding the box and then back to the camera. Clarity shines in her eyes or maybe they're glassy and shining for another reason.

"I did this wrong and asked you before I was completely prepared and that is on me. Like you said, you're the kind of woman who deserves a ring. One with meaning and one that symbolizes how special and perfect you truly are. And Korra," her eyes drag up from my hand to my eyes. The sienna of them capturing me and making me feel emotions that I know I shouldn't right now.

*This isn't real.*

Neither of us are that great of actors but something about this *feels* real.

I wanted it to seem as authentic as possible. To sell this idea and take her mind off of her loser ex.

"Korra, you do deserve all those things."

I get on one knee.

Opening the box, I present the ring I chose for her despite my heart beating up through my ear drums.

She gasps my name again, but this time the shock tugs at my chest.

I'm going through with this.

There's no turning back.

It was my idea and it's still a good one.

*Even if it's fake.*

With a deep inhale, I exhale all those doubts away. We already agreed to do this. All I have to do is ask, "Will you marry me?"

Hands over her mouth, Korra is speechless. She stares and stares at the ring in my hand. I didn't think I'd be on the ground this long and the small pebbles are starting to hurt my knee, even through the sweats I'm wearing.

"Korra," I prompt, hoping she'll say something... and soon.

My nerves in asking her were real.

My nerves now that I've broken her somehow are real, as well.

Maybe I should have talked to her about this before, but I didn't think I needed to. When I went to the store early yesterday morning, I just figured there was no point in waiting. Take her out to pop the question soon as possible.

Bringing her on a hike to a scenic place kind of went with the whole story of what we'd been doing so far. Asking at the photoshoot. Then presenting the ring at the cliff's edge of the most scenic hike I've ever taken.

We'd come here in high school and I take the hike every now and again when I'm back in Harmony Hill. There was a bit of nostalgia and importance here. Mixing the real with the fake to make this engagement as authentic as possible.

She finally moves. Touching my hand, she says, "Stand up, Bryce."

Now I'm the one who's confused. *Is she going to say no to this whole thing?* If she doesn't want to go through with it, I wouldn't hold that against her. I'm asking a lot. I know I am.

"You didn't have to do this," she has to crane her neck back to look me in the eyes. Those huge browns are still shining. In a low tone that the video won't capture she says, "This feels like a real proposal."

I whisper back to her, "It's supposed to…" Holding her eyes, I try to judge if there is hurt there but only vulnerability greets me. "Is it too much?"

She shakes her head minimally, finding a smile to mask that inner turmoil. "Yes! I'll marry you!" Holding her hand out for me, she bounces in anticipation as I slide the ring onto her third finger.

She marvels at the ring for a moment before jumping to hug me around the neck. I hug her back immediately. She's warm and soft in my arms, fitting into my embrace perfectly. Though so much is different about this hug, it's the same.

*It's us.*

*This is us.*

But everything has changed when she releases me.

"You're still the best gift giver. How do you nail it every time?"

"I know you. It's not that hard to do," I say jogging over to the phone to stop the video.

# CHAPTER 16

## Bryce

Honking my horn three times at the person who just cut me off in traffic, I huff my frustration. No amount of squeezing my temples will get me out of the grid I'm stuck in on this highway.

Being back in Harmony Hill was the break I needed.

Leaving the city, even if only for a weekend, was refreshing. I ate great food, had good conversation and got amazing views atop Harmony Hill's namesake hills. Did I propose to my best friend and also live to tell the tale? Yes. But I slept like a baby last night with no dream of her in that damn red lace. That's gotta be a win.

When I went to my closet to pick a suit for my day, I could feel my smile stretching beyond its means.

Brushing my teeth, I smiled.

Making my smoothie, I smiled.

Hell, picking up my heavy brief case and walking out to my car, I smiled.

But now, as I am forty-five minutes into my *should-be* twenty minute commute, stress hunches my shoulders like the long weekend never happened.

I suppose that's why people are happier in a small town.

Thoughts of how this weekend went down end up putting that smile back onto my face once the asshole who cut me off is long gone. I'm one step closer to getting that senior partner slot and that is something to smile about.

My phone rings inside the cabin and I pick up expecting it to be the only person who calls me before work.

"Hey, ma," I say. "How's Singapore?"

"It's wonderful, baby. We went to Bukit Timah Nature Reserve yesterday and it was so beautiful. Michelle just loved the macaques. I thought she was going to try and take one home."

I chuckle at the happiness in my ma's voice. Years had passed where she wasn't anything like this. Joy had evaded her. To hear it now, is truly a blessing. "Pictures or it didn't happen," I say, then my phone vibrates with the messages that I'm sure are the photos I've asked for. "I'll look at them when I get to the office. It's a good thing you called, I actually wanted to talk to you."

A heavy sigh weighs down her voice even as the ambiance of nature makes itself known in her miserable reaction. "Please tell me you didn't get back with that Lisbeth girl. I don't know what you see in her."

"Wow," I say, surprised that she thinks I'd get back with *that*. "Definitely not. I did see her though."

"Okay. What is it then, son?"

Better just rip things off like a bandaid. Her parent knows. It's only fair that I tell mine, too. "Korra and I are engaged."

"To be married?"

"Is there any other kind of way?"

She proceeds to list all the ways in which I could mean. "Engaged in combat. Engaged in conversation. Engaged elsewhere. Engaged—"

"Stop acting funny, ma. I'm being serious. I proposed to Korra this past weekend."

"But," she makes a noise that sounds like coughing on the other end and I wait for her to speak again. "You've never said anything about her *in that way*. I thought—I thought you were just friends. When did that change?"

*I don't know.*

"They say you should marry your best friend and you'll have a longer, lasting marriage. Maybe we've just been doing that. And now, we're moving forward."

"Moving forward?"

"Yes. I got her a beautiful ring. I'll show you when I get to the office."

"Bryce, why didn't you tell me you were having these feelings? You know that I'd be happy for you, right? I'm shocked and a little confused but... Son, you can tell me anything. I miss your father everyday but that doesn't mean I can't be happy with you finding love and loving your life."

My mom had often talked about how close my father and her were. I remember them being that way and knwo that her grief in losing him changer her. How could it not? It changed us both. "It's not like that, ma. I wasn't keeping this from you. It just happened all of a sudden. I didn't even have a ring at first."

"You better be joking, Bryce Idris Hampton! I know I raised you better than that."

"Not the middle name, too," I laugh. "I'm telling you that it was sudden. Korra is happy. We're happy." My laugh dies on my lips as I say the words aloud.

*She is.*

*We are.*

But it's fake and not at all a reality.

We're not actually getting married. So why did it feel good to tell my mom that?

Coming into view is my office and I know I'll lose service when I get into the garage. "Look Ma, I'll call you later. Okay? Kiss auntie Michelle for me."

She agrees, though reluctantly, and now I have to wrap up whatever that clang in my chest was before I'm deep into the fray again.

Caught up in the complexity of emotion I had with telling my Ma about the engagement, I ripped another bandaid off. Telling Phil about the whirlwind proposal turned into all the other associate and senior partners opening a champagne bottle for me. They projected the photos of Korra and I on the back of that truck in the conference room to celebrate my announcement. Someone even ordered lunch that we were all toasting over.

**Bryce: {picture msg}**

Gotta admit, it felt good to talk about Korra like she was truly my wife-to be. We both know it's not real and I suspect that Phil isn't dumb enough to think he had no influence in my decision. Likely, doesn't care about my real feelings toward the woman or not. All he knows is that I'm taking the steps he knew I had to if I wanted to be in the running to fill the spot he would leave open.

**Korra: *STARRY EYED EMOJI* That is a lot of sushi. I'm jealous**

**Bryce: I'm eating it in your honor**

**Korra: Stop pretending to hate sushi to make me feel better**

I had her favorites delivered before I even sent the text so her responding picture message with the three bags for the whole clinic doesn't shock me. If I'm getting anything out of this, I have to pay it forward to the woman who selflessly helped me.

**Korra: {picture msg}**

**Korra: I think some of your sushi parade ended up here**

**Korra: There's tempura, too? No take backs. I signed for it *TONGUE OUT EMOJI***

**Bryce: lol it's for you. *we're* celebrating**

**Korra: this fake engagement sure does come with perks**

**Korra: {picture msg}**

She sent a selfie of her holding the tempura shrimp with her left hand. The ring catches the light as she pretends to attack the food with her mouth. I can't lie. The green of the crystal and gold band look good on her skin.

**Bryce: enjoy it lol**

Several hours pass of me pouring over the merger that landed on my desk. It's with more prestigious clients than I usually work with by myself. I'm already reaping the benefits of being a more *committed guy*. I scoffed at the notion, but I can see how quickly things are improving.

As long as I can remember that this is fake and to not screw up my only real friendship, life is good.

Phil pops his head into my office on his way out, "Don't stick around too long. You won't want that fiancée to be waiting up all night for you."

"I won't," I smile, which appeases him.

With him gone, I'm the last one here on the floor. It's not uncommon, but it's nice to have the silence with how raucous the day was.

When I check the time, my shoulders ache from my hunched position and my back is creaky. It's time for me to wrap this up and get home already.

I'm sure Korra is already at home babying her plants so I call her on speakerphone as I'm packing up my case materials.

"Please don't tell me you're still at your office," she says instead of a greeting.

"Hello fiancée," I respond in a flat tone. "I'm doing well. How about you?"

"I'd be doing better if I couldn't hear silence in the background of this call," she snarks.

I chuff, "What does that even mean?"

"Your apartment's nice but the A/C is so loud in there. Given the fact that you keep it colder than your refrigerator, I know you're not at home yet."

"Okay detective... I just had some things to wrap up before I headed that way."

The sound of water swishes briefly in the background as she must be shifting in the tub. *So, not babying her plants.* I missed that time already. It's later than I thought. "Remember that big picture we talked about the other day at the gardens?"

I check my watch under my sleeve. "Weeks ago, but yes."

"You don't. We talked about you experiencing life. How are you experiencing life at your desk this late? You should be getting ready for bed."

"It's a Monday. Do you expect me to be at the club? I'll have you know that's not the kind of fiancé I am."

She doesn't laugh at my joke. Her focus too laser pointed to the absence of sound. "Not hearing the crackling poor service of someone in an elevator headed for the garage."

Shaking my head, I say, "You just don't get what the pressure is like here. I have to take my job seriously. I don't have the luxury of being in a bubble bath soaking my day away."

She gasps, "There are no bubbles in here." I don't respond while she sputters. "I ran out a couple of days ago. I will not feel bad about my soak."

"I'm not saying you should, Kor." I rub a hand over my face. "Do you know how many Black lawyers there are in this country?" I shake my head again. "I won't make you guess because the number is appalling. Only five percent are Black. A negligible statistic when we make up almost fourteen percent of the population. The numbers were worse then years ago and now that we're in these courts, we're still under-represented and often overworked from that basis alone. There are not enough of us. The fact that I found a mentor who looked like me meant everything. I'm not going to let him down because I dropped the ball."

The weight of that fact looms heavily on me every day. It's not about desire but opportunity. The choices in front of me are unfathomable to a young man looking at the same statistics I am. Why even try when there is so much opposition against you. And as a young Black man, it's a commitment to just get to college to begin with. Then you have years of studying in almost complete solitude. The odd-man out on top of the clubs and societies that just aren't an option for us.

Years, I've worked my ass off to get right here. So that if an opportunity arose, I would be first in line to receive it. But it never works out that smoothly. There is always competition. There is always someone as hungry as you are. Sometimes it's luck. Sometimes, it's connections. This time I'm hoping that it's a combination of all three and I can walk away the victor.

*That is if I can survive to the end.*

"I understand that." She pauses, though her thoughts are loud. "That doesn't mean that you have to make up for the discrepancy. You deserve to be treated fairly, work the appropriate amount of hours. You've earned rest."

"I've not earned anything." I sigh and push away from my desk. The sun has long gone down and my office is dim in comparison. Flicking on my desk lamp, I put my hands behind my head. "I haven't heard a thing from Mozier since he sort of hinted at an opening. I could be in the same place two months from now as I was two years ago."

"That's not true," she says in a small voice. "You have over five years of experience and you've handled many more cases—successfully might I add."

"You're just trying to make me feel better."

"Guilty," she laughs. The sound bounces around my chest several times and I feel like I can chance a breath. "It's not easy being the angel on your shoulder you know? I need a pay raise."

"Isn't that role supposed to be two parts. The devil too?"

"Like I said, I don't get paid enough for that. Besides, your body will make the adjustment for you. When it's had enough, you're gonna shut down."

"I'm fit as a fiddle. The only *shutting down* I'll be doing is of this computer so I can go to my car."

"That's a great start. I should probably get out of this tub before I turn into a prune."

# CHAPTER 17

## Korra

"Now, I wouldn't call myself a prophet. But did I call this or what?"

Bryce stands at his apartment door with a blanket around his head, pulled tight under his face. He doesn't respond, simply groaning and shuffling out of the way to let me in. I had just as difficult a time getting up to his place as I usually do. I swear he's living in the Fort Knox of apartment complexes downtown.

He falls like a log onto his couch, huddled into a ball. "Oh. This looks way worse than I thought it was over the phone, buddy."

"I really thought I was gonna be able to shake it off. But it seems like it's getting much worse," he says in a scratchy voice that makes me wince.

"It's a good thing that I brought basically every remedy and over-the-counter medicine I could find on the way here. So, let's get started with something for your throat. I'll be back in a second."

I really wasn't kidding. I went to the drugstore and grabbed everything for a fever and sniffles that I could find.

It's surprising to me that Bryce even got sick. Especially when he literally only eats for nutrition. He has to be in such good shape. No matter, if my brothers are any indication, whenever a man gets sick–it is the end of the world.

*So here I am.*

I fill the electric kettle on his counter with water and set it to boil. I know where his mugs are so I grab one and get the elderberry syrup I learned to make from my Mom. It's concentrated and just needs hot water to make a drink that's more pleasant than the syrup on its own.

His kettle is quick and I'm back at the couch handing him the mug when he sits up. "Be careful, it's hot," I caution but he sips from the mug, settling deeper into his blanket cocoon.

He's an adorable little couch gremlin right now. His nose is red from where he's been blowing it. I swap the toilet roll he's been using for the box of moisturizing tissues instead.

I open the new thermometer next, taking it out and reading the instructions quickly. "Arm up. We gotta see if you're running a fever."

He raises his arm for me to take his temperature properly. Bryce, of all people, is on his couch in a blanket at mid day. That, more than anything, is a clear sign there is something bad going on. When the thermometer beeps. I look at it and it's at one-hundred and three degrees.

"Definitely a fever. Let's start with this first." I open up the fever reducer and measure out the amount that he's supposed to take.

He makes a face. "I hate cough medicine," but he takes the little measuring cup from me and tosses it back. He hands the cup back to me and I trade him for his tea again. He starts chugging it to get rid of the flavor in his mouth.

"I'll be right back," I tell him, going on the search for a towel for his forehead to try and bring the fever down as well.

"I feel like I'm melting, but I'm also freezing." He whines. "Whatever this is, it's killing me."

"In my professional medical opinion it is the flu or rheumatoid arthritis. Well, I'm leaning heavily in the direction of flu though." I yell back to him from his bathroom. "I thought this whole engagement thing was supposed to mean that you were gonna take some time to rest."

"I feel like this is a poor time to lecture me. Considering I am seconds away from a fever dream."

I'm back by his side, placing the cloth carefully on his forehead. "Oh, my dear friend. There is never a poor time to say I *told you so*."

He makes a face, but is already staring off from exhaustion or the medication. It's hard to tell which one.

Now is the perfect opportunity to heat up the soup I brought from my house. Because it was frozen into a solid brick, as I always do, it managed to make its way from Harmony Hill to Denver. Luck is on my side because I didn't get caught in too much traffic on the drive up here.

I make my way to his extremely organized kitchen, looking for a pot big enough to heat up the soup. I did bring it for him, but I'm gonna have a bowl for myself, too.

"Where are your soup pots?" I ask after checking several cabinets.

"Soup pot?"

"Yeah. You know? A big pot for soups?"

"Pretty sure that I have never owned something like that. Why would I be making that much soup?"

"If you're making any soup, you *need* a big pot. It's not about how much you're gonna eat. There's always going to be a ton."

He scratches his head. "I don't know what gave you the impression that I would have something of that nature in my place. Do I look like the kind of guy who makes a lot of soup?" Well the elderberry is clearly working its magic since his throat is no longer scratching nails against my senses. *But the mouth on him...* Sassy thing when he's sick.

I laugh at the couch gremlin. "You look like the kind of guy who's on his deathbed and needs some damn soup. How am I supposed to heat this up?"

He shrugs. "Microwave?"

I take a deep breath. "Okay, fine. Where are the bowls big enough to hold this much soup?" I hold the bag of soup for him to see it.

Bryce peers over the fluff of his blanket, "Don't have any of those around here."

"You are not at all helpful. I'm going to just find things for myself."

I start rummaging around through his cabinets again. This time looking for any cooking vessels that could hold the amount of soup that I brought.

This has turned into a whole ordeal. *It was supposed to be easy.* But I guess that's kind of been the story of my life as of late.

I manage to find a Dutch oven. Which I'm sure he probably didn't know was here. But it's just the right size to heat everything up. I give it a wash in the sink and empty the frozen contents of the soup into the pot for it to start heating up.

I go back to sit by his side. He's bundled even tighter in the blanket. His eyes drift close, but I don't think he's asleep yet.

Looking down at the ring on my hand, I still can't get over how absolutely perfect it is. "How did you manage to get a ring that I actually love wearing?" I'll admit that I've been proud to show anyone who notices the jewelry.

Clients at work were eager to hear the story of how he proposed and my Dad even joined in once to share his experience with it. Standing behind me at my desk, with his hands on my shoulder, he gushed about how Bryce is such a great guy for me.

I was taken aback by how on board he's been. The emotions were joyous and not once did he sob as I thought he might. I'd seen him cry over euthanasia so often that we moved him to only consultations.

*It was still dicey.*

I think the dam is close to bursting every time he hears someone tell me congratulations. I'm at war with myself in those moments. Both happy that he's happy for me and internally reprimanding myself for deceiving him. Whatever happens, I know I have to keep the fact that this was all fake—a secret. I'm taking it to my grave as far as Wayne Thomas is concerned.

He yawns before saying, "It was easy actually. I just thought of you... And when I saw the ring, I knew it was the one."

My head tilts, some of my curls getting into my face before I grab a scarf from my purse still around my shoulders. "What do you mean, you thought of me?" Tying my hair back with the scarf, I finally take my purse off and set it on his coffee table.

"Micah asked me questions about you. You remember Micah Baird from high school? I was able to narrow down the entire store's worth of rings to just a few, and I thought, 'hey, there's something that Korra would like'. This is what I came up with. It's kind of lucky that the store even had something that looked like it. I don't think I've ever seen anyone with a ring that looks similar." *Me neither.*

I'm still stuck on the first part. "What kind of questions?" I also haven't seen a ring that looks quite like this. I do love a good crystal jewelry moment. I collect quite a few of them. And even now, I'm wearing several pieces. But for him to pick a moss agate, which is one of my favorites... I'm certain I've never told him that.

"Apparently the right ones," he shrugs deeper into his blanket. "If anyone were paying attention, Korra, they would know exactly what to get. A beautiful person needs a beautiful ring. I think it speaks for itself."

"Is that how you managed to get me the very best birthday gift every single year? I don't know anybody who has given better gifts than you."

Seeing the ring for the first time, I was speechless. If I had imagined what the perfect ring for me was, my thoughts would have been completely blank. No one other than Bryce would know what I liked *better than I would.* He is truly the best man and friend anyone could ask for.

That sounds shallow, but it's not just about this ring—that I don't know how much he spent on and frankly I don't need to know—it's in all that he does for me. He pays attention. No matter how silly or long the ramblings of my plant talk get, he'll listen. Or if I'm feeling off, he's the first to notice and try to change my mood around.

But we have always been that way.

The whole proposal was something out of a dream. I was yapping to him about my Cissus and then there he was on one knee, asking me to marry him.

It all felt so real.

*Too real.*

I was close to tears and warring with myself because I wanted it to be real.

I wanted someone to put this much effort into planning things to do for me. Proposing is a big deal. It deserves something big but Bryce is the kind of guy to be this intentional about everything.

That's the kind of friend he is.

It's clearly the kind of lover he would be as well.

I'm cosplaying his doting fiancée. I worry that if I don't keep reminding myself that I'm doing this to help him get ahead with his job and that I'm not building a life with him–I'll be fine.

From what I've seen, the latter doesn't look like too bad a gig.

"Yeah I guess... But—"

His eyes droop as he fights, trying to keep them open with the medicine starting to all hit him with their drowsiness at once.

Guess, I'm eating soup by myself until he wakes up again.

# CHAPTER 18

## Korra

"Korra! Are you hearing me?"

At my twin's annoyed tone, I drop the leaf patterned paper and look up at her. "Oh, yea. Zach's coming by a little later on."

She shakes her head at me. "I know that." She sips her iced coffee and speaks again, "I asked how Bryce was doing. You know? Since you were over there taking care of him."

"He'll be fine." *Me on the other hand?* I'm not all right. Spending yesterday helping him get better changed something for me. Taking care of him and being in his space flittering around like a concerned girlfriend is sticking in my mind and holding on.

I just know that I have a place and that place is not by his side like that. Looking down at the ring on my finger, I know that I've made a gross miscalculation somewhere.

The question of what Bryce would be like as a lover is playing on a large scale over my thoughts. He was a shivering mess. Sweaty, snarky and feeling poorly. It only made me think of how that was nothing in comparison to what he's like when he isn't sick.

"Girl, you have got it bad. Why don't you just go back over there? You haven't heard a word that I've said."

She's right. It's just a curiosity though. I'm just intrigued by the idea. It means nothing. "I'll call him later. I need to make some progress on this spread. Zach said he would help me today. Are you going to?"

Kasey looks at the papers I have strewn about the floor and twists her lips to the side. "I don't know. This was you and mom's thing. I'm not really a paper crafter. Have you heard what Nia prepared for Merry & Bright?"

After Merry & Bright is the scrapbooking competition, so she's got time in between practicing for that I hope she'll use to help me with the spread.

"When will Nia be back from school to keep working on things together?"

"I think she's got final exams this week and then she's coming back. We've just been practicing over video calls."

Sure, I could have still been a part of them preparing for this performance, joining those calls, but what would be the point? The sour feelings of being left out are better kept to myself. Purposefully, I ignore those parts of the family group chat. "How's that going?"

"It's going well. We'll be the best vocals on that stage. I'm sure of it."

I smile in response to her confidence but don't engage with the conversation further. Using a stencil I found, I trace a photo frame shape from the pumpkin patterned paper and cut it out diligently.

My brother startles me when he drops to the floor beside me. "This looks really good." Zach points to the photo of Bryce and I.

I had the engagement photos printed out to go on my spread. Wuying was correct in her assertion that these photos would look great on canvas. My eyes trace over the gentle way that Bryce holds my face and sticks. "He looks so in love, doesn't he?" I ask absently.

"He better. Haven't had the chance to sit down with him, but you bet that we will be having a conversation. Is he treating you right?" Turning from my task, I take in my brother for the first time since he got here. He's wearing a half-zip up pullover with cargos. Nothing unusual there. The crisp tone, very unlike him.

For whatever reason, my face heats. "You didn't have a sit down with Palmer, so why would you with Bryce?"

"Well, that guy was a dunce, minus the hat. I hoped you'd be smart enough to give that guy the boot and you did. He didn't last."

"Right." This is news to me. Of course, I knew Kasey didn't care for him. But Zach didn't? And with such a strong apparent dislike for him?

Maybe I have been a little bit delusional. How could I miss Zach not liking him? He doesn't have a problem with anyone.

My sister's voice cuts into my thoughts again. Am I really daydreaming this much? "Sooo... How'd you know?"

"How did I know what?"

"That you and Bryce... you know? Should start bumping uglies."

Zach splutters. "Kasey gross. Don't say it like that."

"We're all adults here. You may act like a saint, but I know you're not one."

"As far as you know, I am."

"Whatever. No one cares about that right now." Kasey taps on the papers in front of me. "I want to know. After that whole situation with Jillian at the club, I figured something was up because you're usually not so catty. Were y'all already together?" No.

It wasn't long ago that Jillian was still trying to dig her claws into this family. Growing up, I had a dislike of her that was miles long. I never did anything outwardly to show that but Kasey knew. Her talents and attention from my Mom was always something that got under my skin. Her smug arrogance and sneak disses were irritating to me when we were kids.

But as we got older and puberty hit us all, I got acne and she got boobs. *Tale as old as time.* The popular girl becomes more unbearable and the more quiet, quirky one becomes more silent.

Unfortunate for her, she developed a crush on Zach. As a freshman, she wasn't anywhere on his radar since he was a senior. On top of their age difference, Zach had heart eyes for someone else. It never stopped her from pursuing him under the guise of working with my Mom more to be in his vicinity.

Eventually, he went away to school but she didn't stop inserting herself into our lives. Zach was considerate and respectful in turning her down but she never stopped.

She couldn't have Zach and she figured she could make him jealous by being taken by someone else he'd have to see all the time. Bryce. She manipulated and used him for almost two years. He was happy, I thought, so I never said anything. Her plan wasn't truly working since Zach still didn't care about her in that way. Her nastiness towards me was more covert though I was able to ignore it. If Bryce was happy, then I was going to try my best to be happy for him despite his girlfriend's petty misgivings.

That changed when I caught her trying to push up on Zach when Bryce was working late. She was "comforting him in his time of need" after my Mom passed. But I couldn't unsee her searching fingers on my brother's body while she claimed to care for my best friend. I was the one to expose her for the treacherous leach she is.

Zach brushed it off, but it hurt Bryce to find out she was willing to cheat on him to get to my brother. He asked me to keep it between us. I had been fine to keep my comments to myself though Jillian would try her luck with Bryce when she got bored. I knew he'd let her before he cut her off for good.

Seeing her hurt him, after years of dealing with her shitty behavior majorly lowered my reluctance to play nice with her. That night when I was feeling too raw from being stood up on my birthday, opened a rawness inside me that sparked the idea to improvise like I had in front of everyone. She deserved worse.

The origins of my fake engagement had to start somewhere. Maybe it was safe to say that night was the beginning since Kasey had already suspected something. "I guess it kind of did."

"You were pretty drunk that night. I suspected something was going on in your room. Glad I didn't go check on you. Who know what I would have walked in on."

"Kasey, don't be gross."

"Korra, don't pretend that you aren't climbing this man like a tree. He's good looking, successful, plus he lives in the gym. I know that body is doing more than stretching the confines of those tailored suits."

Okay, I'm not blind. *Objectively speaking*, from a *very objective point of view*, Bryce is very good looking. The cheekbones, the jawline, the body... all good. *All very good*. From his tender eyes despite his more serious nature to the straight, white teeth despite how rarely he gifts anyone with a smile. Any combination of all those physical qualities would make him attractive. But it's not those outside qualities that make him a good friend to me or why I'll always have his back.

What's much more dangerous is how he makes me feel.

Never in memory have these things meant anything more to me than the objective observation of *sexy human being*.

Kasey's commentary is taking my thoughts there. Taking them there when I'm trying my hardest to not cross a line of friendship. It was easy to swipe any inkling of that idea away before. But now...

Too much effort is required to rectify my thinking.

"Ah, no," Zach says, finally slamming a hand over Kasey's mouth. "Big brother is still in the room. I don't want or need to hear about any of this. You do this when I'm not here."

I say a prayer that she does not bring the topic back up because I'm hanging by a thread.

"Oh, hush. We all know that you've been running through women. Those calendars aren't just for wall decor. What do y'all do? Put your cell phone numbers in them?"

If Zach could blush, I'm certain he would be beet red right now. "That's not even close to true. The annual calendar is for raising funds for charities and underserved nonprofits. Nothing else."

"It's raising something more than funds..."

I tune her and Zach out as I go back to arranging things on the pages in front of me. I've yet to secure any of the elements I've been selecting. It's all just a shuffle of ideas that I haven't committed to.

When I packed up what I was working on before, I kind of threw everything into the box, choosing to order a new scrapbook online. It arrived last week but if I'm honest, I haven't been doing anything to move the project forward before now. Pulling out a paper punch that's shaped like a pumpkin from the box, I use it to cut some shapes. It's more just busy work and not with an aim in mind for an addition to the spread. I'm lost in thoughts of *hot Bryce, no—friend Bryce* on repeat.

"What is this?" Zach holds up the fabric bundle in his hand. I kept the ID and necktie since I didn't know what to make of them. Returning them would have been smarter but I just couldn't. I'd folded it back up how it was and threw it into the box with everything else.

I don't get a chance to explain what I've found before Zach has unfolded the fabric and is looking it over.

"Korra, what the hell is this?" Kasey asks, snatching the tie from Zach's hands. "Why do you have a bloody tie in here?"

"I found it."

Zach picks up the ID, "You found this? Where?"

"When I was looking for scrapbook stuff in Mom's studio. It was with a bunch of those newspapers." I point to the stack of them in the box still,

"She had these?" Zach studies the ID and then takes the tie back from Kasey. "Why?"

"I have no idea. I've never seen this man in my life. Do you know him?"

He shakes his head, "No, I don't. He looks familiar though."

"That's exactly what I was thinking! I can't figure out why though. Bryce thinks the ID is from the nineties. Why would Mom keep this random ID and tie though?"

Kasey's eyebrows rise. "Do you think he was like some secret love from before we were born or something?"

The idea is wild and so unlike anything I could imagine from Delanna Thomas. "No way, Kase. Be serious. It's gotta be something else."

"It could literally be anything. You don't know what Mom had going on," she replies, looking through the clippings of our Mother in her youth.

Zach shuffles through the news clippings, saying, "You're both ridiculous. Mom was a serial volunteer and choir nerd. Don't jump to conclusions. It's probably just random junk she kept. I've seen the studio. It's full of it."

"Nope, we're on this train," Kasey says. "I love jumping to conclusions. It's what makes me a good writer. Oh, I bet this man's body is like buried in the front yard. That's probably why she was always up there tending to it. Not because she loved gardening but to make sure no one ever found his remains."

"Kasey, stop," Zach warns as my fists ball at my sides. He was often mediator with us arguing at kids. We're right back at that age as Kasey continues running her mouth with zero regard for how she's upsetting me.

"Everyone knows decomposing bodies make great fertilizer. That's why all her flowers grew so well. Maybe–"

"Shut up, Kasey. Seriously stop." I don't recognize my voice as I stand over her.

"Calm down. I'm just spitballing. Joking around," she explains.

"You're not. *This is our Mother.* She didn't have her kids playing in the dirt of some crime scene. You're sick!"

I stomp out of the living room to my bedroom, blood boiling. How dare she say that about my Mom? *Our Mom.* It wasn't funny.

Wiping stupid tears from my eyes, I'm moments away from calling Bryce but he's probably still knocked out on fever reducer. I flop onto my bed instead.

The knock at my door receives a huff from me.

*Leave me alone, Kasey.*

"It's me," Zach says. "Can I come in?"

"Fine."

"Are you okay?" He asks and then rubs a hand over his face. "Obviously not."

I huff again, this time kicking my feet at the blanket to get it off of me. "Why is she so..."

"Everyone is handling this differently, Kor. I'm not defending her but Kasey is... rough. You know that. Better than most. She figures that if she treats this like anything else, it'll keep her shell from cracking. It wasn't fair of her to say those things though."

"She's a dick. Just say that, Zach. She should've stopped while she was ahead but she just kept on going."

"I know," his soft eyes are already apologizing for my sister's inconsiderate comments.

"It's not your fault. You don't have to take the blame for Kasey acting like... Kasey."

He sits on the bed beside me. "Has she been doing this all along?"

Shaking my head, I tell him about what she said at Thanksgiving. "I think she's hurting and handling it poorly."

"Do you think what she said to you is true? That you're not coping." Like Bryce, I appreciate that he's asked me. But again, I'm on the spot answering. Does my brother agree with what Kasey thinks?

"Do you?"

"I can't answer that question for you, sis. From the outside, I think you're okay. But cracks like today say otherwise."

They're all so composed and nonchalant about our Mother while it's tearing me up just to hear Kasey speculate something absolutely ridiculous. I hate how weak and unstable it makes me seem. "Am I supposed to be completely fine now? I'll never stop missing her."

"You don't have to. None of us do. I want to be there for everyone but the more I make time for you all, the more I realize how hard Mom must have been working to love us as thoroughly as she did."

"She really was an angel on Earth. What are we going to do without her?"

"Our best," he says, into my hair. "Stay in here if you want. I'll go talk to Kasey before I head out. Okay?"

# CHAPTER 19

## Korra

Pink and white swirl around us as we walk into the building. There is a Candyland theme in this place. Extra large lollipops and candy canes line the walls. Huge gumdrops sit at the corners of the stage and fluffy white cotton candy clouds hang from the ceilings. A few gingerbread houses serve as photo booths on the right wall. Pink and white tulle are pinned to the back of the stadium style seating.

The auction hall has been completely transformed into a winter spectacle for Merry & Bright. Each year they raise money for the women's shelter that Zach volunteers at. Many of the women who are sheltered there have children. The money usually contributes to a toy fund and general needs of the establishment. To think that most of the extravagant decorations of this event come from donors of the cause is fantastic. Thomas & Friends is on that donor list. I signed that check last month.

Even if my family weren't participating this year, I'd still be here to see what they've done to celebrate the Christmas season and for such an amazing cause.

Bryce sees the photo booths in the room first and is already beelining towards it. "We've got to get a shot before the concert starts."

"I'm glad you're feeling better." In heeled boots and a plaid wool coat that matches my scarf, I toddle behind him. "Slow down, I've got short legs." *He's really on a mission.*

"Sorry," he says, chancing a glance behind him toward me. "I don't want to get stuck in a line. That front row will fill up fast. Hand me your phone, will you?"

I give it to him though I still feel like a tug-a-boat behind him.

A group leaves the tallest house when we reach that part of the display. Bryce hands his phone and mine to the volunteer and hurries back to my side. I'm fixing my curls even though they continue to spring back into my face, getting caught on my eyelashes and scarf.

Bryce gives me a hand, like its second nature for him. In a way, I suppose it has been. Before we made this agreement, I never gave his actions an ounce of contemplation. He's comfortable touching me and I'm not at all uncomfortable being close to him. I would not have said that there is anything intimate about it but...

My body isn't getting the memo.

Thanks to Kasey's crude comments, it's been pulled to the forefront and I am having the hardest time beating them back. I feel like a pervert for checking him out so often.

Video calls at his apartment are completely out of the question now since the man never wears a shirt. I have to save my sanity somehow.

My face heats the longer he looks at the way my hair falls around my head. No more than a minute could have passed, but suddenly I'm too hot in my clothes. When he's satisfied with his arrangement, he turns to the volunteer who directs us to smile.

Bryce's arm holds me close to him, the weight of it warm against my heated body. I remember smiling next to him, but not putting my hand over his chest. The ring is clear to see in how we're embracing. Gotta remember this is all fake.

*Fake, fake, fake.*

"I got some pictures from when he was fixing your hair. It was so cute," the volunteer squeals under her breath as we pass.

*Great, another immortalized photo of Bryce's hands in my hair.*

*I mean… yes. Great. I need further proof to keep our ruse going.*

*But also, not great, because these look like stars in his eyes.*

*Am I okay?*

"These turned out great," he says, swiping through the photos when we take a seat on the first row.

I shrug out of my coat and scarf before I really do start sweating and use it to save my seat. Bryce does the same.

The chairs behind us start to fill and my Dad takes the spot on the other side of me. I recognize the man who sits next to him from Thanksgiving. I think he's Zach's friend, but he introduces himself saying, "I came with Wayne after the grief counseling session today. I hope that's alright."

I know I've seen him with Zach, but I wonder who he lost to be attending those meetings. There are a few other faces I recognize from dinner in the building but none that sit with us. I chance a wave to the Geiers who are a couple of rows behind us, minus Jillian. Hopefully, she and Terry won't be here tonight.

"Gonzalo, right?" Bryce asks, reaching over me to shake his hand. A fresh wave of his masculine scent wafts toward my face and I only barely resist the urge to lean in for more. "It's more than alright. These tickets are for a good cause."

Gonzalo nods and smirks, "I know about kids needing their toys, alright."

"The kids need their toys," I repeat like a loon because my brain is a little screwy at present.

His little girl in a strawberry sweater leans around her dad to say, "I hopes it's not comin' outta mine." Her curly poof making her look like a strawberry herself instead of chastising as her words were meant to be. We chuckle at her commentary though Gonzalo is not charmed at her addition.

"Lucía, behave," he says, setting the girl into her seat beside him. He takes a coloring book out of his bag and hands her some crayons. She busies herself without fuss, coloring a picture of reindeer flying in the sky purple.

Chatter is loud in the room the more it fills up. Time passes with me greeting other people I recognize as clients from work or classmates.

Bryce stands beside me taking the lead on questions of how he popped *the question*. It's nice to hear his side of the story.

I thought mine was convincing, but as he tells the story of how he couldn't help himself in proposing when the light hit me just right on the back of that truck, butterflies do a little dance in my middle. I know the words aren't true. I know he's meant to make it believable. But again, my body is not cooperating with logic.

Standing at his side, looking up into his smiling face, I'm taken by the desire I have for this to be real.

That I came to this charity concert with my handsome fiancé who tells our charming proposal story and holds my waist with a firm hand. The smell of his designer cologne getting stuck in my memories that I will forget that this is fake.

*Dumb.*

*Very stupid.*

*Cut. It. Out.*

This is simply fodder for him to tell his firm. *It's not real.* The feelings I'm having, while problematic, are not important.

After talking with the pastor of Harmony Hill's only Baptist church, who encouraged us to wed at his church, I was overstimulated and not ready for another conversation. He only left because they made the announcement that the show would be starting in ten minutes.

Bryce leans over to ask, "Do you want to go see them before the show starts?"

My brothers and sisters he means.

"No, I'm just going to be a guest tonight," I tell him.

He searches my eyes for a moment, asking, "Are you sure?"

I nod, leaning into his shoulder for a hug. I need one. At this moment, I would normally be backstage, listening to the encouragement that my Mom would have for everyone to perform their best and make her proud.

Instead, I made the executive decision to not participate in the winter concert with the family. It's not that hard to imagine why I wouldn't want to participate. I've spent my whole life being the one who didn't fit in with the rest of the family because my voice was not beautiful by any definition.

My Mom spent hours with me trying to help hone what hidden talent might be there. But the truth is that I just am not a singer. I'm not musically inclined. It is something that stands in stark contrast to my other siblings.

It's not the only thing either.

Bryce puts an arm around my shoulders as we make our way back to our seats at the front when the lights dim. I'm grateful to not be as exposed as I felt talking to everyone before. To be safe under his arm now.

The first performers of the night are a sweet group of kids singing about Santa coming to town. The second is two young men who play *White Winter Hymnal* on the clarinet and guitar.

My brothers and sisters are the third group for the night. They walk onto the stage with applause as the Thomas family is well known in this show. Looking at my siblings getting ready to perform, I'm struck by how different we are.

My oldest brother, Zach, has a heart of gold and aspires to help people in need. Who could be more selfless than him? He runs into burning buildings to get people out of them on a regular basis. I can't think of anybody who is a better person than he is. In his free time, he's usually volunteering at the women's shelter. The man is a saint.

Then my twin, Kasey, the one who's supposed to be just like me. Her and I are exactly opposites. But she's been a successful writer. She has a career. She's getting the deals. She has the recognition from others in her field. She's living the dream that she's always set out to do.

Then my younger brother, Lee, I mean... he's following in Dad's footsteps. He's always looked up to our dad and in a lot of ways I see him trying to become as great a vet as Dad is. My brother did the time. He studied hard, he graduated, he put in the hours. Now, he's probably gonna take over for Dad when he decides that he's no longer interested in running the clinic anymore.

And then my baby sister, Nia, the beauty that's about to take center stage. She's so smart. She's in college. She's graduating with her degree next year in graphic design. I'm just amazed—awed—at how well she's doing. I know that she is going to achieve nothing but big things. And to top all of it off, she has such a beautiful soul inside and out. The sweetest one of all of us. And her voice... Her voice is actually magical.

Then there's me. No ambitions to any of the greatness like my siblings have achieved or are about to achieve. It never really occurred to me to have some big dream like the rest of them. I like my job at the front desk of my family's clinic that I've had my entire adult life. And for a long time I thought that there was something wrong with me because I didn't want more. I don't have these aspirations for grandeur like all of them do. My Mom taught me to see the beauty in slow life, the small joys. She taught me to cherish and treasure my loved ones.

I like my cozy apartment with plants everywhere. I like spending my weekends caring for them coming home to them. I like hanging out with my friends and my family and hearing about what they've been doing all week.

My Mom was the string that tied us all together. She was common ground and the level playing field. She loved us all the same.

She's gone.

There is no one in the wings, cheering my brothers and sisters on. It's just me and Dad down here, to clap when everything is over. There is something meaningful and sharp about the separation there.

They chose a song that I recognize from my mom's favorite acapella group. It opens with Nia and Zach singing harmoniously together. Singing of a box with lights that were passed on for generations and spreading cheer. Their voices are clear over a simple guitar that carries their vocals and the gentle humming from Lee and Kasey behind them. It's so cozy and warm that my eyes prick with tears.

Bryce reaches over to hold my hand when the next verse talks of how a mother's love is evergreen. Nia begins getting emotional, as well. A trail of tears runs, but she doesn't let it affect her vocals. It's hard to talk when crying, so I can only imagine what it would take to sing when you're so emotional. Still her voice is strong, never missing a note.

The lyrics are powerful because they mean something for all of us. The song holding truths specific to us, but general enough to touch anyone who has had a mother that cared for them. Christmas was my family's time to sing together and really settle into the Christmas mood. Though I couldn't participate in this part of it, I still felt the magic of the music they made together.

Lee's voice breaks out from the rest, honeyed and sweeter than his personality. He sings of a mother who never let her family see her struggle and kept the magic of tradition alive. It's brief before the rest of my siblings join in to sing that the *joy is never gone.*

They form a perfect harmony that I have to bear witness to from the outside—as usual. Bryce squeezes my hand even tighter, before wiping the tear from my face.

I don't think that I will be able to make it through the end of this song in one piece.

The performance is beautiful and they are absolutely killing it. I wish that my Mom was able to sit on the other side of me to see what her children have created.

My Dad pats my shoulder after Kasey's deeper, sultry voice sings of spending her whole life trying to be like her mother. The lyrics affecting me like nothing else has so far. *It couldn't be more untrue.*

To see someone who shares your exact face and be so much unlike you say something like that is torture. It's *not her.* It's always been me who wanted to be just like our mother. *Kasey never has.* I didn't get the voice that my mother had and there has always been something unfair about that to me. In this significant way, I didn't get to continue doing what she loved. And now I have to sit here and—

I'm up and moving as soon as the song ends. With my coat over my arm, I rush past the seating area and push out of the double door.

The cold bites at my tears and I'm still on the move. Ignoring the discomfort. Ignoring my perfect family and the absence of my mother. Ignoring all the mixed up emotions bubbling to the surface of my composure.

I shove my arms into my sleeves and wrap my scarf around my neck. Regret over not driving my own car here, hits me hard as I stomp toward the parking lot.

"Korra," Bryce's voice calls from behind me.

*He followed me?*

"Where are you going? What's going on?"

"I'm—I have to... I can't be there right now," I whimper, sounding as pathetic and beat up as I feel.

"I get it," Bryce says. "Will you slow down?" I don't slow, I keep moving further and further from the auction hall. "Korra, please."

I turn to face him, face burning from the cold and my tears. "In what way do I get to honor her name? I shared her with my siblings while she was alive. I've tried to be everything that she was to the world. But they all stand up there, pitch perfect and spotlighted, professing their love for her in a way I never could. She's gone, Bryce, and I don't know who I am without her."

He wipes my tears away, slow and deliberate. His brows knitted in concentration as he attempts to keep me from looking like a completely rabid raccoon. "I know who you are," he says when he's gotten the evidence of my hysteria cleaned up. "You are allowed to feel upset by not being up there with them. Anyone in your position would."

I cross my arms over my chest, hiding my chilly hands under my armpits. "I'm feeling too much. That's the problem."

Snow begins to fall in heavy, fat flakes that flutter to the ground.

"Your feelings are not a problem," he says, stepping closer to me so I have to look up to meet his eyes. "Your big heart and big feelings are the best thing about you, Korra. You care and care genuinely about the people you love. Seeing them on stage without you has to be a hard experience, but it doesn't mean that you loved her less or that you aren't honoring her."

"I know it doesn't," I huff. "My head knows that. It's my heart that won't stop screaming for—" My mouth snaps shut and I look away from him. Blinking at the cold flakes melting against my heating skin.

"For what?" He asks.

I shake my head. "I don't want to live my life like any of them do. I don't have those same dreams. All I wanted from life was happiness and love, the things my mom showed me that I wanted for myself. I was happy before. I *know I was.* I had time to reach for the things I wanted for myself."

His hands return to my face, keeping my focus on him. "What is it that you don't have time to reach for?"

"We're in our thirties, Bryce. As much as I hate to agree with Phil, people are settling down and having kids. We're faking something that I do actually want—a family of my own. A partner. To have my own man I could kiss when he came home-"

"You could kiss me..." he suggests. "If you wanted."

My eyes snap to his and then lower to his lips. His teeth catch the lower one when a snowflake lands on it. He slowly releases it and my eyes find his again.

It's only getting colder outside, but something is burning between us as his impossibly warm finger tips wipe a flake from my cheek and then my lips. His thumb pauses over my mouth and I take a breath in through my nose, hoping the cold air will talk some sense into me.

There is clearly no sense in the air as I parrot, "K-Kiss you?"

# CHAPTER 20

## Bryce

"K-Kiss you?" Korra asks in a breathy voice. The molten brown of her warm eyes taken by surprise with my words.

*I'm taken back by my words.*

*What am I doing?*

It was me who said I didn't want to ruin our friendship and here I am asking her to kiss me...

*What am I doing?*

She doesn't look upset by my suggestion. There's an emotion that resembles hope or anticipation.

*She's anticipating kissing me?*

Snow is falling around us. The ground begins to fill with the cold covering and hide the leaves that are still there underneath. The path that led us to this spot in the parking lot hidden by its presence.

*There is no going back from this.*

I opened my mouth and the words that came out were *permanent*.

I have to say something.

I need to do something to make this better.

*Make it right.*

All evening, I'd been telling anyone who wanted to listen about how I couldn't take it anymore and I needed to ask her to marry me. The words came to me easily and it felt good to say them.

How much of it was a lie and how much of it wasn't is blurry.

As I look down into her face that's hoping for the answer I have to give, I say, "Yea. It's probably something we should get used to..." *If I'm going for it, then I'm going for it.* Never been a half-measures kind of guy before. So no point in starting now. "We never kiss in front of anyone though we're so happy and in love..."

My explanation should sound sarcastic and be recalling the words that I said earlier in a joking tone but that doesn't happen. My brain is still thinking that the words I have been spewing all night are true.

*I don't know if they are or they aren't.*

With snowflakes clinging to her curls and eyes on my lips, Korra's words are all I needed to hear. "You should kiss me then."

And I do.

I press my lips to hers gently. The softness of her mouth meeting mine is a welcome warmth in the quickly chilling temperature around us. With my hand on her cheek, the moment that her lips curl in a smile against mine pulls me up from how I've fallen into her.

I pull away to look at her fully.

*I don't want to miss this smile.*

If I were able, I'd get a photo to immortalize this moment forever. To see her with eyes full of emotions, all chaotic, fighting each other. The smile on her lips that I put there...

She isn't happy with the space between us, though. She leans up, searching for my lips again. This time I am holding her there. My hand travels down her jaw to the back of her neck, holding her in the right position for my lips to meet hers.

Over and over again we find connection in this way.

I can't get enough of the give and take we exchange right here.

At some point, we stepped together, our bodies aligned at the front. Her cold fingers marking a trail down my back under my coat and sweater. A shiver rolls down my spine, but I can't keep my lips off of hers.

*I want time to slow.*

*I need time to slow.*

And if I had my way I'd be able to keep her right here right now for as long as I'd want to.

I nip at her lip. My teeth catching the soft skin, hoping to press this memory into her body the way that it's  burning into mine.

She came here tonight in a sweater dress the same color of that infuriating, red thong. The color never left my mind. It's mere existence causing all these illicit thoughts of the woman who I always knew as my best friend.

The color against her skin is as stunning as I knew it would be.

Her walking out of the house in the coat, I had no idea that she had it on underneath. She was bundled so tight. But as soon as we sat in our seats, she took her coat off. I saw how the red knitted fabric hugged every single one of her curves—I knew I was done for.

I immediately had to grab her, walk around with her and show her off to anyone I could. The alternative was taking her back to my car and explaining to her just how much I had been dreaming of her. How hard it was to separate the lines between what was a genuine desire on my part and what was me pretending for everyone else.

I was supposed to be making a story and adding as many believable details as I could.

But coming to this concert? I *didn't have to do that.*

Continuing to get photos of us? I *didn't have to do that either.*

Telling anyone who would listen about how grateful I was that she said yes and how much I wanted her to? I *certainly didn't have to do that either.*

I questioned before whether or not this was true or if it was fake...

I'm too scared to admit the answer on that.

Finally, finally, I release her and allow her to breathe. *Though I don't want to.* The only thing I want to do is get in my car and leave.

Take her back to her place, or hell, all the way back to mine. Explore what else Korra likes besides my lips. Tell her that I will find out what those things are.

Just like that, we can never go back to what we were before—I can never go back.

*Everything between us has changed.*

She blinks, gathering her composure as she wipes snowflakes from her lashes. "Well I think that's very believable don't you?"

I chuckle at her dazed assessment of what just happened between us. Making light of something that could be nothing other than heavy right now. "I'd say so."

Before I had considered that having it all was a myth.

How could it *not* be?

I've seen it time and time again. When you're working the kind of hours like I usually am there is no way. And then I remember the fact that I had a caveat there. Someone who knows what you're going through. Knows what it takes to get to the things that you're after in this career. If you have someone like that, then maybe you could.

This kiss made me feel like I could have it all.

If that's not a win, I don't know what it is. I take her hand in mine, "We should probably get back inside before people begin to notice we've been gone."

"You're right. Though isn't that the point..." She wiggles her eyebrows at me like I did for her on Thanksgiving.

It's hard to believe that that was weeks ago.

It's hard to believe that so much has changed in just this moment.

Ever since I had that harebrained idea to fake being engaged, the two of us have been on a collision course  that I couldn't see the end of. I knew what I wanted to be at the end of that path, but I didn't think that I would be holding hands with her after kissing us both into a stupor. Our silly faces stretch tight with smiles because of something that was a long time in the making.

Having it all looks one way for someone else, but for me this looks like what having it all *should be*.

We walk into the building and I'm thankful there's a reception area where we can warm our fingers up, gain some semblance of normalcy, before we walk back into the Candyland that set all of this in motion.

We don't get far before her family stops us. Everyone is there except Lee.

At the back of the seating area is where the performers for the night are sat after they're done. I recognize the young kids who went up before the Thomases did. Her family wears varying expressions upon seeing us coming in together, still holding hands.

I don't remember grabbing her hand again, but somehow it's in mine as she stands slightly behind me.

Do we still share a look of giddy excitement that would only come from kissing someone you have known for years in the snow?

Did they see us leave right after the performance?

I don't know how Korra is feeling now in this space again when she was so distraught in leaving before. Looking back over my shoulder to gauge her expression, I check to see if she's doing all right.

She looks up at me and nods once, confirming that she's okay.

We don't bother going down to our seats in the front row instead of taking one next to her family. I sit next to Zack and Korra sits on the other side of me. Kasey leans over the seat to talk to her sister, but Korra pretends that she is engrossed in what's happening on the stage instead. So, she doesn't want to talk to them yet.

I don't know if the two of them are going to have words, but I know that Kasey is not going to let it go. If her personality is any indication, then she's not gonna let it go. For now, Korra can have this moment between us uninterrupted since there are ushers in this auction hall, who would probably kick us all out for disrupting the show over a petty family discrepancy.

I'm thankful for that. I'm thankful for the fact that I'll get to sit here and enjoy what's left of the relief that I feel in finally doing something that's been plaguing my dreams.

I kissed my best friend today.

My phone rings on my kitchen counter. Steam rises from the pour-over coffee I'm making for myself. It's Phil's name on the display.

Weeks had passed where I hadn't heard anything from Phil or the other partners about potentially expanding their team. Long before I went to the concert and shared the kiss that changed everything for me. The firm had been quite profitable this year, so there would be no reason for them to not add another senior partner. It was all a matter of them meeting and deciding on who they thought would be a good candidate. I had made my case with my dedication and the time I gave to Warren, Keesley & Mozier. I've shown up and put the hours in. And I had secured profitable clients along the way.

As much as what I'm doing is about helping other people—this is still a business. A law firm is only as good as the dollar signs it can accrue. Though my firm isn't the largest in the state, or even in Denver, it still has to be on the map in this way.

I'd like to think that the hours that I've contributed to this firm have benefited it in a big way. Five years is not very long. Especially when you think about how much time it usually takes for someone in my position to rise in the ranks.

It's a mixture of the politics and the experience in this firm. I had earned the experience but Phil has been my way to appeal to the better nature of his partners. If I did as he advised well, then I'm golden.

Of all the other senior associates here, I have made strides that outweigh my competition. The only reason why Jackson had even been considered was the fact that he secured more profitable clients. But now with that nod of approval from them, seeing that I was *committed*, the gap is growing even larger between the two of us.

With me in the lead, of course.

To say I was surprised to get the call today would be a lie.

I've been working my ass off this entire time just to be able to receive it. I've been working fifty to sixty hour weeks for the last three years. And that was just when I started to actually pay attention to the numbers. Ending a year with nearly three thousand billable hours clocked is nothing to sniff at.

"I didn't want to call you on a Sunday, but I thought you should hear from me first." Phil says."Tomorrow they're going to open up the discussion. I'm moving out and they need someone to move up. I put your name in that conversation."

*Check. Mate.*

When I get off the call with Phil the first person I wanna call and tell the news to is Korra. After that kiss we shared at Merry & Bright I didn't know what to expect afterwards. I didn't think that things would be awkward between us because I just don't think that we're those kinds of people. I also didn't really know how to act.

When it's all said and done, we don't have to keep kissing for the lie or for fun.

*Kissing her was fun.*

It did not help my little red dream problem at all though. Now that I had actually felt her lips and that curve of her waist the dream had only gotten more vivid, taking depth.

Becoming more real and less dreamlike.

I didn't know what it meant. I wasn't going to think about it too much either. It's been a week of cold showers that turn into reluctant handjobs because the desire has built too much. I know her too well. When she whispers in my ear, *You're not just my best friend anymore, Bryce,* I know it's the moment my tip leaks in my sleep. I know it because when I'm there pumping my dick to release the tension, I hear, *I think about you. Like this. More than I should.*

It's driving me crazy, but there is nothing I can do. These are words I've never heard from her. Just because we kissed doesn't mean anything. There is a huge difference between kissing someone and having them ride your dick.

Fuck, I should not have said that. Now, I'm stiff as a fucking brick. I just need to drink my coffee and get this off my mind before I call her.

*We're still us.* I know because we still talk almost every day.

Despite my thoughts in a chaotic flutter of *am I flirting? Is she flirting? Should we be flirting?*

I don't understand how anyone would willingly live in the friend zone. Is that not a consistent torture?

Things that I had not really given much notice to are starting to stand out in a way they hadn't before. Like I didn't realize how adorable it was that she would put her pen in her hair whenever she wasn't using it. Or in the way that she talked to me about the clients that came in like they are all people too. I suppose the animals do have their own names, but as someone who's never owned a pet, it was not something I thought about.

She started a monthly contest where clients could submit adorable photos of their pets for them to be shared on the social media page for Thomas & Friends. It led to me receiving many photos of the animals. She was either telling me the story of the photo or just making them up. I couldn't tell whether it was a real story or not, but it was entertaining none the least.

*Everything was normal.*

I hadn't broken us because I opened my mouth and said that we should kiss.

But my biggest problem is the fact that I did want to kiss.

I wanted us to keep kissing.

And that was the problem right now. I wanted to go to her place and tell her about what happened and, ultimately, celebrate.

*Are celebratory kisses a bad thing?*

Now I feel like some sort of creep for plotting on how I could pass this *celebratory kiss* off as something that would help me with our pretend engagement.

The last thing I wanted to do was take advantage of her in this situation. Especially when I couldn't truly name what the hell my motives were here.

I'm still in the same position as before. I've been working even harder after getting that bump in recognition at the firm because of this engagement. I don't have time for a romantic relationship. What I do have time for is a friendship. And though I know they could be the same thing—I know that she deserves somebody who could spend more time on her. More time than I have to give.

A call will have to suffice for now.

Korra picks up without a preamble. "Glad you called. I've got some baked chicken coming out of the oven. We got this huge pack on sale at the store, so I made way too much. You should come and get some. I'm going to take it to the house with everyone else. If you leave now, then you'll be able to make it in time to eat with us."

She's talking at a mile a minute. I've barely had my coffee but for some reason, she's going like she's been up for a while. "I don't know..."

"Nonsense. Go ahead and put your cardboard food back into the refrigerator, go through that maze to get out of your garage, and make your way to Harmony Hill. Super easy. I'm not taking no for an answer."

I don't know how she makes me chuckle but she does. "You know you can't just bully me into coming back home whenever you feel like it?"

"I can and I will. Don't act like you don't miss me."

*Careful, Bryce.* Honesty is not the best policy here.

Missing her is not the problem. It's what I'm going to do with that emotion that's a problem. I can't tell her that though. I'm in this unknown limbo of what the hell I should and should not be doing with her.

I called her for one thing and I got distracted by her invitation. "What if I were going to invite you to my place instead of the other way around?"

"Then I'd ask what you plan on feeding me. Because my dad is cooking. All I had to do was bring the chicken which I didn't technically have to bring, but because we had bought so much it was gonna go bad. I thought I might as well. So are you going to be making dinner, or..." She drags out that last word for a long time while I contemplate the merits of staying here versus going there.

I'd be able to tell her my news in person…

But I also know that I'm still going back-and-forth on what a celebratory kiss looks like.

Why I'm still thinking about a celebratory kiss is another good reason to not go.

"If you came to town, then I'd take you to dinner." There's a long silence on the line where we both pause at the implications of what I just said. Sure, *we're engaged* but *taking her to dinner* is undoubtedly a date. "Because I don't cook. Obviously there's nothing in the apartment to make. Unless you wanted to try the falafel and tabouleh that I have."

*There I fixed it.*

"I don't think I need to find out how this company has butchered one of my favorite meals. Just come down. I know everyone would be happy to see you."

"You'd be the only one happy to see me," I correct.

She asks, "Is that not enough?"

*It's more than enough.*

"You win. I'm going to get my clothes on and head that way."

# CHAPTER 21

## Korra

Telling him to meet me at my parents house was a bad idea.

I have zero time to prepare for how I will react to seeing him in person. Though nothing really has changed from Merry & Bright until now... everything has changed.

I've been thinking about his lips nonstop.

Remember how before I was saying that he was objectively attractive and unanimously we would all vote that he is a good looking guy?

I don't think that it's as objective anymore.

Knowing *intimately* what his mouth feels like on mine and how strong his back is...

Dirty thoughts are the only thoughts I have.

It was just one kiss! How could I be this caught up in it? I'd kissed men before. I've had boyfriends before.

But kissing Palmer couldn't compare to kissing Bryce.

My best friend takes the cake. Again.

It's like he can't help but be the best at everything.

*Stupid overachieving lips.*

Why did they have to be so soft and receptive? My toes did not need to be curling in my boots. I had no need for tingles to be tingling in places that tingles were tingling.

*Ugh.*

The snow was falling all around us. I felt like I was set on fire. My mind was screaming for more and more and more.

But that's not what this is.

It could not be that because we are in a fake, *keyword: fake*, engagement. The ring on my finger isn't a real declaration to his romantic love for me.

Everyone knows we're friends.

Everyone knows that we're close.

But no one knows about the fact that I have been daydreaming about his lips while I'm waiting for a client to finish filling out their paperwork at my desk. No one knows about how I'm imagining what the weight of his body would be like over mine.

These are very *unfriendly* thoughts.

I have got to clean it up.

Walking back into the auction hall after having one of the best kisses of my life was a true testament to the strength of my own mental will. My emotions were all over the place and thankfully at the top of it was *oh my God, I'm so hot in this coat.*

I've been playing it off pretty smoothly. Nothing weird and overly sexual has come out of my mouth. I think that's because my mind is running absolutely rampant with all the ideas of where that kiss could have led to.

As I stand beside my car waiting for him to pull up, I have to say a mantra or two about *how we're good friends* and *how we have only been friends for years.* How this whole situation will *go up in flames* if I say absolutely anything about the way he looks so good in that pullover...

I think he's having these knit specifically for his body. At what point did his chest start looking so defined? And what size are his arms that every single sweater he wears shows off the definition of not only his biceps, but his triceps and I don't even know what that muscle is on his forearm, but is that a vein?

He rolls up his sleeve, and I catch the faintest view of veins peeking from underneath the sleeve.

*I have got to clean it up.*

"Finally you made it," my breathless declaration comes out. Have I been holding my breath?

*Jeez, Korra you can do better than that.*

"I had to take a shower," he says before coughing into his fist. I don't catch if he says something else, but it kind of sounds like he said something about rubbing out... I don't dwell on that instead, grabbing him and bringing him to the front door. The sooner we get into the house the more tame my thoughts will be. Nothing like family to nix the fire.

He stops me outside of the front door. *No, we need witnesses!* I need witnesses if I expect to not kiss him again!

"I've gotta tell you something before we go inside."

I shift from foot to foot in front of the door. My hand grips the knob as I respond, "Okay..."

"Mozier called me before I called you. They're gonna bring it to a vote. I'm like a step away from the review which could lead to me getting the senior spot."

I squeal with excitement, jumping to hug him without considering my actions. "That's amazing! So everything worked out!"

Pulling back to gauge's expression, he doesn't look as excited as I thought he would. He's pensive and visibly unsure, I don't understand his reaction.

Dropping my arms around his neck, I take a step back.

His hands find my waist and he stops me from getting too far from him. "I just wanted to say thank you before we went inside. You didn't have to agree to this crazy idea and put your life on hold. What you're doing for me is meaningful and I'm beyond grateful."

"It's nothing." I wave his words away. "You'd do it for me."

"I would," he agrees without flinching. "The politics are not something that is easy to get around. On merit alone, I wouldn't have been able to do this. You don't understand... I'm so grateful..."

He's looking at my lips...

*Alarm bells! He's looking at my lips.*

"Bryce–"

I'm not able to finish my sentence because we're meeting for another kiss.

But this kiss is its own.

The emotions here are not desperate or pleading. The gratitude he has is clear. With his hands on my hips, I'm pulled into him. The space that was there, keeping me sane, is no longer there.

So, I'm kissing him back.

His soft lips taste like mint, and something a little sweeter. The smell of his cologne is tangling up with all my senses that are firing at a rapid pace.

It's unlike before where we were in the snow and it was unbearable having to decide between keeping warm and staying in place to collect whatever was between our lips...

This is like seeing the mountains for the first time.

It's like experiencing the taste of your favorite meal being made by someone who's an expert in it.

This feels like seeing your favorite plant bloom in all its glory for the very first time.

This feels like...

"Oh gross..." Nia says from the doorway that at some point was opened. "They're just kissing outside."

"We were just—" I look back to Bryce and if I had seen stars in his eyes in that photo I was wrong. *These* are stars in his eyes.

He looks drunk on it.

Drunk on me.

It's then that I remember we are keeping this farce of an engagement going. It's not weird for us to be kissing outside.

It's not weird for us to be kissing at all—to *them.*

But for me? I don't know how I'm gonna sit in this living room with a straight face until it's time for dinner. Dinner is a relative term in this house since we'll be eating at three. But there's enough food that people usually eat on the meal for the rest of the day when they get hungry. Even still, there is too much time where I'm going to be keeping my hands and emotions to myself.

"You guys think you can keep it in your pants when you come in?" Kasey says from her spot on the couch with her e-reader in hand.

I take a spot on the loveseat by the fireplace and Bryce sits next to me. The length of his strong thigh pressed into mine. I'm hyper aware of everywhere we're touching. I don't think I've ever been that aware of how much we touched each other. But now it's something different. I look his way and he meets my eyes with a soft smile.

*Damn, he is cute.*

This is not helping my case.

"I'll do my best," I say to her snarky little comment.

I'm glad that she let up on me. After her remarks before the winter concert and then having to deal with her on stage, I've been feeling sensitive.

Our connection is not one like you've seen in movies or hear about in stories. As twins, we are close and for the most part we get each other. Though we're opposites, she is the other half of me. But when we disagree, it hits a little harder. There's not a frame of reference for us of what not getting along looks like. We just fit together. But ever since those comments were made, I've been looking at her differently. I don't like it.

It's made being at the apartment more uncomfortable than it ever is. I need to make up with her and figure out how we can get back to our normal.

All my close relationships are being upended by this fake engagement. It's unfortunate that I am living with her and not him.

As soon as I have the thought, I feel my face heat. A shiver rolls down my spine, and Bryce puts his arm behind my back.

*No, no, no that was not what I needed you to do.*

I cross my legs and try to sit in a natural position as my family talks around me. Could not tell you what they're saying, I'm too busy focusing on *what is he doing to my shoulder?*

I lean over to whisper in his ear, "What you doing there?"

"You don't like it?"

*Is he serious?*

"It's just..."

My dad pops his head into the living room where we're all sitting, "All right. Everybody come eat." One by one we follow him into the kitchen to make our plates.

Sundays are usually our family dinner nights I always look forward to. Right now, I'm not sure if I can handle a family dinner night. Bryce is at my back and I am acutely aware of everything he's doing.

When I pick up my plate to make food for myself. I also pick up a plate for him, as well. Force of habit, I guess. Whenever he would come to these more regularly, I'd make his food too. Now, the action has a different meaning.

He takes the plate from me, saying, "It's okay. I got it, baby."

*Baby?* Did he just... "Oh okay, *baby*." My tone is light though I emphasize his use of the word. I don't know how I'll get used to that. But I guess we're *babies* now.

Conversation around the table is as it usually is with all of us sharing what we've been up to for the week. I'm surprised to not see Malaya here. But not surprised to see Lee is in an even crappier mood than usual. One benefit of that being that he's not nearly as vocal with his offhand remarks.

Kasey catches my eye and I know she's noticed that I've clocked Malaya is not here. She shakes her head and mouths *later* to me.

Oh, I need to know what my brother did.

My dad asked Bryce how he's been since it's been a few Sundays that he's missed dinner with us. "Seeing as how you're about to become family, don't be a stranger when we're having this meal."

"I don't mean to, sir. I've just been really busy with work. I actually got some really good news today." Bryce looks down at me. I take a bite of food, chewing and putting a smile on. I hope it will encourage him to share because it is great news. "I think I'm moving up. It's been a long time, but I'm getting the promotion I've been looking forward to. Seems like a lot of things are coming into place." He makes a point of grabbing my hand and placing the two of them on the table with our fingers intertwined.

*Oh, he's good, making a big show of the perfect fiancé.*

My dad congratulates him. He's happy for Bryce's success and he's happy for me being a part of that success in some way. I know he is familiar with pursuing a profession that requires dedication and there's something there, he probably thinks is kindred to his own fire and ambition. With Bryce losing his own father, I wonder if it makes any sort of difference to hear the congrats from mine.

I kind of hope so.

The conversation picks up when Nia starts talking about her final year of being in college. I have nothing to offer this conversation, so I continue eating my food with one hand still in Bryce's. It burns hot. It's supposed to look how it does. Though I'm not uncomfortable, I do feel like crawling out of my own skin right now.

I'm doing this for him. I'm doing this for us. Ever since Bryce's Thanksgiving announcement came into the picture. No one has uttered a word about Palmer, which I have been pleased about. Damn near forgot all about him.

Everything is going how it should.

That's the thing. He's doing this so that he can get ahead and his job. This isn't real. And like I figured it would, the line is getting very blurred. I don't know when the lies are stopping and starting. All I know is that it's pretend. As much as that sucks because I can't make my brain or my body understand that we are not doing something that's escalating into any real commitment. I've gotta get it through my thick skull.

This is not real.

He is not mine.

Anything I'm feeling is inconsequential. I've gotta keep all that pushed away, tucked tight, not let everyone see that this is for show.

# CHAPTER 22

## Bryce

Nia and Kasey follow their dad into the kitchen to start putting away the food and clean everything up. Korra goes to follow them, but squeezes my shoulder before leaving. I look up at her and she gives me a soft smile, though it's a little tight around the edges.

I don't know what to make of that, but at some point over the dinner her earlier warmth had cooled. I don't know how to explain it, but she felt distant, though she was sitting right next to me. Even with her hand in mine for most of the meal.

It's just her brothers and I at the table now and I feel like I've been stranded here. I should've volunteered to help too. I should've followed her into the kitchen, but instead I'm still sitting here, hands flat on the table because I don't know what to do with them.

Zach is the first to stand saying, "Game's about to start. You coming?"

*Harmless enough.*

"Yea, I could watch. It's the Thunderbolts playing right?" I ask.

Zack nods and takes a spot on one of the recliners. He leans back in the chair, calm and measured. He is the oldest and should be the most protective, but he's much more diplomatic than that. Way too nice.

I had a small amount of jealousy towards him after everything that went down with Jillian. But I really couldn't fault the guy. It's not his fault that my ex-girlfriend was lusting after him. It's not his fault that she made choices that ultimately ended our relationship. I don't have a right to hold any animosity towards him. After all, he is a good guy. Probably one of the best that I've ever known.

Lee takes a spot on the couch with his arms, sprawled across the back like he owns the place. His jaw's tight, a muscle flexing there. I noticed that his girlfriend wasn't here tonight. Malaya is cool people and usually if she's around, he's less of an asshole. But since she's not here, I guess he's going to be a complete asshole.

The only place I have to sit is on the loveseat by myself, which has the worst view of the TV, but I didn't really care about the game to begin with. So I take my seat there and cross my arms over my chest. The TV is on,  it's low enough that conversation can still be had. That doesn't seem like a good sign. There's just one reason for that.

"So, Bryce," Zach starts, "First generation lawyer and you're making your way up the ladder huh?" This is an easy question and I know he has the answer to it. It feels like a trap somehow…

"Uh, yea," I say, clearing my throat. "It's been a big dream of mine. A lot of things had to fall into place for it to happen. Pretty grateful for the success I've seen so far."

Zack tilts his head like he's impressed but Lee snorts. "So you worked your way to the top. Good for you. You seem to work hard for the things you want in life." He jerks his head towards the kitchen where his sisters are helping his dad. "My sister… Did you work your way to being with her too?"

My spine stiffens and I know better than to take the bait. *This was absolutely a trap.* I wonder if Korra knew what was going to happen when she left me alone with these two.

"I'd say so. She is… Korra." I try to keep my answer simple. "She's—" My throat locks up.

How do I explain that she is right for me in ways that nobody else has ever been? As *a friend, of course.* She pulls me out of my head and makes me see what's in front of me. Makes me be in the present.

How do I explain that she's the one that makes me laugh after I've had twelve hours of rigorous work in a day that feels like it won't ever end?

How do I explain that she's the one that makes me believe that I deserve more than just what I thought I could have in life?

How do I explain that she's changed my perspective on what having it all looks like?

"Uh-huh, I know *she's Korra.*" Lee's smirk deepens, and I start to feel uneasy. "You realize you didn't actually answer my question, right?"

"I didn't?" I ask, though I'm starting to feel my palm sweat. *Why are my palms sweating?*

Zach studies me with an unreadable expression. It seems that whatever I did, it wasn't right. I don't know how my mind is not in the game right now, but I have faced much more challenging opponents.

They're not opponents though they're Korra's brothers who I've known for years.

Lee settles back after taking a swig of his beer. "Nah, you didn't. You two move fast. Some might say a little too fast. Wasn't she just dating that Palmer guy? Were you two together while that was going on?"

I knew this was coming.

I've been telling the story of us for a while now. I said it so many times that it should be airtight. Can't lie too small or too big and make it impossible for me to keep my story straight. "We have been friends for a really long time. And I knew her long before Palmer did. We all know that guy was the worst. I've been very vocal with her about how she deserved more."

"Deserved more?" Lee laughs. It's sharp and humorless. "Damn right, she deserves more. That guy was a fucking loser." He looks me up and down. "She didn't mention anything about you two being together though. So were you just lying in wait? Now, you're engaged and you never even dated. Forgive me, but something smells a little fishy about the whole thing..."

I feel the heat creeping up my neck. He's not wrong. I know he's not wrong.

My brain scrambles for the smooth courtroom logic that I'm good at. Though this isn't the office and her brothers aren't a judge that I'll be able to charm easily, they are Korra's family. And though they haven't known me as her romantic partner for any period of time they do still know me. Whatever this interrogation is, it comes from a place of wanting to protect her. I want to protect her too.

"I know it seems fast," I admit, allowing the validity of their accusations to stand in the room with us. Because I know it's true. And I know this is a crazy thing that Korra and I have gotten into. "Sometimes when you know, you just know. And I hate to say it, but Palmer is the one who forced me to figure it out."

Lee sits forward on the couch, his voice dropping low. I don't know if it's for my benefit or because he's trying to keep things from Korra. But the question catches me off guard. "Do you love her?"

The question hits me like a sucker punch. I should have expected it. I'm surprised that no one has asked it outright until this point. Leave it to Lee to be brash in his inquiries. My gut twists and my pulse races. The easy answer should be *yes, of course, absolutely*. But the truth is a little bit more complicated than that.

I do love Korra. I loved her for a long time. But in love with her? Also complicated.

Obviously this whole agreement was for my benefit mostly but it was also to keep them off her back about the failed relationship that she was in. Something that I understand very much so. I wish that I could just sweep everything that I had in my past with Jillian under the rug. Unfortunately, I can't because she had too many parties involved in her treachery.

When I think of Korra, her bubbly laughter like champagne, her hand fitting perfectly in mine—which is something I've just discovered I really enjoyed—the way she looks at me like she actually knows me because she does. She knows me better than basically anyone in my life.

I have to stop pretending like I have not fallen.

I know I have.

"Yes." The word comes out of me raw and unplanned, but honest.

Lee narrows his eyes, searching for cracks in my admission. Zach just watches silently, weighing what he knows.

"Well say it like you mean it," Lee pushes because he will not be satisfied. Though he is the youngest brother he has the worst attitude. The last thing I wanna do is get into an argument with him over something that has nothing to do with him. What Korra and I decided on is between Korra and I. I have to make this work.

Though I wanna snap back, I force myself to lean into this conversation and brace for whatever will come from sharing the truth. "I love your sister." The words roll off my tongue and they're not as heavy as I expect, instead they're light. My chest expanding, something is being set free. "I love the way she makes everything in my life brighter, even when it feels impossible. I love how she sees the world and how she helps me see it from her point of view. I love that she makes me want to be more than I am."

The silence that follows my admission is heavy in the room. I don't feel it. There's something powerful in the absence of a response from them.

Zach blinks a few times and when his features soften, I know I've won him over. Lee, though, just tilts his head, lips pressed together like he's trying to decide if I just delivered the answer he was looking for or not.

"Big talk," Lee mutters finally. "But talk is cheap. If you hurt my sister, Bryce, I'll be forced to show you how the Thomases don't play about family."

"I know." My throat feels raw, but my voice comes out steady when I tell him, "I'll prove to you that I'm worthy of her. And that we have a good life together."

For a long moment, the three of us just watch the football game. I couldn't tell you what's happening on the screen.

My skin prickles with my promise, but I don't say anything else.

From the doorway, Korra's voice comes to me in a tone that's too casual for my liking. "Can you help me with something?"

*How much of that did she hear?* I'm sure I'll find out soon enough. For now I need to get the hell out of this living room. Standing from the loveseat, relief rushes in, but it's tangled with something a little more uncertain. The second that I said those words, *I love your sister.* I realized that they weren't for show.

And now I don't know what the hell I'm gonna do with that truth.

# CHAPTER 23

## Korra

"Apparently, Lee told her that he had zero intentions of having kids. He got a vasectomy." My twin says while scrubbing a pot clean in the sink. I've been drying the last one she handed to me. Nia's putting the plates into the dishwasher.

"No way," Nia says.

"I can't believe it," and I really couldn't. I thought you had to be a certain age and assumed most men opposed the idea. It is completely shocking that he would do the procedure voluntarily.

"Neither can I, honestly. He never told her but they got into a fight about it," Kasey continues.

Still in disbelief, I ask, "Because he got it snipped?"

"Well, yea. He didn't tell her. She found out last week, but it's been months since he had the procedure done."

Malaya is a smart woman, capable of making her own decisions but I'm still perplexed by all of this. "She wanted to have kids? With Lee?"

"Enough to tell him to kick rocks."

Nia takes a sharp inhale of breath. "They're broken up, for real?"

"She said she needed time to think. But I heard her voice. *She's pissed.* I didn't know having children meant that much to her," Kasey says.

"Neither did he, I guess." Nia says, "What did he do when she confronted him?"

She rolls her eyes. "He reacted... Well, he reacted how Lee always does. He started talking first, not thinking, and made it way worse."

"What could he have said?" Nia asks, looking toward the living room as if it will have the answers.

"Oh, my sweet summer child. Your brother is very dumb. He might be book smart, but he runs his mouth like he enjoys being punched in the face," Kasey explains.

"Kasey!" Nia exclaims, putting a plate in the dishwasher.

Indifferent to Nia's offense, Kasey shrugs, "Help me out here, Kor."

I tilt my head from one side to the other, considering. "He says some pretty dumb things. His timing is terrible and he doesn't know when to quit. I love the boy, but I want to strangle him too sometimes."

"He always protected me..." Nia says in a soft voice.

"Well, he's our *baby brother*," I say, though Lee is less than a year younger than us. "We see it differently. And besides, Malaya would have been an awesome sister. But he messed that up. You think he'll win her back?"

Kasey shakes her head. "Malaya is strong willed. He should've known better."

Nia sighs, putting another plate into the machine. "So what about you? Are you and Bryce thinking about having kids?"

The pot in my hand drops, splashing the three of us with the soap and water from the sink.

"Oh my gosh. I'm sorry," I say, looking for towels to clean the mess up.

I'll admit that I am panicking.

*Okay, it's obvious that I'm panicking.*

Thankfully, Kasey is more annoyed that I've gotten the front of her wet and Nia is trying to keep the water from spilling off the edge of the counter to the floor.

"I hate to make this mess and run, but I completely forgot. Bryce and I have plans to... do some registry shopping. You know? Since he has free time today." *That's a thing that fiancés do, right?* I throw a thumb over my shoulder, "We really should get going."

"You set a date?" Nia asks, now that she's cleaned up the water from the counter. She bounces with excitement.

"Uhh... Not yet, but you know Bryce. He likes to be prepared," I say.

Kasey raises an eyebrow, not totally buying the words but not pressing me on this shopping trip I've sprung out of nowhere. "Are you gonna be home tonight?"

"Uhhh..." *Well that is a great question...* "Probably not. I wouldn't wait up if I were you." I rock back and forth on my heels. I need to get out of that kitchen and fast. "I'll see you tomorrow. Okay?"

I hug both my sisters before tossing a goodbye to my Dad who is watching TV down the hall in his room already.

Look at me running away from complicated feelings... Again.

I am only a girl—a woman—with an ounce of self-preservation.

Walking back down the hallway to the living room, I hear my brothers and Bryce are talking. I don't mean to snoop. *I know that eavesdropping is rude.*

These are things that I would have taken to account if I did not hear my name. But I *did* hear my name and I wanted to know what was being talked about.

Looking back at my sisters, who are talking amongst themselves, I decide that whatever it is the men are talking about is more interesting. What I didn't account for was hearing the words out of Bryce's mouth that I never thought I'd hear.

"I love your sister."

*What?*

Did he just say...

WHAT?

And it doesn't stop there. He said things that I didn't know were true. Bryce continues, "I love the way she makes everything in my life brighter, even when it feels impossible. I love how she sees the world and how she helps me see it from her point of view. I love that she makes me want to be more than I am." My heart is a flutter in my chest.

I'm feeling...

*I'm feeling!*

This is bad.

My eyes prick with tears. *I can't cry right now.* I shouldn't even be hearing this. Of course, Lee says something rude back to him, but I'm still stuck in the moments where he said he loved me four times.

*I have got to get Bryce out of there.*

I don't need him saying anything else while I am trying to remember that this is a fake engagement.

*This is pretend.*

*He is my best friend.* Only.

He's just saying this so that he can protect what he has going for him at his firm. It is way too difficult to keep everyone on the same page if you are trying to sell something like this. Right? And who knows what could happen if the truth of what we're lying about got out.

*It doesn't seem like a big deal.*

And of course, Denver is not the same as Harmony Hill. But Harmony Hill talks. And the last thing I need is for one of my siblings to unknowingly out us to someone, who knows someone, who is close to someone, who works at his firm. People love the gossip. You least expect to be met with the truth of your own story from someone else's mouth. It only gets more warped as it travels from person to person.

Stepping into the living room fully, I gather up my mask of calm that I don't feel and ask, "Can you help me with something?"

Bryce hops up from his spot quickly, with a look of gratitude. We walk over to the dining room together and he scrutinizes my face. If he's looking to see whether or not I heard him confess to loving me *multiple times* and having reasons on *why he loved me,* then I am not saying anything.

All I know is that now I am going to have to figure out what I'm gonna do with *that information.* And *that information* is gonna stay right where it's at until it needs to be addressed.

"So, I kind of said that we were gonna go shopping for our registry…"

He nods repeatedly, happy that I haven't called him out on *that information* probably. Not crossing that bridge. "That's fine. It's not like I have plans to do anything else today."

"And I said I was staying the night at your place," I rush out before I chicken out.

His brows slam down, eyes full of trepidation. "You're gonna stay the night at my place?"

"Yes, *baby*," I sass.

"Oh my goodness, will you look at this? They make a charcuterie board that comes with a lid. Do you know how many times I've needed something like this? We have got to add it to the list." I scan the barcode from my phone.

This list is shaping up pretty nicely. I've already found plenty of things that we'd both like. Not that anyone will ever buy it but there is nothing wrong with a good wishlist.

Bryce looks at me like I've lost my mind. And maybe I have. It is actually quite fun to do this kind of shopping. "So, you wanna add a charcuterie board, but you didn't wanna add the Sherpa throw?"

"I think we'll get a lot more use out of the charcuterie board. The lid locks. Look at it!" I wave the bamboo board in the air between us.

"I'm gonna be completely honest with you. I don't even like charcuterie. Why would I want a bunch of little snacks when I could have an actual meal?"

I gasp. "What do you mean?" Dramatically, I look around us to see if anyone heard him. Then, turning back to him I place both of my hands on his shoulders, "Is this going to be our first fight as a couple?" I whisper with a giggle.

He shakes his head at me. "I think you're taking this a little too seriously. We just need to get some things on this list for it to be believable."

"I don't think you're taking this seriously *enough*. I'm finding out all types of new things about you. Who only likes white towels? A gradient of grey ones is not even *that* wild. If I'm supposed to give you a Danica plant to go in the bathroom, she's going to need to have some variety in her life. All that white—it's like she's in a padded room."

"Korra," he says, no longer walking beside me as I go through the aisles of ideal wedding gifts. "I think we need to have a serious conversation about where this *fake engagement* is going..."

That gets me to stop in my tracks and then retrace my steps to where he's standing. There's no benefit in him yelling out this conversation across two aisles.

We came to a department store that's somewhere between Harmony Hill and Denver. It's nice knowing that we won't run into anyone we know here unless fate just really wants to spit on us.

I was hoping that we could avoid any sort of serious conversations for some time. There's only a few things that I could think of that he'd be talking about right now—none of which I'm ready for.

I'm not ready for any more life changes that include losing people who are important in my life.

If it were up to me, I'd like for our feelings to remain unknown. I put *that information* somewhere in a box that I don't have to touch because as of right now we are still friends who have kissed a few times...

Which is not an uncommon thing for people to do if they've had a little bit too much to drink...

Or are out of their minds...

"Korra?" He takes my hand in his, holding it gently. "I don't want to freak you out... Or to ask something of you that I know I shouldn't."

Squeezing my eyes shut, I plead with my hands. "Please don't tell me that you're not gonna take the Danica plant. I was just joking before. They're easy to maintain and have so many health benefits. I really do think that you need some life in that apartment. It's gonna be a lot of weight on her shoulders to carry, but if anybody can do it, it's gonna be an Ellen Danica."

He chuckles and shakes his head at me again. "Can you maybe not think about plants for five seconds? I know it's a lot, but for right now, we're going to have a conversation about two people. Korra and Bryce."

Inhaling deeply, I say, "Okay, fine. I am not at all thinking about how I did not water—"

"Korra, focus."

I cross my arms over my chest, waiting for whatever it is he has to say. Though I have my own suspicions, I have to play it off like I'm not expecting *that information* to come out of his mouth.

"I honestly can't thank you enough. I feel like a bit of a loser for continuing to thank you for agreeing to be my fiancée..."

"And I've told you that it's not a big deal. If this works out for you, then it makes me happy to help you in any way that I can." I meant that. I knew that he had done most of the work. And this was just one small thing. One small thing that was testing me in ways I didn't think it would.

He fidgets which is so unlike him, it's making me nervous in turn. He's always so put together and unfazed by any sort of stressor. Having heard what he said to my brothers before, I can glean what is going through his mind.

He looks up from his hands to my face. His eyes are vulnerable and open with the question he asks next. "How do you know when we're not pretending anymore?"

"Ummm... what?" I whisper.

The air thickens with his question.

It's heavy as sound travels in an odd manner that makes it almost impossible to understand his next words.

Like when he proposed—fake proposed—on our trip to the Hills, I do my best to listen to what he has to say.

"Korra, I know this started off as something that was supposed to be pretend but it feels like we could be something else." Unsure, he asks, "Are you happy?"

I blink several times. "What are you asking me, Bryce?" My eyes find the ring that I have only been taking off for showers and otherwise has lived on my finger.

He covers the ring and my hand with his. "Forget about the engagement for a second. Do you think that we could be more than friends? Could you be happy with me?"

# CHAPTER 24

## Bryce

Uncharacteristic silence is a third presence in the car ride to my place and even the whole ride up to my apartment. I carried her bag with no protest up to my place because she was still so quiet.

I didn't think that my question would cause her to basically shut down. *My expectation was more questions.* Precisely a million of them, but instead she only responded, "Yes." But she sounded anything but happy about the answer. Her contemplation is starting to become worrisome as she sits on my couch with little to no awareness around her.

"Korra," I place my hand on hers and she barely registers it. "Korra, I need you to say something. I'm getting nervous now."

She blinks a few times, "Sorry, I—" Her eyes travel downward to where my hand is still on hers. The two of us have never shied away from physical affection.

In fact, she needs it. It's always been platonic and, at first, foreign to me. But now, I don't recognize when I do touch her because she is probably already doing it to me.

If we're walking together, she is within reach and will often hold my hand or my arm. It's a real need for her to feel connected. I became accustomed to doing the same—only with her though.

Now, as her eyes examine how my hand is covering hers, she can't straighten her brows. They are at war on her face between confusion and contemplation.

"What's wrong Korra?" I take a deep breath in, using a tactic of hers when she is avoiding a ramble… or getting ready for one. "If you're not interested in more, then I have no problem with staying friends. I knew that it was a lot to just spring on you like that." Running a hand ove my hair, I lean back into the couch cushions, "Maybe I was just reading everything wrong."

"Why?" She asks, her eyes still not meeting mine, instead staring at the button on my henley top.

"Why what?" I ask, still watching for any change in her expression.

Her sienna browns hold me with their unapologetic interest. "Why do you want to be more than friends?"

I take her face in for a long time.

Memories of every emotion I've seen on there through the years, vivid in my mind.

We've been through so much and I have never felt like my next words would affect her more than they do right now. The frailty in her gaze is unmissable.

"I've had time to think. To think about us and what I know to be true for us." If I'm honest with myself as her brother made me be, I don't truly want to go back to being just friends with her. I want our relationship to move forward, not backwards. Saying my feelings aloud opened a door that I happily walked through.

Fierce emotion turns her eyes glassy though I know that she is not one to jump to conclusions. Korra likes for everything to be plain and out there for everyone to understand. "Bryce, what does that mean?"

Though my heart is racing I confirm, "You said that you think we could be happy together." She nods once, never taking her eyes off of me when I ask, "Is the point of a relationship not happiness?"

"You sound like Kasey," she says on an exhale.

"Kasey said that?"

"About Palmer," she admits, twirling her thumbs around each other.

I grimace at his name. "Well, if she was saying it in regard to him, then I'm definitely better than him at making you happy." *Right?*

She nods again, but doesn't verbally agree. Doubt blooms in my mind. "Why were you with him anyway? Everyone could see that he was not worth your time."

Korra looks down at her hand, straightening the engagement ring on her finger. "He was there," she says. "He didn't treat me like I was broken or like I was missing the biggest part of my heart. He was happy with what little I had to give. In exchange, I got to fill that hole with... a body. Somebody who had more to talk to me about than the loss of *her* or how I was coping. He never had a pitying look on his face when he saw me."

I can't control the frustration in my tone when I say, "He didn't have a look of *anything* when he saw you. The guy was like a packet of crackers. Bland but filling."

"That's an accurate way to look at it." She shakes her head. "I settled for a bland packet of crackers because he could take my mind off the pain. I was able to talk to him about anything besides myself for hours." Her head hangs lower, "I don't think we ever talked about me."

My palm cups her cheek, urging her to look at me. "How could you want that?"

"To turn off my mind, to be the shell I felt I was? It was easy. I was moving on autopilot and only recently had I begun to see how empty the time I spent with him was." She bites her lip before continuing, "Everyone had something or someone to busy themselves. But most of my free time was spent with Mom. Kasey poured herself into writing. Zach had work which never slowed. Lee had Malaya and the clinic. Nia had school. I had my plants that reminded me of her and yet they couldn't talk back to me or hug me. But Palmer could."

"Korra, you could've talked to me. I asked you all the time to let me in. You would brush me off. You brushed everyone off, saying, 'I'm fine' and we knew you weren't. I could see that you weren't."

Intensity sparks a clarity in her gaze that I had not seen since we arrived at my apartment. "You had Jillian."

Her words cut me deep. Deeper than I could have prepared for. When I finally blink back my disconcertion, I ask the question I should have long ago. From my recollection of their interactions over the past few months, I'm nervous for what the answer will be. "Why does that matter?"

"Jillian and Mom were close. They did have a bond that I didn't understand. Didn't want to understand. She might have been upset by Mom's passing, but Jillian made it clear that your shoulder was the only one that she wanted to cry on. It was *very clear* that you were otherwise committed to comforting her."

When Delanna passed, that time was hard on all of us. She had touched so many lives and her legacy of kindness and love in this community knows no bounds. I was there at the funeral, the wake and the reception. All of which, overflowed with people there to pay their respects. It was more than our small funeral home and reception hall could take. I'm certain she could have filled the auction hall to the rafters if they had held it there. Through that time, I remember Jillian on my arm.

But I also remember searching for Korra to see how she was holding up. Jillian had told me that I *never put her first* and that she was *not important enough to me* whenever I did. Most of the time I brushed it off, but now I see those statements with fresh eyes.

"I was there for you though. I was—"

"She was there too. Bryce, do you not see how awful she is? What did she do to blind you so thoroughly? How could you not see that she is a cruel and hateful person with a personal grudge against me? Do you think that she would let you get close enough to comfort me when it takes the spotlight off of her? Even after everything she has put you through, you still don't see how vile she is?"

My jaw ticks, unsure of what to say. Of course I know now. But then... "Korra, I—"

"That's a no. I care for you Bryce. I really do. But she tried to drive a wedge into our friendship. She tried to use you. Not only to get to my brother but to get back at me." Her eyes glisten with unshed tears as she stands from the couch looking down at me. Her voice is high pitched and cracking when she recounts the things that Jillian said to her. "I can see her snarl clear as day in my mind. 'Stop trying to use your mom's death to get close to my man.' She treated you like she owned you and had control over what you did and who you could talk to. I don't doubt that you wanted to be there for me, but I didn't want to deal with her to seek comfort you wouldn't be able to give. Jillian had no intention of letting you be there for me.

"And before I left the reception, she caught my arms after I had obviously been crying in the bathroom. It was the only time that I had to myself that whole miserable day. I remember her saying, 'Zach is over there dealing with everything by himself and you're in here boohooing by yourself. Fucking pitiful, Korra. You only think about yourself.' An unbelievably shitty thing to say to someone grieving, but not unbelievable that she would say something like that at all. She was always nasty to me, constantly trying prove how she was better than me."

She takes a breath and I do my best to stay there and listen to what she's saying, to not interrupt. My instinct is to try and fix it but there is nothing I can do to take back what Jillian said or how it affected Korra.

"And so I wiped my face and went to stand by everyone's side to support them. When anyone asked me how I was doing, I smiled and changed the subject. Then Palmer saw me getting food by myself one day and I fell into him." She wipes at her eyes, confessing, "Then he left me when I needed him most."

She holds her middle by the time she finishes sharing how I inadvertently allowed my ex to hurt both of us. Her sobs wrecking my resolve and sending me spiraling. Trying to think over every time I had seen them together. Trying to figure out how I allowed this to happen. Jillian had ripped through my friend at her most vulnerable. Tapping into her insecurities about being a part of her family and the value she has in their lives, knowingly or unknowingly. I was too busy working and trying to maintain my relationship with Jillian that I didn't have the mental capacity to see what was really going on with my friend.

I scoop Korra up. Taking her into my arms and holding her close to my chest as she cries into my shirt. Emotions from months of holding this from me pouring out of her. *I should have known that there was more.* That she had a broken heart under all of this. That there was more than just her mother passing. It was all compiled and I had allowed this to happen.

"I'm sorry. I'm so sorry," spills from my lips over and over into her hair. My own face wet with regret and hurt but I can't let her go. I can't let this go.

Everything I know about us is true.

We can get past this.

I'll never let Jillian hurt us again.

When our tears finally subside, I help Korra to the bathroom so that she can shower and get ready for bed. I sit right outside of the bathroom door in case she needs me, with my head in my hands. My heart still cracked, broken at how I let her down.

Then to ask her if she wanted more? When I've given her nothing?

I'm going to make this right.

She comes out of the bathroom, unsurprised to find me waiting for her. Something passes between us as she looks up at me with a bare face and her hair all up on top of her head. She rests her forehead against my chest again for a brief moment before I do the same to get ready for bed.

Coming out of the shower with only my basketball shorts on, I look forward to finally laying down after such an emotionally draining day.

When I meet Korra in my bedroom to grab a shirt, she says, "You don't have to." I look back at her from the doorway of my closet when she adds, "I know you get hot in your sleep. You don't have to put a shirt on for me."

"Right, okay," I say, still unsure about being so bare in the bed with her. We never said in so many words that she would be sharing the bed with me, but I think we both need that closeness right now. The vulnerability in our admissions is raw in the air between us. With her in a tank top and sleep pants, that is enough to separate us at this point.

I join her on the bed, peeling back the blankets and settling in the middle of the mattress like I always do. With only the side table lamp to illuminate the room, it's cozy and comfortable in my room. Tonight is different because Korra is here. She rests over me, her head over my heart, her hair tickling my chin every now and again as she gets comfortable. When she finally settles into place too, I wrap my arm around her back. Pulling her leg over mine to keep her close.

"I am happy with you," she says, answering my initial question but not as the stunned woman she was before.

Rubbing her back, "You're not just saying that because we're upset?" She idly traces something over my chest that makes my skin tingle. The ghost of her touch is more intimate than any way that she's touched me before. It is not at all friendly...

"No," she says after a time. "I think that more for us could be good. No one gets me like you do."

"I could say the same. I'll never forgive myself—"

"You don't have to. I forgive you for the both of us." Looking up at me, she waits for me to meet her eyes. "If you agree to give this a shot, we have to go into it with open hearts. I hold no grudges toward you so you can't hold any toward yourself."

"Korra—"

"Say it," she demands with her voice firm.

"I don't know—"

"We've moved on. We're giving this a fair chance. Now turn off that lamp so we can get some sleep." I don't have to respond because we both know I'll go where she directs us as long as we're together.

# CHAPTER 25

## Korra

Ever had a Monday that didn't quite Monday like other Mondays?

Well, I think I am having a Monday unlike any other.

It's actually good.

I didn't roll out of bed to grumble into my morning routine and scrubs to go to work.

No, I woke up next to Bryce who was already out of the shower and ready for his day at work. We talked about basically nothing while I got ready at his place for work. The traffic out of Denver was as thick as it always is, but I happily hummed to some RnB that made the drive just float by.

I guess that's what happens when you're dating your fake fiancé.

I giggle to myself, rearranging the miniature succulents that decorate my desk corner. The thought of Palmer doesn't make me feel anything as I make them form a little pyramid. The succulents are thriving and I figure that I'll have to take them home to clear out their old leaves with my others before winter weather gets too harsh.

The front door bell tinkles into the lobby and a very welcome client comes in carrying a box under one arm as her dutiful Vizsla walks beside her.

"I've got something a little different for you today." She says without greeting and puts the box on my counter for me to inspect. "The poor little things were terrified and cold. I don't know how they got into my garage. Russell was just barking up a storm and I had to investigate."

Looking over the schedule for the day, I check to see who has time to see the little patients today. Lee has more regulars lined up so I think Zadie will be the better fit for this walk in.

"Audrey, you did the right thing in bringing them here. Zadie will get them all checked out and then we can figure out what else we can do." I page my friend and call her to the front desk.

The little mewls are adorable when I open the top flap with my pen. My heart sinks. Four kittens wiggle about in the towel Audrey set in the bottom of the box. "Have you given them anything to eat or drink?"

"Nope. I didn't know what to give them. Once I got them in the box, I brought them here."

"That's good," I say, letting the box close. The four of them all have sticky faces from eye infections and they're dirty all over. In various shades of grey, black and white, they are in bad shape except for one that looks a little worse than the others.

Russell is sitting dutifully by her side. I show Audrey one of the treats I have by my desk, asking if he can have one. She nods, and I hold the treat out for him to see it more clearly. He perks up but sits even more still. Audrey takes it and places it on his nose. "Hold," she commands. He sits as long as she keeps her hand up. Then she releases the command and he bounces it off his nose to snap it up into his mouth.

Zadie comes from around the patient door to join me behind the desk when Russell snaps up his treat.

A stunned gasp comes from the older woman. "My goodness you have grown up to be so beautiful, Zadie. I remember when you were just a little thing. Now, you're so grown up."

Zadie blushes a little. "Thank you, Ms. Audrey. You're too kind." For an overachieving badass, Zadie is awfully bashful when hearing compliments.

Coming around the counter, she leans against it. "What brings you in today?"

"Oh, right," Audrey shakes herself, "I just can't believe time flies so quickly. I, um, brought those in." She gestures to the mewling box on my desk. "Found some kittens and a few of them look hurt. I didn't know what else to do with them. I'll pay for whatever to get them fixed and healthy, but I can't keep them."

Zadie looks into the box and sucks her teeth. "They're still little so it's usually easier to find a home for them. Well, let's take them back and I can figure out what we can do next. How's that sound?"

"Sounds good to me." Audrey says. "Come," she says to Russell who trots happily behind them, still chewing on his treat.

Korra: {picture message}

Korra: She's the sweetest baby. No one will take her

Bryce: All right. I'll bite. What's the story with this cat?

She mews softly, still a little weak from her surgery. She was the last to get spayed since they had to work on her other injuries first. I've put her into my lap because I don't like the idea of her sitting in the room by herself.

Korra: Audrey Perry found her in her garage. The other three kittens were fine and they've already been claimed. But this one had to have her eye and part of an ear removed. But she's a fighter. She probably defended the other kittens and now she's got the scars to prove it.

Bryce: Nothing's wrong with her?

I look down at the sweet baby in my lap.

Korra: She's just looks a little different… From everything they could tell, she's fine

**Bryce: I'll take her**

I rub my eyes, not sure I'm reading the text right.

Korra: You'll take her where?

**Bryce: To my place?**

I dial his number immediately. I have to know if he's just messing with me or not.

He picks up after a few rings and says, "Hold on a sec." There's a few moments where he is moving around and then I hear the click of the door. "What's up?"

Petting the little head in my lap, I ask, "Did you just say that you were adopting a kitten?"

"Pretty sure I did."

"You do know that a kitten will be staying in your apartment? Your very pristine and sterile apartment…"

"My place is not sterile. " He chuffs, "Weren't you saying that I needed some life in here? I think a kitten will do the job."

"Well I mean, yea… But you do know that a kitten is alive right?"

There is a moment of silence before, "I'm aware."

"Well I'm gonna bring her there tonight. So if you're not serious, now is the time to back out…"

"And you're going to personally deliver her? I'm seeing less and less of an issue." Well, there goes the flutters in my belly. I feel like a teenager. He just casually makes me feel that way and it's not even on purpose.

"Mostly because I wanna make sure that she actually arrives at your house and that you have everything set up for her."

"Good idea and while you're at it, you can bring me that clipping of my new ivy to hang in the bathroom as well."

Bryce meets me in the parking lot to help grab some of the things that I brought. When he sees I kind of went all out with accessories for the little thing, he returns back to the car with a cart that we pile everything into.

Back at his apartment, I'm hit with the memories of what we talked about the last time I was here. Though recounting the memories aren't great, the resolution of having Bryce firmly as mine, is nothing but. It's only been a few days, but I'm sensing a lot of travel to Denver in my future.

He starts looking through the things in the cart, holding up a little pink tutu in question. "What's a cat gonna do with a tutu?"

"Be absolutely adorable... Obviously." I set the necessary items that I got for her aside and grab the most important thing to put into his hands. "This is a guide for kitten care. Plus her outpatient papers are in the back."

He flips through the book before turning it to the back. "This says it's for kids five and up."

"Great. You're old enough to read it then. Super quick. Cats are rather easy once you understand what they need."

He chuckles but sets the book back into the cart. "Well, let's see the little thing."

Sitting onto his plush leather chair in the living room, I say. "Ah ah ah. She is not a thing. You need to be thinking of a name for her."

I open the little travel carrier and take out the sweetest little girl. She has been rather quiet on the drive up here, but now that she's in a new place she starts mewling again.

I'm careful with her as her bandages are still crucial to keep the sutures she has safe.

The little kitten huddles into my arm, trembling, and looking around with her good eye.

Bryce's eyes soften immediately on the small fluffy bundle. Coming to where I'm sitting, he holds a hand out for her to sniff and she does so tentatively at first. Then she brushes her cheek along his knuckles. The smallest chuff comes from him with her affection.

*Oh, yea. He's done.*

Holding his hand out for her, she presses a small paw into it and carefully steps over. "I didn't know that her paws were white." His thumb rubs over one of her front paws.

"Probably because she was a little kitty loaf when I sent you the picture."

He looks up at me, confused, like I'm not speaking English. "Kitty loaf?" He repeats the phrase carefully.

"You know? When they have their paws tucked under their bodies." I mimic the motion with my hands, bending them at the wrist to rest them at my chest. "It's universally the best thing about cats—when they loaf."

The kitten paws at the sleeves of his hoodie. "I see." He removes the fabric stuck under her tiny claws. "Well, I decided on a name."

"Let's hear it then." I didn't realize how dangerous Bryce with a small cat would be to my libido. And here I am watching him maneuver her around like she might break.

"I'm gonna call her Socks." The cat has crawled up his sleeve to rest inside the fabric of his hood. She nuzzles the side of his head and he lets her.

"I think she likes it. And you. Little Miss Socks."

She fully traversed his shoulders returning to her comfortable spot in the hood where she kneads the fabric. "Well that's good considering I just signed on to be her landlord."

"You just had to make it sound so..." I don't get to finish the sentiment, because he's moving around the apartment with the cat in tow. Or I guess I should say *in hoodie.*

"Hey, have you eaten yet?" he asks.

I'm suspicious of the subject change but I answer anyway. "No, not yet. I just grabbed all this stuff and came down here."

"I've really been craving some wings and I haven't had any since your birthday."

"Are wings actually an indulgence? You could have wings whenever," I ask, knowing that he subsists on cardboard meals and protein shakes.

"Yea, they don't really have the macros I'm looking for. Do you want some?"

"I'll take some. You order and I'll hang up your other new pet." I hold up the small pot, showing him the minimalistic design. I could have chosen something more bold, but I think this was a good choice so he'll appreciate the pop of green more. The bonus is that I'll be able to easily hang the one from his bathroom ceiling.

We continue setting up Socks's new things like a cat tree and a round bed that already looks good in his bedroom. With how comfortable she is in his hood, I don't think she'll use the bed at all. Lucky little girl.

We eat our food and Socks eats her food in peace. Sometimes it can be weird ordering wings with someone because you have to do that like divvy up thing. But for us, it's easy. He prefers the drums and I'm a die-hard flats lover. Drums are the worst, argue with the wall. Not me.

As friends, I've never doubted our compatibility. But as something more? That compatibility is just as smooth.

He lets me put on the crime show that Kasey and I have been watching. Though it's not his kind of law, he did admit to liking the first few episodes. He is the least picky about TV though. He's always been that way. On the other hand, I'm extremely picky about them.

*That information* that I've been holding onto in the back of my mind, will stay where it's at. But if I were to think about it, I might say something like... Bryce and I were made for each other.

Since I'm not, I can just acknowledge that this friendship has lasted because we have complimentary interests.

"I have one final thing to show you." I say, reaching into my bag. "I think I finished the spread."

Socks has migrated to the top of Bryce's head now, playing in his curls. It is the cutest thing I've ever seen. He is completely unbothered by the cat moving around his head.

"That's us," Bryce says when I finally flip to the page. Why I didn't start on the first one is beyond me. His finger traces over the pumpkin border I made and the bucket of apples I painstakingly cut from a larger patterned paper. Loads of leaves and acorns are scattered over the page. I even learned how to emboss and get the date embossed over various colors of paper to stand out from the page. It looks very professional. I'm happy with how it turned out though it wasn't easy.

"Do you like it?" I ask.

His eyes search the page before searching my face. "I like it a lot."

# CHAPTER 26

## Korra

"Hold on, Korra. Socks is demonstrating her hunting capabilities," Bryce says when he picks up my call.

I giggle at the thought of Socks hunting anything with those little paws. "What is she hunting exactly? Spare no details."

There's some rustling on the line before a few curses. "This cat is a menace," he says in a droll voice.

"She is a sweetheart," I say, still remembering when she was sleeping soundly in the crevice of his neck. "An adorable little sweetheart.

"Korra, her claws are sunk into my hand as she kicks me to get free."

My giggle turns into a full-on belly laugh, "Oh, is she doing the little kicks? Ahh, I wish I could see her." I sigh. "What does she have?"

"A strip of my sirloin. Her little teeth can barely hold onto the piece and she is still giving it her best."

"Well I'm glad she's feeling active." The last time I saw her, she was sporting bandages over her stitches.

"That's what you have to say?" More rustling and then a picture message vibrates on my phone.

Sure enough, Socks is giving her fiercest little face as she holds onto a piece of steak from her mouth. Tiny white paws attacking his veiny forearm.

Well... I'm not upset about any of this.

"Oh no, take her out of air jail!" I exclaim in mock-offense on her behalf. "She's innocent until proven guilty."

He laughs despite the circumstances, saying, "I just sent you the incriminating evidence. She is still committing the crime as we speak."

"This is not a fair trial! I demand to speak to a lawyer."

"Korra," he says, his voice taking a deeper tone than before. "This is attorney Bryce Hampton on the line. Did you forget who lays down the law?"

A shiver rolls down my spine.

Okay.

*Did he just...?*

"No fair," I say. "I don't have a deep voice to do whatever that magic is."

"What magic?" He asks but he knows exactly what he's doing with his voice still vibrating in that low timbre on the line.

"Quit it," I tease, "Free Little Miss Socks so she can eat her steak in peace."

"I'm only letting her go because she's cute and so are you." Cat parenthood suits him well. "Are you at the house yet?"

I sign at the subject change, "Yea, I got here not long ago but I don't want to be the one to deliver the news."

"What news?"

"They're closing any and all upcoming Brenford events down with the bad press surrounding the company. Apparently, it's a safety concern." The email was bolded as it came through this morning. An email from the Brenford family on a Sunday was definitely a big deal.

Bryce's voice comes through clearly from my speakerphone as I sit in the car. "I'm sorry, Kor. I know you were looking forward to it."

"It was just something that I thought would bring the family together to work on. But only Kasey and Zach worked on it with me. I can barely say that they did." I was proud of the spread. I hoped that it would be as big an homage to my mother as the concert.

So dumb. It was just a small thing. Not her local legacy for music in this town. It was all I could manage and it still failed.

"It looked great to me," Bryce says, trying to cheer me up. "Are you going to tell them?"

"I don't have a choice," I sigh more heavily. Looking at my family home through the windshield. "Are you still coming for Christmas tomorrow?"

"Yea." Socks' little meow is on the other side of the line. "I'll be the one with the velcro cat."

"Oh, perfect! Everyone will be so happy to meet her."

He hums in agreement before saying, "Stop stalling. You need to go inside."

"I'm not stalling. I just don't want to go inside."

Nothing gets past him. "Same thing. You can call me later. Okay?"

"Tell Socks bye for me."

"I will," he says before we end the call.

Exiting the car, I walk up to the porch. Frost has covered the railings and windows. It's getting chilly which is perfect with Christmas coming tomorrow. "Just go inside," I say aloud to no one. It's not a failure. The event was cancelled. *I'm not failing mom.*

Pushing into the house, I'm hit with the aroma of rosemary roast and cinnamon cider. The hum of conversation is already going. The warmth is welcome as I shrug out of my coat and hang it in the closet. Everyone is standing around the kitchen. My Dad, Lee and Gonzalo talk by the stove. Gonzalo's little girl is stuck to Nia's leg, who doesn't seem to mind as she talks with Kasey. Still no Malaya. I think Lee really messed that up. Though I just talked to Bryce, I miss him and wish he were here tonight. I'd like to be holding his hand as I tell the family about the scrapbooking competition.

It's not long before we're all sitting in the dining room. The conversation goes and I add my little bit of input every now and again.

"Well, while we're all gathered around, I thought I'd tell you first." That gets everyone to quiet down. "This will be my last year at the clinic." You could hear a pin drop. "I'm retiring."

It's not that much of a shock for me to hear him say these words. He had been stepping back from his daily duties already. Lee stepped into some of those roles. But then he hired Zadie and she's been taking some of them too. Our clinic isn't large and we don't have that many staff members. It's easy to feel when someone's presence is lessening over time. My Dad has had this on his mind for a while I think.

Lee pipes up, "You're leaving? Who's gonna take over?"

"I don't know yet. I've got to make a decision before I go but that won't be for some time."

Dissatisfied with Dad's answer, Lee charges forward without humility. "You're playing with me? There is only one person who is fit to do it, Dad."

"I said, I'll decide in time, Bentley. Don't take that tone with me," Dad warns.

Hovering over the table is a growing tension from Lee and everyone else not knowing what to say about all of this. I break the silence, "You deserve it, Daddy. I'm happy for you. Whatever you need for this change, I'm here for you," I say, blowing him a kiss.

He pats his cheek to set my love in place. "Anyone else, have something to say about it?" When no one speaks up, he says, "Back to your conversations then."

Somehow, Zach leads the conversation to the scrapbooking competition anyway.

"Next Saturday, huh?" He confirms. "I requested off so I could be there for the judging."

I set my napkin on the table after I wipe my mouth. "Actually, I needed to talk to you all about that."

Now all seven sets of eyes land on me. Kasey speaks first, "What is it?"

"Well... the contest was postponed. Indefinitely."

Lee's face twists in confusion. "What do you mean *indefinitely*? It's a crafting thing."

I ignore his condescending tone and respond, "It's a crafting thing that's held by the Brenfords. They have suspended all their events because of bad press or something. The email I received was vague but this competition and a whole host of other events held by them are not going to happen."

There's grumbling around the table before Nia asks, "What kind of press could make them cancel a crafting competition?" Of course, everyone goes to their phones to figure it out. I don't know why I didn't think to do that.

Gonzalo pulls up the article on his phone. Reading it out loud, "With the decades-old union dispute that was previously settled, the Brenfords have decided not to comment on the Kindrick family's public commentary on how everything was handled." He looks up from his phone to the table. "Apparently the Kendrick's think that it was a coverup and their family was not compensated fairly."

My father looks stricken with the words Gonzalo has said. His hands ball on the table, jaw working.

"Dad? Are you okay?" I ask.

Everyone turns their attention to him. "I wish they would just lay that mess to rest. Who came back bringing it up again?"

"It doesn't mention anyone... Just the Kindrick family." He checks his phone again and then asks, "Do you know something about this, Wayne?"

"Not that I could share," he says.

An evasive response if I ever heard one. Very odd especially combined with his change in demeanor.

"Wait, that name sounds familiar," Zach says. "Let me see it," he says to Gonzalo.

"Wasn't that the name of that guy on the ID?" Kasey asks me.

My brow furrows, "It was..."

"This is the same last name. I've never seen it spelled this way either," Zach says.

My Dad stands from the table, "I'm going to lay down. You all clean this up before you leave." He's out of the dining room before anyone can object or reply to his sudden exit.

"What ID?" Nia finally asks after we've all been staring at the door he's exited through.

"Korra found this bloody tie in Mom's room that had an old work ID from Brenford's mill." Kasey says.

"Okay, the grown ups are talking. Let's go see what's on TV," Gonzalo says, ushering his daughter, who's reluctant to go, out of the room reluctantly. She liked being close to Nia. Nia watches them go and I wonder when she and Luciá got so close.

Lee finally joins the conversation, looking up from his phone. "You found what? Where?"

"I found an old work badge from someone called Aiden Kindrick in one of Mom's storage boxes. It's at the house."

"How come this is the first time I'm hearing about it?" Lee asks

"It's my first time too," Nia adds.

"It's not like we were keeping it a secret. You probably would have known if you came to help with the scrapbook."

Lee grumbles, "Some of us have lives to live." That hurts, hitting a little too far below the belt right now. "I'm going through a pretty shitty break up right now."

"Yea, we noticed. Great job, by the way. We liked Malaya," Kasey sneers.

"I didn't do anything wrong. She just needs some time. We'll be back together. Just wait."

"Doubt it," Kasey says.

"Hey, stop. Seriously. Is no one concerned about why Dad left in a huff?" Zach asks.

"Should one of us go talk to him?" I ask.

"Nah," Lee says. "He doesn't need everyone bothering him if he's ready to lay down." The man is getting up there in years. "You heard him, he's tired and he's thinking about leaving the clinic. Never thought I'd see the day."

The best part about today is knowing that I'll see Bryce later. If it were up to me, I would only stay for a short while. But since his mom is still traveling, I'm glad he could come here for Christmas.

I gracefully bowed out of any preparation for this event, as I barely survived last time. Lee is in charge of food and from what I hear, he's just having it catered.

The morning passes quickly as we have a few visitors from town that stop by to chat. With a smile in place, we accept Christmas treat after Christmas casserole until Dad begins putting them into the deep freezer in the garage. It's a good thing that Lee won't be around til later. He'd be having a field day in expressing his dislike of all the guests.

"Do you think Zach will make it back before tonight?" Kasey asks me when she checks her phone for the twentieth time. Our oldest brother got called in late last night after someone left their Christmas roast in the oven and it caught fire, sending the kitchen into flames that spread. He sent a text in our group message to say he'd be late but it's good to know that he's alright. Even with all that gear, anything could go wrong in a rescue.

"He's probably trying to get some sleep before he comes over. I don't know what time he was done with all that." I hold my middle, feeling queasy at the thought of something happening to my brother.

"I'm sure he's fine. It's best that he gets some sleep and then we'll get to hug him when everyone's gone," Nia says, bobbing her head one toward the five or so people all talking around my Dad.

I only recognize one of them as the bank manager for our credit union. His face is on several benches on Main Street. The others are listening to something he's saying as the three of us hang back in the kitchen to avoid another introduction.

"You think Dad needs to be saved from this one?" Kasey asks, combing her hair over the fuzzy sweater she's wearing. Subtle red highlights peak through the long strands and it really suits her. I'm about to say as much when Bryce walks into the kitchen with a carrier in his hand.

"Merry Christmas," he says, looking like something right off the cover of GQ. His grey sweater somehow looks more cozy underneath a brown leather coat that has a fur collar. The black jeans are sprinkled with white cat hair and I grin to myself at his cat dad problems. I wonder how many times he must have rolled them with a fabric roller to get the hair off, for it to still be there upon arrival.

My sisters tell him Merry Christmas back and the little meow of his guest makes itself known.

He raises the carrier and Socks has her face pressed to the mesh of the front opening.

Many coos of delight come from Nia and Kasey as they take the carrier from him and go to the living room at once. Bryce puts an arm around my shoulder and we follow my sisters. "Merry Christmas," he whispers in my ear. His lips brush the shell of my ear and sends a shiver down my back. My face heats but I don't have time to respond with the commotion his kitten is already causing.

"Oh, what a cutie," Nia says, straightening the little dress on Socks when she unzips the flap. The small cat fights her hand the whole time, tumbling around, so the dress becomes more askew.

"I don't remember getting that one." I say, watching my sisters playing with Socks. Her stitches are still intact but her spirits are high and you'd never know that she was in a bad way not too long ago. I love this for her.

"You didn't," Bryce says. "I got it yesterday when we got off the phone. I thought she'd look cute in it. I was right," He rubs the back of his neck, slightly embarrassed by his shopping trip. It warms my heart that he's taking to his little girl so quickly. I knew he needed someone in that apartment with him.

"You definitely were right." I pick up Socks, kissing her little face and she doesn't fight me like she did my sisters. She leans into me, her scratchy tongue catching my chin before I hold her to my chest for a brief moment.

"So, what made you decide to get a kitten?" Nia asks, watching Socks sniff cautiously around our rug for something to play with.

"Korra," he says easily. Looking toward me, he gestures, saying, "She sent me a picture of her and I couldn't refuse that face." The more he talks about Socks, the more bashful he becomes. It's sweet and if my heart weren't already mush in my chest, it certainly is now. "Then I saw her little white paws and I was done for. She's a menace for sure but she's got good taste." He shrugs. "We've got that in common."

I shake my head at him, grabbing the little one before she starts climbing the Christmas tree in the corner.

"Knock, knock," Zadie says from the doorway. "I brought cookies!"

"Oh, set them in the kitchen and come here."

My Dad pops his head into the living room, "Hey, Bryce. Can you come here for a second? I've got somebody I'd like you to meet."

Bryce looks to me and I shrug. I have no idea who it could be. He kisses my forehead before taking the kitten with him who promptly falls asleep in his hand. I swear the two of them are too adorable.

When Bryce leaves the room, I hear a scoff from Nia who shoves her phone back into her pocket.

"What happened?" I ask, leaning back on to the couch now that I'm no longer on the floor playing with Socks.

"My ex-boyfriend has been texting me. I wish he'd stop because I hate ignoring texts," she pouts.

"I didn't know that you had a boyfriend. When did this happen?" Under her breath, Kasey grumbles, "Everyone is getting guys and not telling me apparently," into her cider.

"I don't know. He wasn't really anything special." Her lips twist to the side as she decides whether to share more. We wait expectantly so she continues, "He just wanted to hook up all the time and I'm not really... I don't do that."

"Don't do what?" Zadie asks when she takes a seat on the couch with me.

Nia winds one of her twists around her hand. It's a nervous tell and I couldn't imagine what she would have to be nervous for. I tell her as much, "We're your sisters... and Zadie. We won't judge you."

"I've never had sex," she huffs. "I didn't want my first time to be with him. That was a big deal for him. I don't know. I ended things because it just wasn't going to work out."

"Your first time should be with someone special. Or at least someone you want to share that time with. It can be really emotional," I assure my sister in the embrace of my hug. She allows my hug with the sounds of agreement coming from around the coffee table.

"That's why I've never done it," Kasey says nonchalantly.

I blink a few times at her words, "But what about Jason or Rich?"

She shakes her head. "Neither. I'm not like *untouched* or anything. My hypothetical hymen is still intact."

Zadie is the next to express her astonishment. "But you write the smuttiest books I've ever read..."

"I was blessed with a vivid imagination and the internet. It's not that difficult to communicate. Like I said," her eyes bugging out at the three of us with our mouths hanging open. "I'm not untouched."

"Okay, but why though?" I ask. "You could be doing the things you're writing about. It seems like a lie."

"Not a lie. Would you ask a horror writer why they haven't slashed a body to bits for their books? It's the same thing."

Zadie holds her hands out in front of her. "Alright, I get it. Sorry. It's just really surprising. You're not missing out on much. I've traveled to several different countries and I can tell you that men are mostly clueless in all of them." She rolls her eyes, "Glad I left Harmony Hill to figure that out for myself. They can be trained but it's usually not even worth the time it takes."

"Don't scare her, Zadie." I hug Nia tighter to me, "With the right person, any work you do on your relationship is worth it."

"Says the woman getting cracked by Harmony Hill's most eligible bachelor." I open my mouth to object but then she corrects herself, "I'm sorry. I meant Harmony Hill's most obsessed fiancé."

"You probably didn't have to train him at all. Bet he came with advanced instruction," Zadie wiggles her eyebrows. "I mean, what's he like crafted by angels? I fear for his sleeves."

"Right?" Kasey high fives her. "I was telling her about how she must be climbing him since she's so small in comparison. I'm grateful I haven't been at the house with them knocking boots."

Zadie turns to me saying, "You lucky witch. I'm settling in for a life of K-pop shipping, animal companions and wine while you're living some cute, fairytale romance. Proposed to on the Hills? Iconic."

"It really is cute between the two of you," Nia says. "I should've known you two would end up together."

"You should have seen them in high school. You were still young but they have always been inseparable. I'd be here to hang out with the twins and Bryce was there. Usually just like chillin', I guess. But it was pretty obvious they'd at least be in each other's lives for a long time." Zadie's words don't surprise me but seeing what she remembers from a different lens is causing me to see it differently as well.

"Explains why all her boyfriends have been shit too," Kasey adds.

"What?" I exclaim. "They have been just fine."

"We won't get into Palmer at all. It is simply a fact that he is not great. But the others... You didn't have to even like them much because you had Bryce to fill in all the gaps they left."

"That's not..."

"Anyway, you righted it," Kasey says. "Gotta admit that I'll be happy to call Bryce my brother."

"Me, too. He's good to you. I can tell," Nia chimes in.

"He is," I agree.

I had thought of what *more* could look like with Bryce. Though, I had moved anything sexual from the forefront of my thoughts. Not that any of the women in the room are conscious of that.

Even with us dating now, I still want everything to flow naturally to that step between us. I'm not rushing anything. When it happens, it will happen. If sex between Bryce and I is anything like our friendship has been, then I know it'll be worth the wait.

# CHAPTER 27

## Bryce

"Hey, Bryce. Can you come here for a second? I've got somebody I'd like you to meet." Wayne says from his spot by the living room entrance. I check with Korra to see if there is something I missed before coming in but she shrugs. Kissing her on the forehead, I grab my little menace and follow him to where he's talking with a few men in the dining room.

They introduce themselves to me from one end of the table to the other. Wayne takes his spot at the head of the table, and to his right is Ryan Spencer whose face is plastered all over the benches on Main Street. To Wayne's left is Robert Voorhis who is the lead realtor in town. I lose track of the other men as on his right is Wynn West, who looks up from his phone to study me standing there with a sleeping kitten in my hand.

"Take a seat," Wayne says, introducing me, "This is Bryce Hampton. He's engaged to my daughter but that's not why I wanted you at the table son." Another *son*, I've become a man I admire. This has to be good. "Bryce here is vying for a senior partnership with Warren, Keesley & Mozier in Denver." There is a level of pride in his voice as he nods around the table men make noises of approval.

My firm isn't world renown but in Colorado, we've definitely earned a reputation for ourselves.

So has Wynn West. Especially in this town. He used to represent the Brenfords and all their interests. Now, he protects citizens from the massive corporation's failings. You could say that he's kind of a legend around here.

His tone is firm even as he asks, "Is that right? Corporate law then."

I nod and sit up a little taller. "I've been there for just under six years. We're in talks of the promotion as of late."

"Impressive. My team's expanding now that all sorts of cases are coming to the forefront. We could use someone hungry like you."

"Hey, Bryce. Give us a hand will ya?" Lee says going into the dining room with his arm full of catering trays.

Zach is directly behind him with his arms full too. "He caught me right when I was pulling up. Join the great unloading," he jokes walking around the table to place food there.

"I think we've talked business enough anyway. Are you staying for the meal?" Wayne asks the table and I take that as my cue to go help Lee get the food in the house.

Before I'm able to leave the dining room, Wynn stops me. "I'm sure you like where you're at and climbing that ladder is always a big accomplishment. I meant it before when I said we could use guys like you." He holds his card out for me.

"Guys to do the work for you. I know the Brenfords are causing a stir with the reemerging evidence."

"Not at all. Look, I won't be able to tell you everything about what we do here. But if you find yourself wanting to fight for the people of this town, give me a call."

Looking down at the card, it's embossed and sleek, belying how charitable his work appears to be. "Okay," I respond simply, not wanting to agree to do something I have zero desire to do.

A warm hand presses to my shoulder blade, before Korra's voice interrupts Wynn's proposal. "Let me have Socks so you can help them get everything in the house."

I turn, Socks still sleeping in my hand. Korra looks so relaxed in her house with her sisters falling behind to set the table. The last time we were here, she was a little cold and unsure before we went back to my place. I like the content looks she has cradling my kitten to her chest as she makes her way to her spot beside her Dad who's already talking to her about the sleeping kitten.

The guys and I make quick work of getting all the food inside and Christmas dinner is uneventful as the family talks about their hopes for the new year and their plans for the holiday. There is usually a firework display at the town park that hosts the rodeo and carnival in the summer time. It's been a couple of years since I've watched it. Getting ahead never stopped for a holiday that wasn't family oriented.

I called my Mom earlier yesterday since she was still traveling. I didn't want to mess up the time zone difference since she's almost a full day ahead of us in Colorado. I'm grateful again that I have somewhere to go for the holiday instead of being at home and lonely.

Watching the Thomases around me as dinner carries on is pleasant. I've been a part of this family without knowing just how close we really are. The guests that are here have come and gone but it's just us now. They chat leisurely as Socks tires herself out getting to know all the people here. I watch her playing and though she comes to me when she gets tired she finds her way back to Korra more times than not.

It's starting to get late and I lean over to Korra to whisper in her ear, "You ready to go back to your place? I think Socks is getting to that point." I'm sure Socks doesn't actually care, but I want to have time with just Korra alone.

She looks beautiful tonight. Her curls all around her face with a green cardigan over a cream dress that hugs her body. I never noticed how enticing her winter wardrobe was. I may not have incorporated more green into my closet like she wanted but she has enough for the both of us. She looks radiant in the color, no matter the shade. I'm dying to have her to myself.

"All right," she agrees with a small smile on her face. She sees through my attempt. Korra stands from where she was sitting on the floor so that Socks could have easy access to her. Scooping the cat up, she says her goodbyes to her family.

I'm grateful for Harmony Hill's mostly quiet streets so it takes no time to get back to her apartment.

With the next three days off, I've got time to chill at Korra's place. Kasey decided to stay at their family home to "give the couple some smashing time". Not that I don't appreciate Kasey giving me time to be with my girls, it's not helping how all of this is playing out in my mind.

Korra says,"You would think that he'd figure out that running from Superguy is not going to happen…"

I have to pause for a second to decide whether or not I'm dreaming when Korra says those words. They're almost identical to the ones she always says in my dream. Then I shake myself out of it because she asks the same thing almost every time we watch this one.

Korra has a habit of talking through almost every movie. Even if it's one she hasn't seen before. The talking is more question based and reactionary. I'm perfectly happy to have that conversation with her about the movie we've both seen a hundred times or are watching for the first time. I never really understood why people get so upset about that. In a theater, I get it, but if you're watching something with friends at your house? *Makes no sense to me.* Of course Korra has more to offer than I do. Her opinions on the villain in this one is more than apparent.

Another difference from my dream and what's happening now is the fact that she's not only wearing a sweater and panties. As soon as we got back to her place, she changed into some flannel pajamas while I set Socks up for a night at Korra's.

She laughs at something particularly ridiculous to her and looks over at me with a big smile stretching her face. My dream did nothing to communicate how her joy really makes her glow, even in only the light from the TV.

I'm not able to focus on the movie, instead, I'm aware of how close she's gotten to me now that the kitten has settled to sleep in the corner of her couch. She might have moved over to give the kitten space but I'm going to take advantage of how close she's gotten to me.

With my arm around her, she presses tight into me. The smell of her hair is strong in my nose. The feel of her soft body warm against mine.

I can't actually take this anymore.

With my hand on her waist I move her and she follows my lead, straddling my lap. I'm already hard for her as soon as her ass is pressed tight against me. In this position we're looking each eye to eye.

"Kor—"

She doesn't kiss me like I think she will. Instead her lips find my neck, trailing from the sensitive skin there to bite my collarbone. What was I going to say? Doesn't matter. Her lips are on me. Sparks from her attention shoot straight to my dick and it's by sheer will that I don't buck into her.

"You're sensitive here," she says, then rolls her hips over me. It's a slow grind at first before it becomes insistent.

I find her lips, biting the bottom one and it stops her movements over me. Helping her find her rhythm again, my hands hold fast to her hips. She moans unabashedly into my mouth.

"You know this is something I've dreamed about," I say and she pauses again.

Fuck.

Why did I open my mouth? "I just mean—"

Her eyes flick back and forth between mine as she tries to find the meaning there. "You dream about me?"

"How could I not?" I admit. "It was kind of a problem. Couldn't tell you how many close calls I've had when I think about them."

Her head tilts. "What was I doing in these dreams?"

My face heats and unprompted, my dick twitches between her thighs. She smirks but doesn't comment on it.

I shrug, going for nonchalant. "Kinda this."

Holding my chin to look at her, "Don't lie," she says.

It doesn't take much to make me tell exactly what I had in my mind for these past few months. With her in my lap, the heat radiating from her core straight to my hard length. The dream seems less salacious than it was all along.

No matter, she doesn't stop touching me while I recount it. I'm drowning in her scent. It's not the time for me to figure out her motives right now. "So you do think about me, about this?"

Her smirk is smug as all hell but I like it. The way she's already riding my length tells me that I'm gonna be the lucky one, even if her smugness is at my expense.

"I'll be a good boy and take the teasing you're doing but just know that it can go both ways."

"You have been teasing me this whole time," she whines. "Never wearing shirts, using your deep lawyer voice and then getting a kitten. It's like you're reading the other team's playbook. Cheating for sure."

I chuckle, smoothing some hair back from her face. "You had every power to change our circumstances." My other hand slides under her top to that deep curve of her spine.

So many close calls I've had. I didn't know whether to flirt or hold her close. The thoughts I'd had felt out of place and every desire I had to touch her like this was inappropriate. But now...

Holding my stare she says, "Fine. I want to change it now then."

# CHAPTER 28

## Bryce

Don't get me wrong I had plans when I encouraged her to come back to her apartment with me but...

Damn.

Once she said she wanted things to change, she's mine.

I don't think it will ever get old. I'll never get tired of being this close to her.

"Bryce," she says, "I don't want to wait and make this awkward. We're both adults."

Our eyes meet and hold for a moment until I can't stand the wait any longer. "Me neither." I hold her face with both of my hands. My thumbs tracing over the fullness of her cheeks. How they taunt me with all her smiles.

I want to keep them all.

I want to hold them all.

But this isn't as close as I can get.

I take her mouth with mine. Our lips slanting over each other.

Each time I kiss her there's something new.

I think that's why this will never get old. I never get bored of her or with her. She always takes my attention.

My tongue traces the fullness of her lower lip and she parts for me. Our tongues meeting, not for the first time, but this time is wholly new. She tastes like everything that I shouldn't have. More than I deserve.

Those lines are nonexistent now.

My fingers comb into her curls, so I can keep a firm grip on her face as I ravage her mouth. She's taking as good as I give.

It's making me grateful all over again that I am able to be here with her.

Her fingers hold me close. Hands clutching into my skin over my shirt.

I need to take this off. I'm feeling the heat rising between us, a fine sheen of sweat making its presence known.

When we part for air, both panting, chests rising. I know I'm where I'm supposed to be.

She takes her top off, and I take mine off. My bare chest exposed for her.

Her bra must match that infuriating red thong on full display for me. Red lace holds the fullness of her breasts. It's slightly sheer, the hint of her nipples are hard and begging for my mouth.

A little gold star hangs from the center. I take it between my teeth, using my thumb to rub over her stiff little peaks. My teeth find those points, taking one then the other while I keep the pressure between us.

I've been away from her mouth too long.  Returning to kiss her, my fingers tracing down her neck, down her chest, down her waist, and back up to squeeze a handful of one breast and then the other. I can't stop squeezing and touching her. The little sounds of pleasure she makes as I explore her body are addictive. I want to hear more.

Peeling one strap down her arm, and then the other, both of her luscious tits are exposed to me. Perfect teardrops that my imagination didn't even come close to picturing. My tongue laves over the flesh there. Plump and warm and soft and...

*Fuck, I'm hard.*

Insistent and stiff, but I can't stop exploring. I want to know every single part of her. As much outside as I do inside.

I suck on one breast and then the other. Her head falls back and her mouth hangs slightly open. I can feel the beat of her heart from my hold on her. It's quickening and lures me in.

Her hand finds my waist and rolls down my pants. It's slow as she's not really focused, but I'm hyper aware of how close she is to my dick right now. *I'm already weeping for her.* Hell, I've been weeping for her for months now.

Never have I been this close to getting what I had been dreaming of.

She's careful with my zipper though. As careful and considerate as she is in doing most things.

I'm still kissing a path down her body, memorizing the softness of her tummy, the curve of her belly button, the firmness of her skin over her pelvic bone.

I curse when she finally meets the stiff ridge of me. I'm not small and being in these pants as hard as I've been is torturous. But I can't let her take me out just yet.

Dropping to my knees in front of her, I make quick work of removing her flannel pants. I can finally see the image I'd been fantasizing about for so long.

I wonder when she changed into these just for my benefit.

She hasn't asked me about what I said in the living room to her brothers. I don't know if she heard me or not. But to add to that list of things I love about my best friend it has to be how she looks in this thong right now.

Four lace straps hang on her curvy hips, the little star charms slightly swinging with her movements. My hands wrap around her body to cup her ass in my grip and... it is glorious.

I can't think of another word to describe how plush she is in my hands.

I press my face into the soft red fabric at her center. Taking a deep inhale, I try to memorize the smell of being so close to something I've wanted.

Call me an overachiever.

Call me a workaholic.

But if there's anything I'm going to be putting overtime into—It's going to be this sweet pussy that I have been waiting to finally see.

I pull the fabric down her hips, and she helps me with the sexiest sway I've ever witnessed. As soon as she is exposed, I tap her thigh. "Put your leg on my shoulder."

She doesn't make me wait. With one hand on my shoulder and the other on the back of my head, I take an explorative lick of her inner thigh close, but not where she needs me. "Oh shit," she sighs. My sweet friend is already dripping for me.

*She's ready for me.*

Dragging my thumb down, I part her lips, my nose buried into the trim and soft curls above her sweet little bud. With a soft tongue, I flick over the hood and feel how she trembles, thigh pressing into the side of my head. Slipping my thumb inside, I feel her clinch around me. So, I lick her clit again. Finding a rhythm between thumb and tongue, I'm moving back and forth with my face pressed deep into her center while she rocks over me.

"That is so good, Bryce," she whimpers. "So, so good. You're so good..."

I hum over her and let her chase the orgasm that I'm helping her find. I'm smiling like I'm high or drunk, maybe a mixture of both, off this woman.

She deserves to come.

I'm blessed to be the one to help her do it.

When she can't take anymore, she drops to her knees in front of me and our lips meet again. I am obsessed with how we taste together. She's reaching for my dick again, but I'm not done with her yet.

I pick her up, placing her on her couch. "Sit back. I wanna see something."

Before, when she was over me, I didn't get a good view of what I was feasting on. But now I've got the full view and holy shit. This pussy I could eat and eat on.

Damn, I am a lucky man.

At this point, I am making such a mess in my pants that I need to do something about it. She's so blissed out that when I lean over her, I don't know if she can focus on what I have to say. But I need to ask her.

Of all the questions I've asked her in our friendship—this is one that holds the utmost importance. *Especially right now.* If I thought anything had changed our relationship before, this is the actual end of what could be considered *only a friendship.*

"Can I fuck you?"

She nods her head, "Yes, yes, please..."

It's been a while, but I've got a condom in my wallet. I pull it out and check that it's not expired. I roll it over myself, taking care of both of us in this way.

I know it will feel good to be bare inside her, but right now I don't need to have that conversation. My mind is on one thing and one thing only.

*How deep can I get inside her right now?*

She slides down the couch so that her head is on the armrest and I'm leaning over her again. She looks beautiful, just like this.

Naked as all hell and a little bit sweaty.

With the fullness of her cheeks all round with a silly smile that I put there. This time it's not from some joke I said. It's from the bliss of coming close and falling right over the edge.

I line the head of my dick up at her entrance. *It's gonna be a tight fit.* Korra's body looks too small to handle what I'm packing but I know she can.

She looks down at the place where my length is just about to enter her. "Oh God. It's gonna hurt."

I smooth a hand over her stomach. "You can take me. Don't worry, I'll make it fit." With a hand on her cheek again I say, "Don't worry. I'll make you feel good."

Her sienna eyes hold a trust for me that turns molten with heat. "Okay, I'm ready," she whispers.

My hand gripping my shaft, I go slowly. Sliding in until finally the head of me disappears inside her.

Just that little bit is doing my head in. Korra feels so good already.

*I can hardly think straight.*

I want to pound into her, so tight and warm and wet.

Damn.

I wanna pump faster, but I take my time.

Gritting my teeth, I move slowly, feeding her more and more of me. Her hands are on my chest. Not pushing me away, but keeping the connection between us in more than one place.

It takes us some time but finally, I'm fully inside. Our thighs are touching, her skin so soft there against my legs. I marvel at us.

We're really doing this.

I'm really here.

I'm awake for this.

"Korra, baby. You took all of me so well. God damn you look good on my dick."

She moves around on me, her hand trailing down my chest to her clit. "You said you were gonna make me feel good... So be a good boy and fuck me."

*I don't have to be told twice.*

Holding her by the thighs, I pull out to where my head is the only part of me inside of her and then I let her have it in one go. The leather of her couch squeals in protest when she takes all of me again.

Her head bounces up on the armrest until she leans up on her elbows. Her eyes on me as I thrust into her. I'm slow at first just letting her get used to the girth of me.

All I know is that this is too fucking good. And I need to make it last.

Her breathing is heavy, a mixture of inhales and gasps on the exhale. It sounds like music to my ears.

I pay attention, finding out what feels good and what she likes most.

"Oh my God. That's so good. Just like that. Just like that," she whines, meeting me thrust for thrust.

Her voice has never been sweeter. I'm thankful for the acoustics in this living room because it's like I'm getting to listen to her say it in surround sound.

She grabs her tit while I'm stroking into her. My movements are careful but deliberate, once I find the spot that's making her moan over and over again.

At a loss for words. I know I've got her.

She holds my gaze, her words do me in. "Oh, I'm gonna come. Come with me, yes. Ohhh..."

She doesn't need to tell me. I could feel her tightening around my dick. But I love knowing that I make good on my words. I keep up the same rhythm, but at a little more force to every stroke. Really hitting that spot over and over again.

She cries out. But this time it's my name.

It's Bryce on her lips when she's squeezing the hell out of my dick.

It feel so fucking perfect that I'm definitely going to come right along with her.

Her breathing pauses, her body taught, as her eyes are squeezed closed.

She looks like perfection.

Korra is the only thing on my mind as I let go. Spurting while I'm inside her. Each throb of cum, a shiver of pleasure down my spine.

When I finally soften and slip out of her, we're both panting into shallow laughter that is full of wonder and disbelief.

"Well, that went..." she starts, from under my body.

"Perfectly," I say, finally rolling off of her.

I'm lightheaded from finally climaxing, but I carry her to the bathroom to get us both cleaned up.

"Stay right here," I say, getting a bath running. I toss the condom and check the water.

She's already slid to the floor, plopped on her bath mat against the wall. "I'm potatoes," she says.

I chuckle. "C'mon, potatoes. We need to get you cleaned up."

I step in first and she lets me help her into the water. We both instantly relax in the warm water around us. My arms around her and her hands on my thighs.

My arms stretch around the sides of her tub, my finger brushing the extra long vines crawling down her bathroom organizer. "So, I was thinking. I could stand to have another Danica in my place. Where do you think it'd look good?"

# CHAPTER 29

## Bryce

The elevator hum is too loud, or maybe it's just the pounding in my ears. By the time I step onto the top floor, my palms are damp as I smooth them down the front of my suit. It's a nervous habit and I'm not one hundred percent sure where it came from. But I need to calm down my senses before I walk into this meeting.

After spending the holiday vacation with Korra, I didn't want to leave Harmony Hill. I didn't want to leave her place or do anything else besides being close to her. But I knew that with this new year approaching, the only time that this meeting could logically occur would be now. So I brace myself in at the back of the elevator car to see exactly what awaits me.

The firm's conference room looms ahead with its polished doors and frosted glass reserved only for important exchanges like this one. Stepping into the corridor from the elevator, it ding behind me to return down the floors again. The doors to the top floor always feel heavier, like they know not everyone belongs up here. And for a long time, I was only just a guest here. But as I approach them now, I swipe my badge and step into the room that is buzzing with the conversation already happening inside. It's different from being outside the doors where I could hear the tick of my watch when the elevator door closed. Inside the room smells like leather and polish. I just need to focus on something else besides my thoughts racing.

This room is far more lavish than any of the conference rooms on my floor. It's well loved with a warm chandelier that hangs from the ceiling. A big contrast to the January gray clouds that hang low in the massive windows behind the table. I stand just inside the doorway, taking in what might be the very last time that I am only a senior associate.

This is everything I've dreamed about. The long table with its cherry wood is buffed to a high shine. All the leather chairs are tucked in neatly except for the three at the opposite side of the room that I stand on. The two walls of windows that open to the Denver skyline where snow sits on top of the peaks that are just visible in the distance. Off to the side, a credenza gleams with multiple crystal pitchers, some with liquor and some with just water. Everything in here announces its stature without having to flaunt that there's so much money made here.

I straighten my tie and step further into the room, needing a glass of water and soon.

Regardless of my feelings on the men sitting here, these partners are the ones who shaped this firm from the very beginning. Phil, the one who pulled me up as a green scholarship kid and told me I had more grit and determination than half of the other students that were all pursuing the same dream is sitting at the very middle. Though his name comes last on the title, he's still the most vital part of this place. To think that I'm going to have to fill his shoes is a heavy weight. But it's one that I've worked hard to withstand. I fought tooth and nail for every inch. I've gotten closer to where I stand right now. I've stayed later, read longer, worked harder, and today I'm hoping that it pays off.

Phil sits with his back straight, hands folded, as I take a seat at the table. "Let's get started," Phil says. He glances at me and then back to the other others. "We're here to discuss the final vote. Bryce Hampton has shown what this firm needs – discipline, ingenuity and loyalty. He's proving himself case after case and year after year."

My pulse is hammering in my ears, but I keep my face neutral. It's time for me to call on the experience that I've gathered in working in these courtrooms. I am a professional and this might be the happiest time of my life, but it is still important that I maintain my composure.

Kyle Warren and David Keesley make sounds of agreement as Phil speaks.

"Let's not waste any more time. The vote was unanimous," he continues. "Effective immediately, Bryce Hampton has been elevated to a role as junior partner at Warren, Keesley and Mozier."

I hear the words. These are not the words I've been waiting for. For a second the room tilts.

Junior partner, not senior like I had hoped for.

It echoes in my head, a title, not the title I've chased for years. It's all crystallizing at this moment.

"Congratulations," Warren says, offering a tight handshake. I shake his back, not bothering to match the tightness of his grip. I don't have anything left to prove. I'm standing next to him as close to equal as I ever could've been, apparently. His face is stoic until it breaks into a wide smile and he claps me on the back. "No need to be so formal with us now. Isn't that right, Dave?"

Dave nods. "Exactly. But we need to get started on business. It'll be a transition for you and Mozier but I'm sure he'll have no problem showing you exactly what to do next."

It's Phil's quiet glance, and small but certain nod that makes my chest unlock. "You earned this," and he is the one to clap me on the back. "Don't forget that."

I won't.

*After everything, it wasn't enough.*

They all file out of the room, and I'm there alone in the empty corridor. I let my shoulders drop. My tie feels too tight, and my skin is still a little hot, but underneath it all the dissatisfaction of not making it to my end goal slogs heavily in my blood.

I pull up my phone before I can fall into this any deeper. The number I dial is Korra's. And that action alone does not surprise me.

She picks up on the second ring. "Hey you. How'd it go?"

"Well, I think…" I don't know why I'm being vague, but I don't want to hear her reaction so I drag this out just a little bit longer.

"Well, you're on the phone with me, so I suppose you survived right?" I can hear the emotion in her voice rising as she is unsure whether to be excited or not. Korra on the precipice of glee is probably one of my favorite things to hear in her voice.

I don't think I've ever been the kind of guy who preferred talking on the phone to texting. But knowing Korra, she is one person that I always want to hear on the phone. Though we do text, I enjoy the same things that she's shown me is better in phone calls. The emotion in someone's voice can completely change an interaction from being mundane and average to being integral and intriguing.

I can't help the laugh that breaks out. The sentiment behind it is muddled in my mind. "More than survived. I, uh… I'm a junior partner."

There's only a moment of silence and then, "Bryce!" Her voice burst through the receiver as bright and genuine as I knew it would be. "You're kidding," I open my mouth to respond, but she cuts me off, "You're not kidding! You did it!"

The knot in my throat tightens. I've heard congratulations before, plenty of them. Over the course of my career and even just now from the other partners I'll be working closely with. Hell, even hearing congratulations from the opposing council can be very satisfying. But no one's voice has ever cut through to my heart as effectively and acutely as hers does now.

"Yea," I say. My voice is rougher than I mean for it to be. I can't help the emotion on my own now. Just talking to her makes it that way for me. "They voted. It's official."

"You worked so hard for this. I am so proud of you! I know that I don't have a right to pride as I didn't do anything to help you get here… Besides agree to wear your ring but this is huge, Bryce. Look at you doing everything you thought you could. "

I close my eyes, leaning back against the cool wall. My earlier disappointment from not getting a senior role stings a little less with her excitement. I still haven't pressed the elevator button to take me down to the floor I normally work on. "Coming from you, that... Means more than I can explain. You did more than just agree to wear my ring. In a lot of ways, I always thought that you were the person, the entity, that kept me grounded over the years. You stopped me from becoming a soulless robot who only had work in their life. I don't want you to diminish that."

"You don't have to explain it to me." Her voice is soft when she says, "I was there. I saw it. The fact that you never quit on this is monumental. You deserve this."

Her words ground me more than any title could at this moment. *And I want that title on my door.* I want a nicer office. But she's right.

She's seen me underneath all of the things that most people would shallowly admire. Without the title she would care for me. And with it now she's still proud. "Thank you," I murmur. My thoughts are swirling around a little bit too quickly at the moment. I think about how I should tell her I love you. Now would probably be a good time to tell her that I love her. But I don't get that chance.

"You can thank me later with a super fancy dinner. I'm talking—I need to be rolled out of the restaurant because everything is so delicious and I can't stop eating fancy." There's a smile in her joking. But then she says, "First, call your mom. She's been waiting for this almost as long as you have."

A lump catches in my throat, "Yea, you're right."

And something that could only be described as a yodel, "I'm always right." Then she says, "Now go make Tara cry happy tears. And I'll see you tonight, counselor. Oh wait, I'll see you tonight, *partner*." She emphasizes my new title and it sends shivers down my spine.

I wonder if she'll call me partner Bryce Hampt if we end up at my house alone. That would certainly make me feel a lot better about this whole disappointment.

# CHAPTER 30

## Korra

The kettle is just starting to hiss when I set my phone down. My stomach flutters, it always does when it's him, especially now, but there's something in the way talking to him and celebrating with him just hits a little bit different. Bryce is too hard on himself but he is always trying to do more and achieve more. Makes my admiration for him burn brighter somehow. Staring at the phone for a second longer, I finally get up and go grab my kettle off the stove. My heart is a mess. It's full and shaky and excited for him. Before I can dive into that thought much further I decide to text my sisters.

> **Korra: Just got off the phone with Bryce! He made Partner! *BIG SMILE EMOJI***

I've barely set my phone down again before another voice creeps in a little louder. This one's a little meaner. And insecure.

*What does that mean for our arrangement?*

That's where all this really started. He was my best friend and I was just helping him out with a fake engagement. The performance of us being in some tight knit whirlwind romance to get him to the spot he's in right now. Lying to the firm. Lying to our family. But then it turned into sharing real feelings. I know that he cares about me. *Care is not even the accurate word.* I still haven't talked to him about the fact that he confessed to loving me to my brothers.

He hasn't said the words to me.

So I can't be sure that any of it was true.

And now–here we are. We're dating, and there is real kissing. Real affection. Real intimacy. The way he makes me feel is unlike the way anyone has ever made me feel. In his eyes, I could be the most important person in this world. Maybe be the most important person in his world.

I look down at the ring on my finger. Doesn't matter how stunning it is. It's still a fake promise.

I twist it absentmindedly, the crystal catching the light in my kitchen. I decide to go ahead and fix my tea before my water goes cold. Even though my heart feels heavier than it ever has, I can't imagine that it's just because of what I've realized.

What am I supposed to do now that the lines are tangled up so tightly? I can't find the start of one to pull it apart. When the day comes around that he no longer needs to look respectably committed does that mean that what we have is done?

He could've just called me as a part of the show for the partners. After all, wouldn't you be calling your fiancée with the good news? That insecure part of me has been too afraid to ask if having a commitment that looks like the one we're pretending to have is not a possibility.

If we admit the truth about our feelings to everyone else, will that be the end of us? Three months is coming up very soon.

I'm terrified to bring the subject up, but for now I have to just put it at the back of my mind. If I think about what it would mean then I really won't be able to untie the knot forming low in my chest right now.

Sitting with my knees pulled up to my chest on the couch, I sip from my tea and stare at the ceiling. It's starting to snow outside, but the cold isn't seeping into this space. It's just me and all these questions. I want to believe that I can untangle the story from the truth. That the act can fall away and leave only me and Bryce. But I've lived long enough to know that wanting and getting are rarely the same thing. I just wish I could talk to someone who would know the full truth of all of this. If my Mom were here would I be able to talk to her about this?

I end up putting a movie on and sipping my tea until I check my phone again.

It's a good thing that I do because my sisters are there to brighten my sullen mood.

> **Nia: *CRYING EMOJI*x3 THAT'S HUGE! omg omg tell him congrats for me!**

> **Kasey: Rich lawyer climbs higher up the money tree. Love this look for you sis. Mrs. Moneybags sound good on you**

I roll my eyes at Kasey's voice in my head. Her dry and unimpressed delivery as clear in my mind as it would be in person. Nia's reaction is the appropriate one.

> **Nia: Kasey **EYE ROLL EMOJI** seriously?**

> **Korra: Could you find it in your heart to maybe not be yourself right now? This is a big deal. He's been working hard for this.**

> **Kasey: No can do. I is who I is. I'm real and that man is definitely racking in the dough. I'm proud of you for locking him down.**

> **Nia: Ignore her. We know that it's love that ties you two together and not money. That's what matters.**

I cringe at her assumption, but I know it's what's expected of us. I do love him and I know he does too. If it's in the way they're talking about is the one unknown.

> **Korra: Exactly, love. He called me first to share the news**

**Nia: *TEARY EYED EMOJI*x3 if that isn't LOVE, idk what is**

**Kasey: It's something. He knows what matters most, my sis**

**Korra: Exactly...**

**Nia: Korraaaaaa I'm so happy for you two *HEART EMOJI***

**Kasey: Time to celebrate with some tree climbing of your own *WINKING EMOJI***

After talking to them, I do feel better, despite Kasey's unhinged commentary. No matter why he chose me—he did. He could've picked anyone else, but he chose me. We've connected in more ways than just the lie. We spend time together. We shared each other's space.

*That means something.*

Even though I've been afraid that my needs were too much and were too heavy, I've never had to swallow those ones and ignore them around him. What might've been too much for even the people I love was never too much for him. I was convinced that I should settle for scraps of attention because that's all I needed.

Bryce would never hand me scraps. He'd be offended by me even thinking that I would get them from him.

He doesn't recognize that he's doing it. It's just a natural reaction and response for him to make sure I'm comfortable, to make sure I'm good. And though I was in a bit of a spiral earlier, I can only imagine that he called me because he truly did want to share his accomplishment with me first.

Maybe I was only waiting for someone who understood that love isn't measured. That it has no bounds. There is no scale. If you pour into each other then there's always enough to go around.

No one is too much.

Not even me.

> **Bryce: I made reservations for 8. You'll join me to celebrate?**

> **Bryce: {{Map Location}}**

I tap on the location and I admit that I was kidding when I said we should celebrate with a fancy dinner. I text him as much.

> **Bryce: Are you going to make me eat this sushi by myself? It's a tasting menu...**

Unfortunately, I can't turn down raw fish and seaweed, it's just too good. So here I sit across from him in an intimately lit restaurant in Denver. The salmon and yellowtail tartar between us is barely touched. Far nicer than the restaurant in Harmony Hill that serves Japanese.

Bryce is halfway through telling me about the firm's latest client which seems to be a development deal of some sort that's been giving the four of them a big headache, though securing it is gaining them major bragging rights. At some point, I stop hearing the words, caught up in my own mind. I'm watching the way his tie is slightly loose around his collar and the tightness that used to be in the creases of his eyes is not really there anymore. He looks so much lighter tonight. Like finally reaching that end goal has lifted a weight off his shoulders.

I should be happy for him. I am happy for him. But that knot that's been in my chest, that I've been so careful to not allow to tangle more, is still sitting in the same spot. It hasn't loosened at all and even seeing him now, I feel like it might be getting tighter. I have to find the right moment to say what I'm feeling. After all, our friendship was built off of our honesty with each other and the willingness to be vulnerable and open.

"Korra?" His chopsticks are still over the yellowtail that he is about to grab. "You're... not saying anything. Are you all right?"

I take a deep breath and grab my own piece of fish to pop into my mouth. Instead of meeting his eyes, I swallow and say what's been in my heart. "I've been thinking about us a lot."

Our next course comes out. It's aji nigiri sushi and one of my favorites. The smoked mackerel is not enough to make me move away from our conversation at present.

He leans back in his chair, studying me. It's careful, his examination of my person. Crossing my booted legs under the table, the unsure emotions from earlier are hot on my face. I'm wearing a long sleeved green blouse and A-line skirt that goes perfectly with my brown coat that sits on the chair behind me. If he doesn't stop, I'm libel to sweat through them both. I pulled my hair up into a curly updo on the top of my head and I regret not being able to hide inside my curls right now.

"Okay," he says carefully. "What have you been thinking about us?"

"I've been thinking about our engagement," I say finally. The words fall between us. "I've been thinking about what it meant before and what it'll mean in the future."

His jaw tightens, but it's not in anger. He seems uneasy more than anything else. "Are you worried about people finding out how it started?"

"I'm worried *we'll forget* how it started," I say with a sharper tone than I intended. My nerves are getting the best of me, but I try my best to lower my tone when I continue. "We agreed to fake this, Bryce. That's how all of this began. You got your promotion. We have just a couple more weeks left in this agreement. And now we're… More. *This is a date.* Not a friendly hangout. All I know is that every time someone calls me your fiancée, I don't know what I'm supposed to do with that. How I'm supposed to feel."

He sets his chopsticks down with his eyes steady on mine. "What do you want to feel about it?"

The question takes me by surprise.

I expected reassurance or I don't know.

But it's not the response that I thought he would give me.

"I want it to mean something," I admit with my voice barely louder than a whisper. "I don't want to be a fool who thought that it was real when it was never supposed to be. We are just dating or whatever we're calling this, but I need you to know that I'm—" Snapping my mouth shut, I don't continue whining about my feelings and miscommunication failures.

For several moments, the restaurant noise fills the silence between us. It's busy here and there are plenty of other people enjoying their time, commenting on how good the food is and swirling wine in their glasses. I look down at my plate, feeling like I am asking for more than I should. But Bryce leans in, his elbows on the edge of the table as he reaches for me.

"What do you think it meant that I called you first today?" He doesn't give me an opportunity to respond to that question. "I called you first because I needed you to hear what *we* had accomplished. I don't know at what point I failed in showing you how much you meant to me. Or where I went wrong in communicating that this engagement was in no way going to end with me leaving you. Even if the three months came and went I was not taking that ring back."

My throat goes dry. I grab my wine glass and sip deeply from it, hoping that I can calm down my racing heart. I don't even like red wine.

Too many thoughts. So many thoughts are going through my mind right now.

"So what happens now that we don't need this deal? If you're not leaving and I'm still here..."

"Then we stop calling it fake." There's steel in his voice as he continues, "We stop pretending that there's a line between what was a friendship and what was more. Because for me there isn't a line there. I'm in a relationship with my best friend and I wouldn't have it any other way."

I blink at him, my heart beating rapidly in my chest.

He doesn't look away. "I'm not interested in letting go. I've never met anyone who I thought would be a better match for me than you. If that scares you then I understand that too. Because I'm scared ten times over. I'll be the friend that gets his plant-obsessed friend to experience something new. We'll do it together."

My vision blurs as emotion warms my face again with him recalling my previous words. I glance down at the ring on my finger and back up to his face. "Together," I agree.

# CHAPTER 31

## Bryce

My new junior title should feel monumental. After years of all-nighters and weekends lost to case prep, I should be proud of where I'm at.

Now that I'm standing in it, the title feels smaller than I imagined.

Formally receiving the acceptance into partnership with Warren, Keesley & Mozier is one thing but sitting down with the paperwork is another. I've been looking forward to this for so long and now that the papers are in front of me, I don't know... That word *junior* hangs heavy like a qualifier.

*Not quite.*

*Almost.*

Each syllable tasting more and more bitter.

Or maybe that's just me for feeling like I should have received more.

Maybe that makes me entitled because I had hoped that everything I'd done would result in more. From Phil's talks, I thought I had my in. But that couldn't be more wrong.

Instead of becoming a senior partner, they only promoted me to junior. There aren't any other junior partners at this firm. The biggest perks of being a senior partner would have been voting rights, a much larger profit share and far fewer hours every year. Yes, those things are still within my reach but under more years of the same and barely making more money than I am now.

I sit at the desk, looking at the door that will soon hold my new junior partner title and wonder what am I doing?

And for what and this point?

This is what I had been working toward for most of my life and here I am feeling like I've been trampled. At this desk, I've felt like I couldn't have it all. I couldn't have a full life. But now that I've been with Korra as more than what we once were, I know that I need to have it.

My dinner last night to celebrate was great after Korra and I were able to come to the understanding that we both wanted more. I just wish that underneath all of that, I was happy with my promotion. We both had work early this morning so I had to let her get back home though I would have preferred to hold her into the night instead.

With our truths laid bare, a new problem has arisen.

The distance between us.

There is an even greater distance because I don't want to settle for just a couple of dates a week or to only communicate with her on the phone.

I haven't tried to make a relationship work with anyone before. I'd give a little as I could to maintain the life I've been pursuing. With Jillian I didn't give as much as I could have and I'm glad I didn't because she was never the one for me.

With Korra, I've seen how good my life can be. She's shown me. There has to be something that can bridge the gap between having a career that I feel fulfilled in, having a woman in my life who appreciates me and being a person.

I open my wallet and call the number on the card I've been keeping there. He picks up on the third ring. I didn't expect it to be him, but instead a secretary or something. It's his direct line.

"Hampton," Wynn says. "You actually called. I was starting to think you'd gone corporate for good."

"I guess I did," I say, though I try for something light, it comes out sounding as weary as I feel.

"Well, we all sell a piece of our soul to the machine at some point," he says. "The trick is buying it back before it's worthless." He laughs at his own joke and I can picture the white of his hair and beard clearly.

I'm not laughing though. His words sound too much like the truth I was trying to move past.

When Wynn finally stops laughing, he asks, "How is that promotion? Big city life and all that positioning. Enjoying it?"

"Somewhat."

He makes a sound that is half grunt and half sigh. "You're too smart for that rat race. I read up on you and saw the cases you worked. Pretty big for a guy your age. Can't say I was that impressive back then."

"I didn't realize I was being vetted."

"Not vetting," Wynn replies easily. "Call it curiosity after Wayne talked you up. He spoke highly of you and I figured it was worth paying attention to that."

"What need do you have to pay attention to me?" I ask, waiting for whatever Wynn has to say.

There's a challenge in his voice as he says, "What I do, it's not glamorous like you're used to. There are no fancy catered lunches, bonuses that could be down payments on a condo or those skyscraper views of the city in a corner office. Our team is small and the building is too. But the work we do is real. We take on whatever the courts spit out when it pertains to the Brenfords. You know the people you're helping. You grew up with them, and saw them around town. Harmony Hill is who you're helping."

Thoughts of Korra lead me to say, "This sounds like the introduction for a hero's action movie."

"Maybe in some ways we are small town heroes. You ever miss that? The drive that's stronger than billable hours?"

My throat is thick as I swallow. "I don't know if I ever had it to miss."

"Sure, you did." Wynn booms. "We all did. When we were in school looking at those stats, hoping to make a difference. Before any firms got to you. Before any promises they could have made led to you signing a contract."

He's not really even selling me at this point. Just telling me the facts that I could come to on my own.

Part of me can see that quitting a high-paying position to chase after some sort of small town justice is laughable. Anyone would tell me how this is logically not the next move for someone in my position.

Then there is a different part of me that wonders if there is any real value in a high-paying position if I'm not happy.

"You're not saying yes," Wynn interjects my thoughts, "and you're not saying no either. I can hear you thinking about it."

"I'm not—"

"You are. You wouldn't have called me if you weren't. That's all I need anyway. Think about what I've said. Just keep in mind that the longer you stay up there, the harder it gets to remember why you started climbing in the first place."

"What makes you think I'd be a good fit?"

"You already sound tired, bored," he says. "The law is not an exciting topic but when you're fighting for something that could save people's lives or make it better, there should be a fire under your ass. Especially if you're getting real justice for people who deserve it."

"I'm not saying yes," I say.

"Well you haven't hung up so that's something." Then he chuckles. "I bet Korra would appreciate the thought, as well."

"Yea," I respond noncommittally. Not that I don't think that Korra would agree but that I haven't hung up on his wild proposition.

"Coming from somebody who's experienced it, hear me when I say that sometimes the life you thought you wanted is just a draft of the one you're meant to live. You only get to do this once so make it count." There's a click before the line goes dead.

I look down at my phone but he definitely hung up on me.

The chilling quiet of my office grows larger as Wynn's words play through my mind. My aspirations have always been aligned with helping people. I thought that I had to get as far up as I could in this game to achieve that.

Justice can be made on any level though. And how could the quality of my life improve like he's suggested it might.

My empty life is no longer empty.

My empty apartment is no longer empty. *I have Socks.*

My empty weekends are no longer empty. *I have Korra and her family.*

My nights? *Well, they're not consistently full but I could do something to change that.*

This line of thinking unsettles me because it's impossible to ignore that I am having a shift in thinking. I can't explain just how but I know that something has to change.

Walking away from Warren, Keesley and Mozier is not just about her. Korra wouldn't be behind that idea. But she's part of the reason why the idea doesn't sound as absurd. She was the one to tell me that I deserve rest and that I don't have to carry the discrepancy of this industry on my back.

I lean back in my chair and look at the stack of folders on my desk, waiting for me to begin reviewing.

Though I don't want it to be, I think the answer is more obvious to me than it once was. Work my ass off, be underappreciated, and lonely or work my ass off, be an asset and have a full life.

Having it all is within my reach. Maybe my hand has just been facing the wrong way all along.

# CHAPTER 32

## Korra

"I haven't had a chance to tell you, but I'm sorry the contest got cancelled," Zach says.

I pull another one of Mom's scrapbooks from her shelf and look at my big brother. "It's okay. No one saw it coming."

"Even still, we could all help more with it. Right?" He asks my other siblings, minus Nia who's back at campus again.

Lee interjects, "I don't know about that. I've got a lot on my plate right now with Dad trying to step down." My Dad's news about stepping down shouldn't have been a surprise but with Zadie there, I know he's feeling the pressure since they are evenly matched. Her teasing him has not helped his general insecurity about it either.

"C'mon, Lee. We've been finding out all kinds of things about Mom through these," Kasey says, holding up one of her journals. "The scrapbook might not be for you but the journals are much more interesting. Like see here," she points to the page she's been reading. "I'm finding out gossip from the town side people were more than comfortable sharing all their business with her. Sometimes she includes photos."

"Yea, hard pass on the small town gossip."

Kasey chooses to ignore him, going back to her reading instead.

I place a hand on my little brother's shoulder. "It's fine. Just you spending time like this with us is more than enough. That was all I wanted anyway. For us to keep spending time together."

Zach agrees, "Exactly. With her gone, I feel like it was already happening."

"We're adults. It was bound to happen even if she were still alive," Kasey adds, unhelpfully. Her views are so cynical sometimes, I wonder what exactly it would take to make her happy. Truly happy. Learning that she's never let anyone close is a harrowing thought. It's clear that she doesn't make it easy for someone to get close. Whoever it is, will have their work cut out for them. I'll wish them luck.

"Point is that she would have wanted us to try. *Trying* is the most important part."

Lee takes a spot at her piano. Without any thought, he begins playing a song that I remember him playing often. I forget sometimes that Lee was able to play many instruments growing up. He picked it up easily. My Mom had gotten him into several classes out of town until he thought that it was uncool and stuck to the activities that remained in our house or for special occasions.

"If you're taking requests," Zach starts but Lee holds up the middle finger to him. "Anyway," he moves on smoothly, focusing his attention back on me as I go through a different album. "Did you finish the spread you were working on? I never saw it."

"Oh! I did," I say with newfound excitement. Popping up from the ground, I walk over to the box I brought back to the house when I realized that I didn't want to work at my apartment on the scrapbook. We may not have had the competition this year, but next year could be our time to shine.

Dropping the box between where Zach and I are sitting, I lift the lid and flip to the page that I was working on.

"This turned out so well," Zach says genuinely impressed. His fingers trace some of the extras I added. Looking back at me, he asks, "Will you help me with a spread?"

I beam back at him. "Of course. I'd be happy to. I'm not an expert, but I could lend you a hand in what I've learned."

Kasey comes over to look at the completed spread too. "This does look good. I think Mom would be proud."

An honest complement from my twin. I'll always take those.

"Didn't you say there was a murder weapon in here or something?" Lee says coming from the piano.

I sigh long and hard to gain some patience and not curse my brother out. "No one said anything like that." Pointing toward the box I got the scrapbook out of, I inform him, "There was a tie and an ID that has a stain on it. We just speculated that it could be blood but it could be anything at this point. Who knows how old it is or what the stain is from."

Kasey grabs a different journal from the shelf and begins reading it. Offhandedly she says, "Don't go down that line of thinking, Lee. Kor got really pissed when I tried to think of what it could be."

My hands fly up in exasperation. "As I should have! You implied that our Mother was a murderer." How is that hard to comprehend?

"Did not. I just said that there could be a body in the garden," Kasey informs Lee.

Zach is the one to break up the argument again. "Alright, let's not do this again. There are no bodies and we don't know what any of that stuff means."

"Let me see it." Lee says, taking the box and digging through the crafting supplies for the suspicious content we've been talking about.

When he finds the little bundle of fabric, it's folded as neatly as it was before. For whatever reason I had gotten into the habit of returning it back to the state I found it. Probably because it hides the stain the best.

Lee unfolds the tie, making a disgusted sound when the stain appears. "Oh this is definitely blood. C'mon. You are seeing this right?"

"Whatever," I say, going back to the scrapbook with our middle school photos in it. Maybe I can find some inspiration for a different spread.

Then he coughs loudly. "What the hell is this?" Lee stares at the ID in his hand with his brows furrowed. He's tense and it's immediately alarming. Zach stands to go to him first.

Lee turns to me though. "What is it?" His voice is louder now, far more distraught than I think it should be.

"Calm down, Lee. It's just an ID."

"Just an ID?" He questions at max volume. "This man looks just like me. Why does he look just like me?"

That gets me and Kasey up. Both of us going over to where Lee and Zach stand to have a look at the ID again.

The breath whooshes out of me.

Kasey lets out a yelp.

Zach covers his mouth in disbelief.

"Oh, my goodness," I take the ID from Lee's hands with a bit of resistance as he blinks and blinks over and over again at some point in the distance. "I knew there was something about this that reminded me of someone."

"Wait, what was the name?" Kasey asks. She looks over my shoulder to the ID and then grabs the journal she was reading. "Aiden?" She flips to the page she was reading. A little newspaper clipping with a group of men and women standing in front of a building is tucked in the page. "Is that Mom?"

We all look at the page. It's undoubtedly our Mom standing next to Aiden. Closely. They are standing very close together. They're on the second row of people but there is no mistaking that her arm is either in his or they are pressed tighter than they should be.

"What does the journal say?" Zach asks. Lee is still basically catatonic, holding the tie in one hand.

Kasey skims the page. "Honestly nothing about Aiden or her... It's about a singing contest that she was taking a bus to Denver to participate in."

Holding the ID up to the clipped picture, I compare the two. "He looks much older in the ID. The picture must have been from when they were younger."

Lee snatches the ID from my hand. "Can you three stop blabbing? This man is identical to me. These are my eyes, my cheeks, my mouth, fucking hell, I think our ears are the same as well."

"Well, I mean..." I start sure that I'll find an reasoning along the way, I don't.

Lee waves the ID around. "This is no coincidence. You don't accidentally look exactly like someone. There is only one reason that could happen."

"You don't think—" Zach says.

"Come on. This is volunteer of the year we're talking about. Mom wouldn't have an affair. She loved Dad."

"I'm going to ask him," Lee says, already making his way through the boxes on the ground to leave.

Zach grabs him by the arm. "You will not. This is not the way, bro. You need to calm down."

"Easy for you to say. You've never been the *other* brother," Lee sneers.

He's not giving Lee any room for this line of thinking. Zach holds Lee's eyes when he says. "Neither have you. Mom and Dad loved us all the same."

"Psh," Lee says, tugging out of Zach's hold. "I'm owed some truth if this has been kept a secret from me all this time."

"What if Dad doesn't know?" I ask in a whisper.

Everyone faces me, the same looks all mirrored around me.

"Holy shit, you're right. What if he doesn't know? Is this really how he should find out? By you waltzing in there waving an ID around. We don't even know for sure that there is anything to—"

Lee's eyes drill into me. "Do you think that this is a game?"

"I don't, Lee, but maybe take a minute to calm down and think more clearly. You're not the only one who could be hurt by this information."

"Who could be more hurt by this than me?"

"You have always been our brother. This doesn't change anything," Zach says. "It hurts to hear you say that you think we've treated you any differently."

"I'm not saying that you have. Everyone sees that I don't look like you all. Come to find out that it's because I'm only your half brother is saying a lot."

"You're not our half anything, Lee!" I rush to my brother's side, tears in my eyes. "I know this is not the way you'd want to find something like this out but know that we're here for you. We're your family. Nothing has changed."

Lee doesn't accept my hug. He pushes out of my arms, storming from the room without a look back.

"Well, that blew up," Kasey deadpans. "Who's going to go after him?"

Zach's already walking to the door, when he says, "I will. You two try to get this cleared up. We'll have to figure out what to do about Mom and this Aiden person at some point."

"Mom's got a lot of explaining to do."

"She can't exactly do that. Guess I'm going to be reading far more of these journals than I thought," Kasey says, scooping a bunch of them up into her arms. "I'll see you at home, right?"

"Yea... I'll get this cleaned up."

She leaves and I get started on what I said I was going to do. When I put things back into the box I had originally packed for my things, I notice that the tie and the ID are both gone. I don't know what could possibly be going on through Lee's mind but I know it can't be anything good.

My heart goes out to him. This kind of revelation could foil anyone. I just hope that he is not going to be too upset by the outcome of his digging.

# CHAPTER 33

## Korra

The heater hums from underneath my window, trying to keep up with the cold. Outside, snow falls in slow spirals, settling against the glass. Winter is not letting up anytime soon and I've been happy about how cozy it is in the apartment when I can watch the scene from indoors. We've eaten dinner late tonight since Bryce came from Denver. I have so much on my mind and Kasey had made a point of holding up in her room after everything went down in Mom's studio earlier today.

After I have taken care of all my plants, I needed something to do with my mind. Thankfully, I had roasted some chicken, tossed together some greens and opened a bottle of wine. Something told me that this day was going to need it. When Bryce called me, I knew that I had the right plan. Kasey might come out to eat later, but there's no telling with how she dove headfirst into the journals that Mom left behind.

Now I'm watching the snow gather on the sill while Bryce paces in the small walkway behind my couch. His reflection moves back and forth in the window, making it seem like he is a ghost in the snow outdoors. He's still in his shirt with the sleeves rolled up from being at the office all day. His suit jacket sits over the arm of one side of my couch. It's hard to believe what went down on this couch not that long ago. I try not to think of that since I can tell that something is obviously agitating him. He was quiet over dinner, but I was too. I just have so much on my mind. Apparently, we both do.

Finally, he stops walking. "Korra," he says in a low steady voice. "I need to tell you something. And I need to get it all out or else I might not be able to get any of it out."

Whatever he has to say, it must be pretty important. Though Bryce is very serious, and in general not very talkative, something is affecting him and I'm curious to know what it is. "Okay...."

He exhales through his nose and steps closer. The tension in his jaw is tight, exaggerating, the sharp edge. The pulse in his neck is thumping at a rapid pace when he speaks. "When this started, everything between you and me, it was supposed to be about getting ahead. All of it. I had convinced myself that all of this was just another play in the greater strategy of making partner. I knew that it would be smart for me to help my image at the firm."

He runs a hand over his curls and they spring back into place. I still haven't figured out exactly what he's using in them to look so good. I need to ask him what it is, but not right now. His voice is rough as he continues, "I only had one goal. But I didn't know what any of it really meant. I just knew that I was chasing something. That I had my eye on the prize. And for a while here, I thought that wanting you was just a part of wanting that prize."

I look up into his eyes as he looks down at me from behind the couch. His hands are braced on the back, clinching on for dear life it seems. I don't know where this is going, but I ask, "And now?"

His eyes are sharp as he focuses on me. "Now I can see that it wasn't ever about the firm. There's only one reason why your name came up when the idea popped in my head. There's only one reason that I would do something so drastic. It was about you. When I thought about what would make me look better—it was you. Everything about our relationship has made me a better person. And I contributed that to my success in this industry and my own drive, but the fact of the matter is that you encouraged me along the way. You made what I did every day, not as menial and mundane. I didn't believe in the idea of love changing anything. I didn't believe it *could*. But you consistently showed me that I was wrong."

The words hang between us and I am in no hurry to pick them up. *That information* that I have been holding onto is so close to breaking free. I didn't know what to say, so I just looked down at my hands.

"Somewhere along the way I figured out that I love you, Korra. And I think I always have. But I never thought that I deserved you. The life that I was leading wouldn't allow me to be the kind of person that I wanted to be in a relationship with you. I thought I couldn't give you enough. I wasn't willing to make the sacrifice that I would have to make in order to be the person I want to be when I'm with you. When I asked you if you could be happy with me, it was selfish. I wasn't willing to make the changes that I needed to in order to be there for you. But now I see that maybe I should."

The heater clicks off and the silence feels deliberate after what he's just shared. I still don't know what to say. And I hate this about myself. I just freeze. I already knew his feelings, but him telling me in this way is overwhelming.

"I'm sorry," he says into the quiet space. "I'm sorry for thinking I could separate what was real from what wasn't." He looks into my eyes, and finally, the words hit me.

"I'm not," I whisper.

He pauses, his eyebrows raising high on his head.

"I'm not sorry because if it hadn't started this way, we wouldn't have figured out what was right between us. We would've still been going along like there wasn't potential for more. I wanted the opposite. I wanted everything to stay the same. My routine, my predictable little life, but then I lost my Mom. I thought I could keep things steady and if I did, I wouldn't have to feel the loss anymore. But when you asked me to be your fiancée, it disrupted everything that I thought I knew. I had to see the world differently because your words made it so. You didn't leave me any room to hide behind what was normal and regular. You cared for me in a way that made it impossible for me to pretend that what I was doing before was enough. You made me see that I deserve more and then gave it to me."

I stand from the couch, rounding the corner to stand in front of him. "I love you, Bryce."

As soon as I'm within reach, he pulls me close to him in a hug. "I don't know what comes next. I just know that I don't want it without you."

Stepping toward him until I can feel the warmth radiating off his chest, my arms wrapped around him, trying to make contact and hold onto something solid. Because Bryce is solid. "I don't know either," I whisper. "But all I know is that I love what we have."

After a while, his arms loosen, and we both settle on the couch. He is much more relaxed now. I pull the blanket over both of us.  Folding up my legs around me, I lean onto his side so that he can put his arm behind my back.

"I called Wynn West."

I glance up at him. "You did?"

"Yeah," he leans back on the couch cushions. "He offered me a job."

It takes a second for his words to register in my mind. "At his practice? Isn't he the one who is fighting the Brenfords now?"

Bryce nods. "He did say that they are taking on the Brenfords. It's a small firm with only local work, but what he had to say really touched me."

"It's not exactly a safe fight. The Brenford's are notorious for being protective of their name and assets. Look at all the events they postponed this season for the bad press."

"Exactly," he says quietly. "But it's the kind of fight that I'd like to be a part of." He looks at me and there's something honest and true about the desire there. Not for me, but for what he wants next in life. "I know it's not a safe move. Leaving my firm is not financially or professionally recommended. And I know I'm crazy for you considering it."

"But you are?" I ask. "You're considering taking him up on his offer?"

He meets my gaze. "I am," he says simply. For a while, neither of us speaks as I study him. "If I do this, it'll mean that I can be closer to you."

"I know."

"If I'm closer then it means that I can be with you every night."

I raise an eyebrow at the suggestion in his voice. "Is that right?"

He nuzzles my neck, "Mmh," then he places a kiss behind my ear, "We should go to your room so that your sister doesn't walk out to something she doesn't want to see."

# CHAPTER 34

## Epilogue: Korra

In many other places in the country, I know snow is more predictable. Some experience it earlier in the year. Some never get snow at all. In Colorado, it's always a surprise. A reminder that what's necessary will happen when it's ready, not when we want it to.

Rubbing slow circles over Bryce's knuckles, the two of us sit in his sedan in front of the small brick building. I look over at Bryce, unsure of what he's feeling right now. A few ideas of how he could be feeling after the call that set him on a brand new course for his life are clear. My hope is that they lean more positive than negative.

"He said that I could give him a call if I ever changed my mind." Bryce finally says into the silence of the car. In front of us is the private firm that Wynn West works out of. The Harmony Hill Defense Group sign is dusted with snow.

"Phil did?"

He nods. "I won't." He looks down at our joined hands, using his thumb to straighten my engagement ring. "For years I thought the glass walls, suits and skyline view from the top floor were what I needed to feel successful. But now I see that success looks different when you change your point of view."

I smile up at him. "Working with Wynn will bring a whole new set of challenges, but I know this town will be grateful to have you at it's defense. Besides, you clean up really nice. It's almost unfair that you're already taken."

"A challenge that I am ready for. Signed the papers last night and sent them over, no turning back now."

"They'll love you. Not as much as I do though."

He makes a sound of agreement, taking his eyes off of the building in front of us. "Not as much as I love you. Speaking of taken..." His eyebrows wiggle on his forehead as he leans toward me.

I hold him back with my hands on his chest and a giggle. "Oh, no. Is this going to be another terrible segue?"

He chuckles, scratching the back of his neck under the wooly scarf around his neck. "I hope not. I was thinking that we should set a date."

Blinking a few times, I ask, "For our wedding?" With a hand covering my mouth, I murmur, "I'd almost forgotten."

"I was hoping that you'd bring it up first. I didn't want to seem too eager." He buries his face into my curls, "Especially since I have something else to show you."

"More? What is it?"

"We'll get to it. Tell me this first." He takes my hand again, "What do you think about a summer wedding on the hillside?"

"Are we talking June summer or August summer?" That is a critical decision. Being outside for prolonged periods of time in August is begging for heatstroke. I could not settle for a wedding where I'm drenched in sweat while hugging people and still trying to look nice for photos. Bryce would look so good in a linen suit as well...

His head tilts to the left, "June summer."

"It's a date then," I say, pleased about the wildflower blooms and the pleasant warmth of early summer. Unlocking my phone, I scroll to next year's calendar and decide, "June third looks good. It's a Saturday and that will make it easier for everyone."

"That won't do," he says. "Saturday is good but I'm thinking the second is better."

"Why?" I question, brows furrowing as I look up into his eyes. "That means it'll be on a Friday. Those things don't make sense."

He cups my jaw with his warm hand to say, "I don't want to wait until next year to call you my wife. What if we got married this year instead?"

I don't hesitate when I lean across the seat to kiss him. Our lips meet in a passionate agreement that neither of us want to wait another moment longer than we have to.

I still take the opportunity to tease him about it. "You were right. This does make you seem rather eager."

He nips at my bottom lip, warm hands holding the back of my neck to deepen our kiss even more. "I don't care if it does. I know I've waited long enough already."

"We might have to compromise on a hillside venue then. Those kinds of locations book out quickly. I could start calling to see who has availability, but there is no telling what I'll be able to find." His cheeks stretch into a breathtaking smile that lures me in but confuses me in the same measure. "Why are you smiling like that?"

"Put your seatbelt back on. We're gonna go see what else I have to show you."

I raise an eyebrow at him but concede in securing my belt again. He makes the familiar drive down Main street until it becomes unfamiliar with two left turns that go down a county road. I sit patiently as he taps along the steering wheel to the music playing on the radio.

The narrow road is bracketed by barren trees that still provide a bit of shade and conceal the shapes of what's to come. I get my first glimpse of the Hills before a two story farmhouse comes into view. Sitting forward in my seat, I get a better view of the property. It's not too far from the smaller access road that leads from the west of the land. "What is this place?"

Bryce doesn't answer me. Instead, he gets out of the car to open my door and hold a hand out for me. I let him lead me to the front porch.

"Are these rosemary and lavender? They still smell amazing." There's several of them that wrap the front of the house, making it feel warm and welcoming. Picture frame windows and sage green siding lure me in. The porch steps are a dark stained wood that lead to a front door of the same color. To my complete surprise, Bryce flicks through his keyring and unlocks a door with one of the keys.

"Watch your step," he says, since there's a plastic tarp on the ground and the smell of fresh paint in the open floor plan. He's far too familiar walking through this place as he shows me around. We end up in a mud room that has a large window overlooking the backyard that already has a fenced in raised plant bed garden. "You think this place would make a good location or a wedding. In the back, I mean."

All the open field space beyond that lead to the hills beyond, most of it is white with previous snow. "It does feel like some sort of scenic bed and breakfast." Looking out the window at the enticing features of this property, I demand, "Okay, who's house are we in?"

"Mine," he says simply. "Closed on it last week."

I spin, gawking at him and this information. "This is your house?"

"Well, I was thinking that it could be our place..." He holds a hand open in front of me. In his palm is a small Monstera frond keychain with a golden key on it. "Together."

My brows lift even as my eyes prick with tears. "You mean... live together?"

He shrugs, "I guess I could rent out the spare room upstairs." With an unsure chuff, he adds, "Yea, live together. We could have something that is wholly ours."

I snag the keychain from his hands. "Only if I can have the bamboo charcuterie board and those gradient towels. Oh! And all my plants will need—"

"Korra, you can pick and do whatever you want with the house—as long as you're in it with me and the menace."

We have a lot of news to share with the family come Sunday night. Everyone is gathered including a few who have become a part of the Sunday gathering like Gonzalo, Luciá, Zadie and Socks. It's a full house with yummy smells and laughter that fills the walls for the most part. We're just waiting on Lee to arrive.

It's an exciting time and I'm grateful that my grief has become quieter now. It's not gone, just softer around the jagged edges that used to get caught in my heart. I used to feel like I was trying to outrun it. I thought if I kept busy enough, loved hard enough that I could trick myself into feeling whole again.

But grief doesn't work that way. The empty spot beside my Dad at the dinner table doesn't sound like the missing note of a song anymore. It's the moment of silence before the crescendo. Mom is still here and in many ways she never left. We are who we are because she was who she was. And now I can be the glue of this family. The even playing ground. The one who loves everyone the same.

Maybe one day, with a family of my own, too.

With our news, Dad asks with a contented smile, "Set a date? Bought a house? This is all wonderful news."

Zadie squeezes my hand, "Oh, that is so good! Congrats you two! Someone call Nia."

"Already on it," Kasey says. She turns the speakerphone on Nia's excited voice joins the table and it's almost perfect until the front door comes banging open. The sound is so loud that we can hear it from the dining room. It makes a few of us jump in surprise, but Lee is clearly in a bad mood. Not good for the celebratory one that we have in the room right now. Bryce puts an arm around my shoulder, kissing my forehead. His attempt to smooth the wrinkle of my forehead at Lee's entrance.

"Why would you invite her here?" Lee exclaims upon entering the dining room. "Don't I see her enough as it is?"

Well, I can't say that this is a surprising argument as our work environment had become more tense with Dad's also telling the clinic of his retirement plans.

If you add in the fact that Lee has been having strong emotions about the ID I found in Mom's things. He's angsty because he hasn't confronted Dad or made plans to do anything else beside stew in his ignorance on the subject. He hasn't talked to any of us after that fateful day, but there is too much he isn't talking about that sits like an elephant in the room. With Malaya also firmly done with him, he is an absolute pill. I'd feel bad for Zadie if she wasn't the person she is.

Zadie, pulling red curls on top of her head with a clip, is completely unaffected by Lee's rudeness when she responds, "Relax, *Broken*. I can be friendly if you learn to use your indoor voice. What's with the yelling?"

"Don't you have your own family? Must you infiltrate mine?" Not one animal pun as he delivers his snark her way and takes a seat between Kasey and Zack.

"Lee, watch your mouth." Dad says, fed up with his attitude like the rest of us. "You're acting like a child. Zadie is always welcome in this house."

Pushing his plate from in front of him, he glares at our Dad head on. "This woman has come to take the position that I've been working my whole life to have. She bounces in here with her 'sirs' and smirks. Now, she's welcome where I'm meant to have at least some reprieve from work stress? You don't care about me at all! What's up with that, *Dad?*"

"Okay, this dinner is not about either of you. It's for the family. Do I need to send you both out of the house?" Zach chastises though he says it with a lighter tone.

"You know what? I'll go." Zadie says, standing from her seat glaring at Lee.

Now, it's Dad who stands. "No one is leaving. I'll clear this up right now." Looking toward Lee, he says, "Yes, I did bring Zadie in because she's qualified and will be an amazing addition to the clinic if we're lucky enough to keep her. The decision to leave my life's work is a hard one to make, but

I know that there is someone who can fill my shoes and make me proud. Tonight is a perfect example for why I have my doubts about it being you, Bentley. I'd been vague before but at this rate, you are making the choice to promote Zadie even easier. My legacy is about more than following procedure. It's about ethos." Throwing a hand in the air, he continues, "You disrespect our guests, a colleague. You have a bad attitude with staff. You've been a loaded canon, ready to blow at any point. That is not the Thomas way."

Lee is already rearing to explode again, but Dad holds up a hand, silencing him. "I'm sorry that you were made to be part of this problem, Zadie. I wouldn't blame you for wanting to go and if that is what will make you more comfortable, I won't hold it against you."

"It's alright, Wayne. I should probably get going anyway. Thank you for dinner," Zadie says. He nods, but is clearly still upset. My friend hugs me, congratulating Bryce and I before getting her things and leaving.

The room is tense with silence as Lee eats his food unbothered by the awkward vibe now. "What?" he asks when he feels all our eyes on him.

"Okay, I see what you mean by Lee wanting to be punched." Nia says, still on speakerphone. "I'm disappointed, big brother."

Zack takes Lee's plate. "You need to apologize to her. You were beyond rude. What the hell was that?"

"I'm not. She's a big girl. She's fine." Lee says.

"Look, I know you've got a lot on your plate right now—" I say before he cuts me off.

"Is that supposed to be funny?"

"No, it's just an expression. Lee, you're better than this. Whatever you're going through, we're here to support you. This is not the way." I continue, "I know you're hurting. Hurt people hurt people. You're stronger than you're doubts. Taking it out on Zadie is not the way."

Lee's jaw ticks a few times. "Fine. I'll go after her, but it won't be to apologize." He storms out of the room, ignoring all the raucous protests of everyone at the table.

"Well, I don't feel confident about that at all," Bryce says with a sigh and we all have to agree.

**THE END**

Thank you for reading Perfect Harmony! I hope you enjoyed it! The series continues with Lee's rivals-to-lovers, workplace romance coming up next!

## FIERCE HARMONY : COMING 2026

Preorder it now on Amazon!

Please don't forget to leave a review as it helps other readers find my stories and enjoy them as well!

Thank you so much for reading Bryce and Korra's story. It truly means so much to me that I get to share a softer side to the kind of romance that I enjoy writing. If you've read any of my previous works, then you know that it can get a little rocky in my pages. The Thomas Family Saga is meant to be a bit of a comfort write for myself and hopefully a comfort read for you.

This story would not be possible without the love and support from my best friend, and our epilogue baby. I love you both more than words can say.

A huge thank you to my PA, Kelsie. You hold me down and keep me sane! Thank you for coordinating all this chaos. (I really put her through it)

Without my wonderful BETA readers, this story would not be. Thank you Brooklyn L., Faith H., Jessica N. and my other BETAS!

I'm so grateful for my Street Team and ARC readers. You all help spread the joy of my stories and give me so much love! I'm hugging you all! Thank you!

And to you, reader, THANK YOU for picking up Perfect Harmony! I'm so happy that you gave Bryce and Korra a try and I hope that you will stick around for more Thomas Family shenanigans.

For more romance and to keep up with future releases, consider joining my newsletter and following me on socials!

https://zeakayleighgalan.com/news

www.instagram.com/ZeaKayleigh

www.facebook.com/ZeaKayleigh

# Also by Zea Kayleigh Galan

## Alpenglow Ridge

**Saddled with Finesse** — Can their unexpected kiss ignite a love strong enough to overcome the shadows of her past and give him the fresh start he's been searching for?

**Verse to Acclimate** — Years after heartbreak tore them apart, a broken small-town girl and country music's rising star must face the scars of their past to find out if love is worth a second chance.

**Whisk til Peaked** — Trapped by a snowstorm in a luxury resort with only one bed, a single mom and her loyal best friend must confront unspoken desires and buried secrets that could shatter everything they hold dear—or finally bring them together.

**Hope by the Horizon** — When a guarded hippotherapist clashes with charming ranch hand, their undeniable chemistry ignites a journey of trust, healing, and unexpected love—if they can overcome their pasts. (Read FREE https://zeakayleighgalan.com/free-novella )

**Roped on the Ridge** — She woke up with no memory, a past full of secrets, and a cowboy who refuses to give up on her... even when the truth threatens to destroy them both.

## Shades of Vengeance

**Into the Blue** — A cold-hearted crime boss discovers that he can't let go of a dancer at his nightclub after she is attacked by his rival.

Written in Red — A dark stalker romance coming 2026!

## Thomas Family Saga

**Perfect Harmony** — An ambitious lawyer needs a fiancée to climb the ladder and his best friend agrees, but somewhere between the ring and their kiss, pretending starts to feel like the truth.

**Fierce Harmony** —  A rivals to lovers small town romance coming 2026

# About the Author

Zea is a passionate storyteller who brings romance to life with heartfelt emotion and unforgettable characters. A lifelong lover of love stories, she weaves her background in anthropology into crafting tales where swoon-worthy heroes fall hard for their strong, relatable heroines.

Living in the picturesque mountains of Colorado with her husband, daughter, and a spoiled, posh cat, Zea draws inspiration from her surroundings to create warm, vibrant settings readers want to escape to. When she's not writing, she's indulging in her other loves: cooking, hiking, designing clothes, or curling up with a romance novel and a plate of sweets.

Zea is dedicated to connecting with her readers and invites you to join her on this journey of love, laughter, and happily ever afters.

Want to be the first to hear about new releases, exclusive content, and special offers?

Sign up for my newsletter at

www.zeakayleighgalan.com/news

www.instagram.com/zeakayleigh

www.facebook.com/zeakayleigh

Signed Book Shop